and friendship and Twitter bios. It will warm your heart. You should really switch off your computer and read it'

Matt Haig, author of *The Humans*

'*Meatspace* is the greatest book on loneliness since *The Catcher in the Rye*'

Gary Shteyngart, author of *Super Sad True Love Story*

'Totally original and funny and humane'

Sathnam Sanghera, author of *The Boy with The Topknot*

'*Meatspace* is, simply, one of the finest novels I have ever read about modern life and modern living, terrifying, beautiful, hilarious and powerful; about how loose we are with ourselves and our personas when we step online; about how technology moves faster than us, and will drag us in its wake if we only let it; and about friendship, love and family. Both brilliantly written and artfully structured, it is a tremendous – and unexpected – follow-up to *Coconut Unlimited*. It is so achingly relevant to whatever zeitgeist we're currently undergoing that it's almost like reading through an instagram filter. Douglas Coupland, Junot Diaz, Chuck Palahniuk and Jennifer Egan: stick them in a blendr, and out comes this amazing new novel by one of the UK's most distinct voices'

James Smythe, author of *The Machine*

'Our messed up times dissected in as funny, tender and suitably weird a way as possible'

David Whitehouse, author of *Bed*

'Shukla writes with precision, humour and honesty, about the isolation that social media can bring. *Meatspace* is a novel with many laugh-out-loud moments, break-dancing to the arrhythmia of its existential heart'

Nikita Lalwani, author of *Gifted*

'If the purpose of a novel is to make sense of how we live now, Nikesh Shukla's *Meatspace* fulfills that promise #ennuiisananalogueconstruct'

Niven Govinden, author of *Black Bread White Beer*

'*Meatspace* is a weird and wonderful novel that brilliantly captures the soul-sickening fun of a life lived on social media. Read it then move to the woods and repent for your wasted youth'

Jenny Offill, author of *Dept. of Speculation*

'As a fellow writer/internet addict/human being, *Meatspace* really touched (and chilled) me. It's not just a brilliant story in itself but really a front-runner in terms of examining how our relationship with the internet is impacting our real lives'

Kerry Hudson, author of *Tony Hogan Bought Me An Ice-Cream Float Before He Stole My Ma*

'*Meatspace* is fun, funny, and moving when you least expect it'

Emylia Hall, author of *The Book of Summers*

'If you replaced the Wizard of Oz with John Fante's protagonist Arturo Bandini, and then made a world crazier than the Emerald City could ever dream of being, you've got something close to *Meatspace*. Because, in the end, nothing's more unexpected and strange than real life. And there's a certain valiancy in trying to manage the rocks life throws at us, whether it's in the stories we tell ourselves, or the stories we tell online. We all filter our lives in one way or another, just as Kitab does. Funny, slightly mad, but deeply sympathetic and relatable, *Meatspace* has the biggest heart'

Rebecca Hunt, author of *Mr Chartwell*

'*Meatspace* could really be an alternative instruction manual on how to get out of the habit of living life online and start actually living. It's funny, desperately funny at times, but also terribly sad'

Culturefly

By the same author

Coconut Unlimited
Generation Vexed (co-written with Kieran Yates)
The Time Machine

Meatspace

Nikesh Shukla

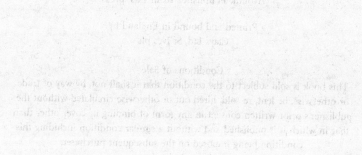

The Friday Project
An imprint of HarperCollins*Publishers*
1 London Bridge Street
London SE1 9GF

www.harpercollins.co.uk

First published by The Friday Project in 2014
This paperback edition first published 2015

ISBN: 978-0-00-756507-8

Set in Minion by Born Group using
Atomik ePublisher from Easypress

Printed and bound in England by
Clays Ltd, St Ives plc

For Nimer, who introduced me to IRC in the mid-nineties

WHY I SENT A LAMB CHOP INTO SPACE

Whenever my best mate and I have stood in line at Tayyab's in East London, our nostrils tingling with burnt mustard seeds, we've ogled the wall of fame – from Daniel Craig to Talvin Singh – and wondered, how in the name of all things sacred do we get on here? I mean, a novelist and an artist, we may not be in the same league as James Bond or the guy who won the Mercury Music Prize in the 90s when being Asian was last cool – we knew whatever we did had to be a cut above.

So it was lucky that I had a book called *Meatspace* coming out.

Meatspace is what people who live their lives online call real life. Meatspace. There's something so strange, odious and fleshy about the word. It shows that we're just a collection of wobbly brains living in meat pods. Nick (Hearne – he's an artist) and I thought it would be funny to take the word literally. And send some meat into space.

We were sat waiting for roast dinners at Hackney City Farm, enjoying the faint, malt-y mist of pig shit and chicken feed seeping through the windows when we had the idea. What could be more ridiculous than sending some actual meat into actual space? And how easy would it be?

Pretty easy, it turns out – all we needed was a weather balloon, some helium and permission from the Civil Aviation Authority and we were good to go. We bought a GoPro camera, made a makeshift pod out of its packaging and forked the sizzling lamb chop.

We took the lamb chop 88.8 miles from Tayyab's in East London and out to the Cotswolds, filled the air balloon with helium and let go. The original idea – sending some meat into space – was just the tip of the iceberg, though. What followed was a lesson in endurance.

The plan was: the chop would rise at 325 metres a minute, for 95 minutes, before the balloon was predicted to burst 50 miles away over Hungerford, West Berkshire. The payload would then parachute back to earth with a predicted landing near Andover, Hampshire, 68 miles from the launch site. We would ping the GPS, go and collect and film a little retrieval skit with a 'stunt' chop we had in a coolbox.

We drank coffees in a supermarket car park and waited for the GPS to start pinging when the chop re-entered the atmosphere. But it never pinged. We waited and we waited. We had a little sausage sandwich barbecue in a park (in a designated barbecue area), ran into Lucy and Russell, whose farm was going to be the original launch site until predicted journey simulations put the pod in the sea. And nothing.

We returned home broken.

The lamb chop was lost.

We launched a local campaign to try and see if anyone had found it. Amazingly, someone did. Nick got a call from a farmer who had found the pod in his threshing machine. The farmer said he was near Yeovil, which was further south than predicted, and sounded like a straight up dude.

Except, he never returned the pod. He wasn't a straight up dude.

The farmer made arrangements to meet at locations in Dorchester, a service station in Bridgend, and Weston-supermare, but failed to show every time. He dodged between different phone numbers and locations, every time giving excuses why he couldn't return the camera. By this time the launch team began to believe that this was life imitating art. The main theme of *Meatspace* is the lies that we tell ourselves and others in the modern social media-obsessed universe. Was this a case of elaborate catfishing? Or purely somebody attention seeking? I mean, we weren't dealing with a case of rare diamonds here. It was a bedraggled lamb chop.

The weird part was, in the book, a stray fact from a character opens up a Google search hole of all their social links, and private information. And with this farmer, an accidental text he sent to me – meant for his girlfriend – lead me to his rugby team, Facebook, LinkedIn and more. It was bizarre. It was life imitating art.

After five months of book promo and having babies, Nick and I called the rozzers. And, amazingly, the camera reappeared. A few weeks ago. We were mentally exhausted by this point. So much so that the irony of the handover, in a KFC, escaped us till afterwards. When we saw the footage, it was unbelievable. Utterly unbelievable. We'd sent a Tayyab's lamb chop into space.

And the thing we gained, apart from the footage, apart from the promotion for my novel, was an absolutely ridiculous adventure that genuinely bonded Nick and I for life. Sounds cheesy, but besides the bizarre achievement of sending a bit of meat hurtling towards the moon, chasing the tail of a farmer who refuses to give the camera that filmed it back to you does great things to a friendship.

Oh, and we made it on to Tayyab's wall of fame.

This article originally appeared on Vice.com

Meatspace
Pronunciation: miːtspeɪs
noun
[mass noun] informal
the physical world, as opposed to cyberspace or a virtual environment.

'Technology proposes itself as the architect of our intimacies.' Sherry Turkle

'Have you ever had that moment when you are updating your status and you realise that every status update is just a variation on a single request: "Would someone please acknowledge me?"' Marc Maron

History:

Which alcoholic drink has the most calories? – Google
Hayley Bankcroft – Facebook
Olivia Munn – YouTube
Olivia Munn nude – Google
[109] – Twitter
kitab_balasubramanyam@gmail.com [4 new]

The first and last thing I do everyday is see what strangers are saying about me.

I pull the laptop closer from the other side of the bed and press refresh on my inboxes. I have a Google calendar alert that tells me I have no events scheduled today, an assortment of Twitter and Facebook notifications, alerting me to 7 new followers, a favourite of a tweet thanking someone for liking my book, an invite to an event I'll never go to, spam from Play and Guardian Jobs. Hayley Bankcroft has sent me a direct message about an event we're both doing next week. Amazon recommends I buy the book I wrote. There's a rejection email from an agency I'd applied to do some freelance marketing copy for. I didn't want the job, but now I haven't got it I feel annoyed and hurt. I think about tweeting 'will write copy for food' but decide against it.

There's an email from my dad. He doesn't usually send me emails; he prefers text messages. It's a forwarded message from a woman on a dating website. In it she's written 'Would love to meet your son and be his new mummy'. In bold at the top, Dad has written 'Kitab-san, Wen u free?!!!!' I ignore it. I never want to meet one of his girlfriends. Ever.

The only other 2 messages from actual humans are a friend request from the one other person with my name on Facebook, which I ignore when I see the next one is from Rach: an email letting people know her new address. I wonder why she wants me to have this information. Am I supposed to think, 'Oh, she's moved out of her parents' house, which even being in Zone 6 and involving interacting with her racist brother and the cat that hated me and her dad's collection of plaid shirts with effervescent sweat patches was still preferable to living here with me? Or, more realistically, 'Why is she moving out of her parents' house *now*, 6 months after dumping me, 6 months after moving out, 6 months after she told me she couldn't bear the way I lived any longer and that I was draining her enthusiasm for life? Is that what I'm supposed to think?

She's moving to North London, where she lived when we first met. I used to like meeting her at her flat. It overlooked a park and had a big kitchen I would sit in while she made coffee with the landlord's Gaggia filter coffee machine. There was a disused railway line we'd take walks down. I haven't been there in years.

That flat was amazing. We cooked all the time, she didn't own a television, just stacks of books, a balcony where she grew tomatoes and a posh coffee machine. It was a middle-class idyll. None of the furniture pointed at an entertainment source. We were those people. For the life of me, I can't work out why we chose to move her to my place instead of me to hers.

She was clinical in collecting all of her things when it ended. The only trace of her was a t-shirt of mine she took ownership of while we were together but I got full custody of in the break-up and the chutneys she left in the fridge. I notice them every time I open the fridge.

I hate chutneys. They're a painfully white condiment, a colonial response to the spicy Indian pickle. I keep meaning to throw them away. When she'd first moved out, I spent a drunken night spooning onion chutney into my mouth because that was the closest I could get to what she'd tasted like.

2

The related Google ad next to her email is for 'house-warming gift ideas'. I click out of my emails and think of things to tweet. I've got nothing to say. I look at the account of this other Kitab.

I've known about his existence for a while now. Around 6 months ago, his Facebook profile had started showing up in my self-Googling. I was surprised at first. Another Kitab with my obscure surname. Another one. Another me. He kinda looked like me too. He had fair brown (what I call caramel, ex-girlfriends have called 'dusty') skin and the hairstyle I had in the 80s, swept up into a Patrick Swayze cowlick of quiff and oil. He had eyes like mine, almond-shaped and -coloured and he had my mouth. Full kissable lips. Or at least this is how I would describe myself on an internet dating profile – caramel-skinned, quiffed black hair, almond-coloured eyes and big full lips.

He wore a white turtleneck sweater, like a Bond villain. His location was listed as Bangalore, India and the avatar photo itself looked like a warped driving licence scanned on a low-resolution photocopier. I was immediately disappointed that my namesake was so Indian-looking.

The related Facebook ad on the search results page for Kitab Balasubramanyam is an identity theft-solving app. It's 69p. I don't buy it.

I wonder why he's decided to add me.

I tweet: 'Feet hurt. Too much bogling last night. #boglingrelatedinjuries'

This is a lie. I was in bed by 10 last night. I had 4 beers on an empty stomach, felt pissed and irritated, shouted a lot in our front room about Rach and how I was better off without her and was put to bed by Aziz, who complained I was too drunk to take out on the town to find some trouble. He'd sighed, I was never up for getting in trouble now I was single.

I clear my throat. It stings like I've been singing too much.

The air in my room feels thick and musty. I try to remember the last time I left the flat. It hasn't been often since Rach moved out. Except for the pub and for supplies. If it wasn't for Aziz, I probably wouldn't talk to anyone apart from online. I left the flat yesterday. It was to go to the pub. And the big shop. I did the big shop after the pub. It consisted of Budvars, bread, and frozen pizzas for emergencies. Now Rach isn't here to fill the fridge with fresh sustainable organic food and chutneys, I'm taking full advantage.

I sleep with my quilt rolled and bunched up into the sausage of a human body. She's my bedtime girlfriend now I'm newly single. I call her Quiltina.

As if he can feel me stir, Aziz opens my door and comes and sits on the edge of the bed.

'Watching porn?' he asks.

'No.'

'I never want to catch you wanking again.'

'Then knock,' I say as he checks himself out in my mirror.

'Actually I do want to,' he says, turning to me and grinning. 'I'm not going to lie, I think you have an interesting wank-face. It's somewhere between "this sweet is too sour" and "my knees are hurting from old age".' Aziz contorts his face into a pained cry and simulates juddering hand thrusts. I turn over onto my side and close my eyes.

'Did you and I go out bogling last night? I really don't remember that,' Aziz says.

I try to cover myself up. Just to annoy me, Aziz pulls the cover off.

'That was just for the internet.'

Aziz pounces on me, pulls the cover over my head and cuddles it. I can feel him humping my body. I try to push him off but he's too strong.

'Mercy?' he cries.

'Mercy,' I say.

'Seriously, I can't hear you. Mercy?'

'Mercy,' I call again.

Aziz pounds away, but I manage to get a knee up to connect with his side. He falls off me laughing. I allow myself a smile. I'm awake now.

'I love you, idiot brother of mine,' he says. He pauses. 'What are you up to today?'

'Writing.'

Aziz laughs sarcastically. He pulls the cover off me entirely. I go fetal. 'No, but seriously, ladies and gentlemen,' he says in his 1930s stand-up comedian voice. 'What are you up to today?'

'Job-hunting.'

'So you'll be on email?'

'Yeah, probably.'

'Cool. I'll send you some pop culture gifs to keep you company.'

'Won't you be busy … you know, working?'

'That's how I'm so swag, my friend,' Aziz says, scratching the dark scar on his neck. 'That. Is how I'm so swag.'

Aziz heads to the door. 'Hey man,' I call to him. 'What were we doing last night? Singing? SingStar?'

He turns his head and looks back at me. 'Do you even remember last night?'

'Yeah.' I feel my phone vibrate in my hand. A Facebook wall message. I don't look at it. 'A bit. I think I had too much chutney. And rum. There was definitely too much beer.'

'Remember what you promised?'

'Yeah. To forget about Rach, move on, stop whining about her and get some writing done.'

'You kept going on about "keeping the wolf from the door".'

'Yeah. Money is fast running out, my friend.'

'That's not it,' Aziz says, smiling.

I'm beginning to remember bits of last night: 4 big bottles of Budvar in, I was standing on our sofa, clutching 2 jars of chutney, while Aziz held my leg like he was Princess Leia on the cover of the *Star Wars* poster, and I was Luke Skywalker.

'I am a golden god!' I was shouting. 'I am the golden god of literature. I am the golden god of this front room. I am the golden god of fucking chutneys.'

'I thought you hated chutneys.'

'I do, I fucking hate the white man's chutney. CBE. Chutney of the British Empire. I'm going to get "I H8 CHUTNEY" tattooed on my arm so future girlfriends know where I stand on the chutney thing without even having to ask.'

'Wait,' Aziz had said. 'You want a tattoo? I want a tattoo. Let's get tattoos. We're getting tattoos.'

'Yes,' I'd shouted back at him. 'The golden god will get a tattoo. I want a tattoo. Right now, there is nothing I want in the world more than a tattoo.'

'Maybe not "I H8 CHUTNEY".'

'No,' I'd said. I hesitated and thought. In that second silence, Elvis Costello came on the iPod, on shuffle. Aziz joined me on the sofa. He was all the Attractions and I was Elvis, crooning through the gap in my front teeth.

'Chapt-uhhhh waaaaa-hun … we didn't really get along …'

'I'm going to get "Everyday I write the book" on my forearm. All the way up. I bloody love this song. It's perfect. It can be a reminder to do my job. And Rach hated that song,' I said, turning to Aziz as he switched from bass to drums.

'Me too. I prefer "Shipbuilding". Remember "Shipbuilding". Always remember it, man,' he said, bopping his head, his hands tight in the air.

'Chapter wuuuu-huuuun,' I sang.

'Do you even like that song?'

'Doesn't matter. I like it. It's good. It's like … you know … analogue … like … write, mate, innit … It's a wicked song. I love this song.'

'I prefer "Shipbuilding".'

6

'Nah, that's shit. This one. Chaptaaah toooooo-wooooooo …'

'Get it then!' Aziz had bellowed. 'Get the bloody tattoo.' He'd jumped off the sofa and pretended to be a screaming fan, reaching up to touch me. I let him pull me down. We sang out the rest of the song like we were in the terraces and it was our club's anthem.

During the fade out, I said, 'I'm getting it. I'm bloody getting it. I can be impulsive too. In your face, Rach. Not so "a-fray-duh-of-uh-chay-nudge" now am I?' I looked at Aziz. 'I miss her.' Aziz nodded. He scratched at the ugly scar on his neck, from the bike crash. I looked at my hands.

I threw the 2 jars of chutney in the bin defiantly. We shook on the tattoo and then, when Aziz was in the loo, I rescued the chutneys and put them back in the fridge, hiding them in the vegetable box where he would never think to look.

That was last night, I think. Today's going to be different.

Aziz has left the flat and I'm checking through Twitter – no replies to my bogling tweet, just some chatter about a recently dead obscure musician, everyone's coming out of the woodwork and saying they love her – and then through Facebook, to see what my wall message is – it's a reminder from the organisers of the event I'm doing with Hayley Bankcroft to increase numbers by promoting it to my networks. I ignore it. I DM Hayley back and say, 'It's been ages … since I got fresh air. Expect barnacles on ol' Kitab.'

She DMs me back almost immediately: 'Till then, Barnacle Bill the sailor. I'll see you down by the docks. Xx.'

No other new interactions. My cousin Veena has just bought a new car. The numberplate says V33D33 – her initials, and accidental comment on her lifestyle.

I need to get up and write something. I check my bank balance on my phone. It's not what it was yesterday, which was not what it was the day before and so on. It's still the most I've ever had in my account. I am burning through the inheritance and when it's gone, and that is a matter of 3 months away, 4 if I live off leftover chutney and force Aziz to actually buy some food, there's nothing else. I'm not a privileged trust-fund boy. When I told my dad I was quitting the job that I hated to become a writer, he said he was going to give me my share of my inheritance now, as insurance that I didn't become destitute. I took it. The sad truth was, I had been caught printing my book off to send out to publishers. This, coupled with my internet usage, meant I was asked to leave. Luckily, I'd finished the book by then. I wrote the whole thing at work on a Google Doc.

Dad worried about steady income and, being an accountant, made me work on 3 or 4 cash scenarios with him, covering every income-related eventuality. I was able to convince him that I could always find bar work while I looked for a job if I needed to. He wasn't disappointed, he was apprehensive and mentally prepared himself to lend me emergency money if ever I needed it. When he transferred over the chunk of my inheritance, he specified that it was for a rainy day, in case the writing full-time thing didn't happen. I was immediately grateful because I was days away from getting a bank loan or a secret job in a pub. It couldn't have come soon enough. The book didn't really sell. Thank god for Mum's life insurance policy. I live off my inheritance. Not for much longer.

In the absence of having anything new to write, I spend 20 minutes looking at my CV, last updated 3 years ago. I have nothing new to add to it except a link to my Twitter profile. Which I take off an hour later, because if they looked, and saw the amount I tweet, they might not see me as a solid bet.

I scroll through Facebook. I click on the photos of someone I used to work with, Anne. She's just been to Majorca. I'm hoping for some bikini shots. There's one but it's a selfie so not too revealing. The rest of the photos are her looking sunburned next to her boyfriend. She's still hot. Hayley has changed her profile picture from her beautiful face to a picture of a cartoon penguin. Hayley's book came out the same time as mine. Her book was on a big publisher, mine on my tiny one, but we were booked at a few events and got to know each other. People want her attention all the time because her book was funny and cutting about male/female relations in a digital age and she gave good banter and probably a little because she's beautiful. She has approximately 3 times as many Twitter followers as me.

I head to YouPorn and look up 'plump' and 'chubby' till I find someone who looks real enough to watch. I don't want cartoonish today. I want real. It may be my, the entire world's, daily tick, but I can retain some sense of diversity. I watch as a static camera records a couple 'doing it'. They start off by looking at the camera in an approximation of what they think porn stars do. They awkwardly remove each other's clothes and fall into the patterns, Porn Grammar. But because the camera is grainy, this feels more like watching 2 real people. It feels like an actual rendering of the infinite intimacy at the heart of a couple making love, in tune with each other, in love and unable to contain themselves. The video finishes and asks if I want to watch a related one called 'Anal fisting POV'. I close the window.

On Facebook, today's context-less motivational message from my dad's brother, a mustachioed former disco dancer who has sent me 47 invites to join WhatsApp in 3 months, is an Aum symbol with: 'WHEN the sun is over your head, there will be no shadow; similarly, when faith is steady in your head, it should not cast any shadow of doubt.'

It links to www.inspirationalvedicquotes.com. I delete it from my wall.

My cousins and aunts and uncles all signed up to Facebook en masse, so they could turn online into one endless family reunion. I've met 20% of them. And that 20% I see less than once a year. They spam me with messages, invitations to apps, endless likes and 'hilarious' videos. First they had mobile phones, then they had Myspace and now Facebook. My cousins signed up in the first wave and were slowly joined by aunts and uncles. Now they interact with me because we're family and it's supportive of them to 'like' what I do. I cringe because once I'd written a book, I'd tried to be a bit more about selling myself, and that's hard to do when you're reminded you're a son, a nephew, a cousin.

There's a private message from a friend I rarely see called Cara. She asks how I am. She's messaged me to say she's annoyed I missed our Skype dinner. She knows I was online because I was live-tweeting a rant about chutneys and my Skype was on but set to 'busy'. Cara lives 45 minutes away by tube but doesn't meet up unless it's on Skype. She does this thing called Skype Dinners, where you cook some food and eat together online. It's supposed to be like a dinner party. I didn't do it because I feel weird about knowing someone has a full screen of me chewing. Cara's developing a site, like ChatRoulette, but for the dinner party aficionado. You create a profile, listing things you like to talk about, what you're looking for – a date or a conversation or to meet interesting people – whether you want politics, or humour, or life-affirming and then you're matched with someone you have dinner with. It's still in beta test because she can't attract funders.

I click 'hide request' on the other Kitab's add friend notification.

I have a job interview with an American internet company. It's for a community manager position. I would work from home and get to travel to Portland once a year for a global team meet-up. I've been asked to look at their website and be brutally honest about it, because part of what I will be doing will be working with developers to create a better user experience. After we've done our pleasantries and I've tried to impress the American interviewer, Lou-Anne, with my English accent, she asks me to tell her a bit about the website and my thoughts. I'm nervous. I don't know how to talk intelligently, sell myself, make me seem like a viable candidate. At the same time, I need the job, so I have to. I try to be as enthusiastic as a Skype call can allow me.

'Well,' I say. 'I like the way the interface allows for a granular approach to the user experience.'

'Mmmm,' Lou-Anne says. She wants me to keep talking. I don't know what to say.

'The thing is, with the landing page, there's a real need for authenticity. Authenticity is important online. People feel like they trust you more if you're authentic. And this feels authentic.'

'What's authentic about it for you? Tell us what we're doing right and maybe tell us what we could be doing better.'

'Well,' I say. 'The whole thing feels like ... like, I logged into this website when I was having a look and the first thing I see is an empty shell. That empty shell is a reminder that we're alone online unless we make connections ourselves. We have an innate desire to create our own immersive journeys. But to do that, we need a proactive approach to content aggregation.' I'm saying words at this point. I applied for this job because I can use Twitter. I don't know what I'm saying.

'Right,' Lou-Anne says. In a clipped way. 'That's interesting. Great to hear your thoughts,' she says with an inflection that makes me think she doesn't care for my thoughts. There's a silence. And then:

'What else? What about the filter mechanism – is it aspirational enough?' I look around the screen for a filter mechanism. All I see is the empty shell of an account I signed up for 20 minutes before the interview.

'Well,' I say, nervously. 'The greys are very slick.'

'Kitab, I'm going to stop you there, and let you know: we just spent a quarter of a million dollars redeveloping our site ... for a chewier click-through matrix full of snackable content. In terms of the ideation and its agility in the marketplace, I suppose, yes, that is a nifty grey ...' She stops talking. I smile into the calendar and stare at the picture of me, my dad, Aziz and Mum on my noticeboard till it blurs. Lou-Anne waits for me to respond.

I spend an afternoon tweeting in-jokes with other writers. Mostly with Hayley.

We're trying to write out the plot of *Midnight's Children* using only gifs. So far, we're only on chapter 2.

I trawl Facebook for what's happening with my supposed 'real friends'. They have been out to places and taken photos of what they had to eat and drink. Who knows if they really did, or perhaps these are stock photos. I 'like' a random selection, just to keep a presence.

I check Dad's account. He's recently added 6 new females and has been tagged in a photo by his brother, in which he's falling over in the garden, drunk. I post a comment on it, saying 'Ahhh, my role model', and my uncle replies. We go back and forth about my dad's antics – dating and drinking – until it turns nasty and I'm accused of being judgmental. My uncle comments: 'Your father has worked hard in his life. Why can he not relax without his son getting high and mighty? We are all on a journey, Kitab-beta.'

I look at the fridge and know there's nothing in there I want. Beer. Cheese. And the chutneys. Those fucking chutneys. Aziz eats all his meals out. He doesn't have anything I can steal.

I notice that Rach has decided to join Facebook. And add me, I might add. I look through her feed. There are a few photos and I'm in attendance at all the events they were taken at; they were when we were together. We look happy. We're smiling, laughing, dancing, cuddling, in one we're kissing, but this captured intimacy doesn't feel like something I've experienced. I stare at the photo of me kissing her and it doesn't look like me. For one, this Kitab looks happy. I remember that night. It was my birthday 3 years ago and we had ended up at our flat, shoes off, dancing to reggae. There was a limbo competition. I won. I'm surprisingly good at the limbo. I think about tweeting 'I'm surprisingly good at limbo', but I don't.

There's a few comments from people welcoming her: 'finally?!?!>>!'. That's it. She has made no declaration of her reasons for joining or what she likes or dislikes. She is simply there. Lurking. Watching. It's weird that she's on here. One of our main arguments was her 'Black Ops' aversion to technology, meaning she didn't have a mobile phone. She couldn't understand why we couldn't make a plan and stick to it; she wasn't signed up to any social networking site. She didn't have email or Facebook. 'Why can't we just phone each other on a landline and make an arrangement and keep to it?' she would say. She worked in a job that didn't require constant email access. You had to be present with her. And bloody hell, that was hard.

I go into my Documents folder, into Admin, and then into CV. In CV there's another folder called D323. It's got all my camera phone nude photos of Rach that I promised I'd deleted. I look at the one of her with her bra hanging off her knee, her foot up on the bed. It's a sideways shot. She covers her right breast and down bits with this angle. I zoom in until the pixels blur into flesh-coloured squares.

I get a Facebook event invite from Rach reminding me about her birthday then a private message from her apologising for including me in it. She asks me 'How are you?', and even written down I can hear the emphasis on the *are*. I don't reply because fuck her for not understanding how social media works. She was constantly irritated that I spent my time self-promoting on the internet and living off my inheritance instead of giving her any attention.

She once told me, 'I hate how you're never in the room with me. Even when you're in the room. You're just on that bloody phone making lazy self-obsessed quips about nothing.'

'It's just fun, this big online conversation.'

'What about our conversation? I'm in the room.'

'I just think it's amazing, having this global audience to interact with.'

'What? And tell them all the stupid things I say?'

'You are funny.'

I used to mock her on Twitter. I thought she didn't mind. People found it funny.

Example tweet: 'My girlfriend pronounces the B in subtle but calls submarine sumarines.'

I had changed the focus of the tweet slightly to make her look stupid. At the time we had been walking through a village in Devon, making fun of words with silent letters, saying them to each other slowly, like 'E-NOO-GUH-HUH' and 'GA-HOST'. We were falling about laughing, and it kept up for another hour till during lunch, when, while Rach slowly finished her sandwich – she was such a slow eater, it was almost cute – I tweeted.

My dad replies to my text asking if he's okay, saying: 'Of course Im ok. seeing you tonight. Please shave. I would like to see my son's face.'

Aziz, sensing my inert hangover, emails me a motivational message to get me writing. 'If you are the Captain of a sinking ship, the best example you can set is to get off that ship as soon as you can. Really, you should be the first off.'

I shave. As my stubble comes off, I remember why I've kept it thick in recent months: it's to disguise the bloating of beer and pizza in my cheeks. I look at myself in the mirror. Apart from the bags under my eyes and the beer gut, I'm doing okay,

I think. I compose an email to Rach. I don't send it.

Eventually, I've wasted enough time to justify opening a beer. As I close the fridge, I see another chutney that I've never opened before. It has Rach's handwriting on it. It says mango, lime and cumin chutney. I close the fridge on it.

aZiZWILLKILLYOU episode 2
Aziz vs Tattoos
[posted 8 September, 11:02]

People, there are 3 rules that apply to all tattoos ...

1. If you get the name of a loved one tattooed on your body, you will break up with each other.
2. If you design the tattoo yourself, chances are it's not good enough to go on your body.
3. If you think your tattoo is unique, it definitely isn't. If your tattoo is unique, it's most likely shit.

AMIRIGHT?

Take it from Aziz. This shit is gospel. Matthew, Mark, Luke, John and AZIZWILLKILLYOU gospel.

So guys, something weird happened last night. I was talking to my brother, Kit, about getting a tattoo. I want one. I've never had one before. I'm definitely the kind of crazy motherfucker who needs a crazy motherfucker tattoo to make him look like a crazy motherfucker. But those 3 rules I listed, they always stopped me. And, why mess with perfection? Innit? My bro Kit's already declared he's going to get an ironic 'job description' tattooed on his forearm, the sensitive artist. But anyway, we were chatting.

I was saying I should get a random word like 'sparrow' or 'erudite' tattooed on my bicep as a talking point. Conversational lull? Wanna mystify some beanie in the pub with something vague but talking-pointy? Flex your biceps and wait for the enquiries to pour in.

Because, then people'll be like ... why does it say that word? And I'll have this amazing story prepared for them. So, Kit and I are discussing words.

'Sparrow,' I was like, yeah, weird word.

And he was like, 'Why?'

And I was like, 'It doesn't matter. That's not the point. It's a talking point.'

'Yeah, but neither of us know what to say about it.'

'True. Erudite?'

Then Kit was like, 'And what?'

'And what what?'

'No ... and what?'

'What do you mean?'

'I mean ... and what?'

'What the words ... "and what?"?'

'Yeah ...'

'That's pretty cool. What about an ampersand and a question mark?'

'Pretty cool.'

'Not cool enough.'

And then, it hit me. When he came back from the fridge, I was like, 'I have the answer.'

'Hit me,' Kit said.

'I'll get my favourite t-shirt. On my chest. That way I'll never lose it, shrink it, or ruin it. Think about it, I'll always be dressed. In my favourite t-shirt.'

Kit laughed.

'Imagine,' I said. 'People who confine their tattoos to where they can't be seen when you're wearing a suit – what if they got a tattoo that smartened them up?'

'Like workwear tatts?'

'Exactly. You gotta be smart for work, right?'

Kit said, 'I wonder if you could get a tattoo of a tie? That way you're always smartly dressed.'

'Nah, man. That would be annoying over your belly. Especially if you put on weight. It'd look stupid,' I said back.

'No, mate. A bow tie. Imagine a bow tie tattoo. You would be so dapper, mate. Do you think anyone has ever had a bow tie tattoo on their neck?'

We Googled it. Why not? We're modern men. And what

is the smartphone if not the thing that means conversations never have to descend into bullshit? We have every answer at our fingers. I'm only too happy to look up bow tie tattoos, because if there is one out there, that person is my new hero. All my heroes are either stupid or brave. I typed 'bow tie tattoo' into my phone's search engine and tapped 'GO'.

I hit the image search and there, courtesy of the internet, were photos of a surprisingly diverse selection of people with bow tie tattoos. Some with bow ties on their breasts, some with bow ties on their forearms but only one where an actual bow tie would be.

'That's me,' I said.

I handed the phone to Kit. Fourth picture into the image list there was a thumbnail of a man who looked remarkably like Aziz. This guy was wearing sunglasses I might wear (aviators in a new rave hue), a black wife-beater, a wicked shit-eating smile, Chico Dusty chocolate skin and the same spiky hair that's been poking up between girls legs round my way for the last 15 years. The same nose. The same wide-eared 'YESSSS BLUUUUUD' grin. And a red bow tie. Tattooed under his neck. Where a real red bow tie would be. I clicked on the thumbnail and it took us to a larger photo. Kit moved to sit next to me. We stared at the screen, dumbfounded looks on our faces.

'Are you thinking what I'm thinking?'

'No,' Kit said.

'I'm doing it. That's me. I have to do it. I owe it to this

19

me.' I pointed at the phone. I pointed at the scar on my neck. 'It's time to cover this malarkey up.'

'That's not you,' Kit said.

'It could be me. From the future. Apparently they can do that now with the internets.'

We examined the contours of the bow tie tattoo man's face. The closer you look, you realise it isn't me.

'It's bloody odd how similar we are,' I said.

'That's the power of the internet,' Kit said.

'What do you mean?'

'The more we're allowed to Google search stuff, the more we realise we're not special.'

'Oh, shut up. There's no one like Aziz. And I'm getting a bow tie tattoo.'

What do you think?

There are 8 comments for this blog:

Muderation: DO IT

Philo Savvy: Yes, cosssssssign. DO IT.

MichaelMcArthur: Seriously? WTF> You cray, Aziz.

Decarp: Someone just tweeted this blog and it's nuts. Wait

– you're gonna get a bow tie tattoo cos someone else who looks like you has one? Yes.

Philo Savvy: Pics or STFU.

AZIZWILLKILLYOU: I've been thinking, this is definitely happening people. Not only am I getting that tattoo, but I'm hunting that fuckface down.

KITABWILLDESTROYYOU: Go to bed. Stop stalking people online.

Decarp: Go Aziz!

History:

Tattoo disasters – Google
Spying on people's Facebooks – Google
Best Asian author – Google
Jhumpa Lahiri hot – Google

It's Friday night (my dad's usual slot for me – Friday for the children and friends, Saturday for the ladies) and I'm sitting in our favourite Indian restaurant waiting for him to arrive. When Dad shows up, he is dressed in a silk pink shirt, a leather jacket that goes past his waist, and black trousers. The only thing missing is some crocodile shoes. Instead my dad is wearing the omnipresent black Nike Air knock-offs he's been wearing for the last 20 years, which keep his now-mangled feet breezy and comfortable. I once bought him some proper Nike Airs but they're boxfresh, unused – 'unused to my feet', Dad said. His feet are now moulded to the shape of the inside of these cheap versions. He is holding on to the remnants of his sparse, thin, silky silver hair by growing around the bald crown a fine mane as long as possible.

'What's new, kiddo?'

'Rachel wants to be my friend on the Facebook.'

'She wants to be back together? Good, I like that.'

'No, just friends on Facebook.'

'Why would she do that? Unless she wants to be back together?'

I don't reply. We both snap poppadoms.

Dad spoons onion onto his shard and I stare at the bubbles on mine, before dipping it in the raita and crunching down, grimacing at the sugary yoghurt.

'Thank you for shaving. You know? Your face looks fat. Why is your face so fat? I need to work on this beer belly so I can get more dates, eh kiddo?'

When my mum died, when I was young, he went through a decade of wearing a fleece jumper and tracksuit bottoms, going to work in the same warehouse and coming home and eating the same food watching the same DVDs of the same Bollywood songs he and my mum listened to. It was a decade of mourning. Then he retired, and quickly realised how much of a social animal he is. He goes out 4 nights a week, wakes up in the early afternoons hung-over and watches old films till it's time to go out again. He is basically me in my early 20s. Wednesday and Thursday nights, he props up the bar in his local Indian pub, watching cricket and counting masala peanuts (finely-chopped onions and chillies mixed in with dry roasted peanuts, drizzled in lemon juice and chilli powder) as dinner. Fridays and Saturdays are date-nights for him. He only ever has dinner with me or with a lady. And because he's the type of guy who stands on old-fashioned ceremony, he will never let his child or a lady pay for dinner. We eat for free.

'Son, I am happy to see you because you are my son, but going out with guys is no fun,' he says to punctuate a silence.

'What do you mean? You can talk to me about football, girls, whatever you want ...'

'I go out with people to have fun, not talk. I want to flirt, to dance, to eat with a knife and fork.'

'You can do that with blokes. Why do you need to date girls?'

'These are not dates. They are my friends. The girls are all my friends. Because I take them out, we eat good food, listen to the music, and dance. And they laugh at my jokes.'

'Because you're paying to take them out.'

'Why must you make me feel like they are my prostitutes?'

'Because you make it sound like you pay them to let you take them out.'

23

'Well, kiddo … I'm old-fashioned.'

'And it is the oldest profession,' I say, spooning onions into my hand and throwing them into my mouth.

I feel, as I always do at these dinners, the unsettling pressure to be my dad's best friend as well as his son. Dad used to have 2 close friends whom he did everything with. They watched every sport going, from cricket to the World's Strongest Man, drank together, played cards, even worked together. Now those guys have retired and moved to Dubai, leaving my dad to date and take me out for dinner. And be a barfly.

He finds friends of friends, divorcees or widows who want to be taken out for dinner and a dance and he uses them for company. He pays to take them out and they give him company. He has rules for prospective partners. He's trying to protect himself from history repeating. He doesn't want to outlive another partner.

My dad doesn't ever want me to come to see him in our family home, probably because he thinks the sight of all the kebab cartons and empty beer cans, dirty bathroom and unwashed dishes will probably send me into a panic. I think of the state of my flat … Rach's chutneys filling the fridge are the only civilised things left about me.

Dad will dress up to visit in one of his 3 silk shirts and come and see me in my part of town because he thinks it's buzzy (he describes it as a 'carnival atmosphere') and filled with beautiful women. He's always disappointed to learn that the crowd is rarely, if ever, middle-aged single Indian women looking to be wined and dined, only thin boys and girls not bothered by our presence in the slightest. Still, he pays. And it's near my house, so I'm happy.

Dad, when first looking for a new girlfriend, set himself some rules and parameters. He laminated them on a card to stick in his wallet as an aide memoire. They were: she must be younger than me; healthier than me; Gujarati Indian but, not

24

too traditional or religious; able to dance; tell jokes; know how to cook (and he goes on to reel off a list of my mum's signature dishes). I repeatedly told him in the last year that he's not going to find a replacement for Mum, not least because his parameters are too defined. He thinks, why mess with perfection?

'How is your book doing?' he asks me, placing his hands together in prayer formation, to show me he's listening.

'Okay,' I say, not looking up from the table, as if enthusiasm would indicate failure. 'Sales are slow, but you know, at least it's out.'

'But what is your marketing strategy?'

'I let the publisher deal with it.'

'How can you trust them to market you? You need to determine your market and sell the book to them.'

'Sure,' I say, to shut him up.

'You better be writing a bestseller. One with police detectives in the countryside. One with murders and car chases. Something you can buy in an airport and a supermarket.' He pauses. 'And don't talk about the past this time. No one wants to hear about the past. Talk about now, kiddo.'

'That's not my thing, Dad.'

'You should though. Don't think you have another inheritance coming to you. I'm spending it all now on enjoying myself. So, write a bestseller.'

'Okay, Dad.'

'In fact, you better not be spending Mum's inheritance. You better be earning, kiddo.'

'Yes, Dad,' I lie. 'I've been doing great. Really great.' He doesn't need to know about my job interview. Not until I have news. News that ultimately proves he's right.

When he first signed up to Facebook, as a way of keeping tabs on all the women he fancied in his life, he didn't understand how to phrase sarcasm nor that if he left a comment on my status update, everyone could see it. He used to sign off

25

with 'lots of love, your dad' thinking that each comment was like a letter or email. Then he decided to use my self-promotion on Facebook to remind me that ultimately I had to make money from writing.

Kitab: 'Hey guys, if any of you are in the Luton area, I'm reading from my book tomorrow.'

Kitab's dad: 'Son, I hope they r paying yr travel because this is an expensive ticket. R U getting paid? I saw yr bk is £2.46 on Amazon. What % r u making frm this? Lots of love, your dad.'

When I put up a link to my novel on my status, my Facebook friends would 'like' it or maybe even say 'congratulations' and 'can't wait'. He'd troll me by saying, 'Can I buy this in Tesco? Tesco is the only bookshop worth its salt.' Then when my book came out, he said, 'You should make something that can be adapted into a film. Maybe I will read it then.'

A couple of years ago, when the film version of *The Girl with the Dragon Tattoo* came out, he left me a comment on my wall saying, 'I read this Girl with A Dragon Tattoo book in 3 days. I still have not read your book. What does that tell you, son?'

His Facebook comments get 70% more likes than mine ever do. People prefer him to me. When Dad first joined what he calls 'the Face Book', it was all he talked about: its politics, its new language, its potential for stalking, and it bothered me how much he wanted to converse with me about its intricacies. I hate talking about social networking in conversations.

'Kitab-san,' Dad says, playing with his new smartphone. 'While you were in the toilet, I just *liked* this photo of a girl on Facebook. She's in a bikini. I cannot unlike it. She looks too porky. I don't want to give her wrong impression.'

'Dad, do we have to talk about Facebook?'

'Come on, Kitab-san. I joined the Face Book because it's the only time I see you.'

'Do we have to talk about Facebook though? My father is the one person I hope I'm free from that rubbish. You didn't add me. So, I added her. Are you following me back? What's on your mind? What are you thinking? LOL. ROFL. "Like". These words mean nothing anymore.'

'What is a ROFL? I have not come across this.'

'Dad, don't you worry our language is changing? That we're as concerned with how to socialise with people digitally as much as physically? That language is dying? That everyone is using these bullshit words to mean new things they don't?'

My dad looks at me, chewing.

'It means rolling on the floor laughing.'

He swallows, nodding to himself. 'This would have to be a very funny thing. To laugh out loud, we have all done this. But to be rolling on the floor. I am happy that at least it means you now speak the same language as your Indian cousins. You don't have to pretend you know Gujarati anymore.'

I watch him funnel shard after shard of poppadom, slathered in chutney and onion, into his mouth, chew loudly and talk slowly at the same time. He keeps his nails long, and years of turmeric abuse have turned them yellow. He starts telling me an anecdote about his Friday night. The anecdote boils down to, I went to this bar and it was full of people half my age and the beer was expensive and I couldn't hear anyone talk – but the way he tells it, I get the s-l-o-w version. I stop him mid-story so I can check my phone, which has chimed with a Facebook message. It's from the other Kitab. Kitab 2. It says 'Did you see my add request dude? What's taking so long, same-name-buddies!'

Why is he messaging me, the weirdo? I stare at it trying to think of an appropriate response. I don't know what to say. Can I just ignore it? Dad berates me for ignoring him.

'What is on that phone all the time?'

'Nothing – just messages from the world, telling me they love me.'

'I got a new phone. A Samsung. You should try it. Better than this iPhone crap. Cheaper too.'

'I'm fine.'

'So, tell me about you, Kitab-san.' Dad once worked for a Japanese company. He now calls me and all his male counterparts 'name'-san. Unless he's giving me advice, in which case, I'm 'kiddo'.

'Oh, you know … I have this book reading this week where I …'

'You know, I found this restaurant to go to with one of my lady friends. It's called Strada. Heard of it?'

'It's a pizza chain.'

'Any good?'

'It's a chain. They're all of an equal standard.'

'No, this is Strada of Knightsbridge.'

'Yeah, Dad, it's a chain.'

'Well, I'm going to take Roshi there for dinner.'

Our food arrives. I Instagram the curries in their steel dishes and upload the photo, adding the caption, 'Dinner with my dad. He pays for the food. I pay for my lack of achievement. We both pay for the over-indulgence in the morning.' Dad hesitates and then dives in. Hayley comments on the photo: 'Delish x.'

I reply: 'I'm with my dad. Rescue me.'

Dad is rarely keen to know what's going on with me, and that's fine because half of it he wouldn't be interested in (emails about things that don't emerge; short stories for magazines he'll never read, that I never read; ideas for self-promotion) and the other half is not for his ears (my lack of earnings, my lack of social or sex life, my lack of consistent happy mental state). Whenever I used to talk to him about my sadness about my mum, he used to tell me I had no right to grieve as much as him because I've only lost a mother, whereas he's lost a life partner. I argued that a life partner was replaceable while a mother wasn't. He would say, 'Wait till I introduce you to your new stepmother.' Since the last time, we don't talk about my mum anymore because I don't want him to know about my grief and he doesn't want me to think he's a depressed alcoholic anymore. He drinks a lot. And not just quantity of booze, but quality too. I worried for years he was a functioning alcoholic. Able to go to work hung-over and not able to enjoy an evening till the first whisky and soda had been downed. Every night sat listening to his iPod of sad Bollywood songs, a bottle of vodka next to him. He told me once, 'I try to drink enough so I don't dream. Because my family is in my dreams all the time. I don't want to see them. I don't want to see what I've lost.' He lived on vodka and whisky, and takeaway food. Along with the various medicines for his ailments, every morning, he'd take 2 ibuprofen for his hangover. My concern led me, in the darkest part of our grief, to take him to an Alcoholics Anonymous meeting and depressed by the stories from people indistinguishable from him, he laminated a card that said 'Remember to no longer drown your sorrows in a bottle' and stuck it on his liquor cabinet. Which was effective because it got him to go out more. Which pleased me no end because I had bought him the laminating machine as a Christmas present 7 years ago and he'd finally found a use for it.

I laughed to Aziz that what I'd done was effectively said: getting drunk every single night and crying is not good; going out and getting drunk every single night, on the other hand ... well, that's just the rest of the country, mate. Aziz's attitude was, 'Leeeeeave it, bruv. Let papa have fun. He worked 7 days a week for 50 years.'

'This one girl,' Dad says, laughing. 'She is violent. I tell you. I said to her, if you want us to go out again, maybe lose some weight, eh?'

I can see chunks of naan in his teeth.

'Dad, you can't say that, it's horrible. It's sexist.'

'It's true. She asks to share a garlic naan with me then eats all of it? No way, kiddo. No more sharing for me.' Dad shoves a large piece of garlic naan into his mouth to illustrate his point.

'Maybe she was being romantic.' Dad laughs with his mouth open.

'Why did she punch me in the stomach for calling her a fatty then, Kitab-san?'

'I don't know.'

'Look her up on the Face Book. Her name is Pinky Marjail ...'

I am part disgusted and part intrigued. What if my balding-fatter-older-version-of-me dad is North West London's premier player, swimming in 60-something gash. What a guy.

'Should I be on Tinder?' Dad says, looking around. I don't answer him.

I swig from my undrunk glass of red wine. Dad insists that a dinner isn't complete without an accompanying glass of red wine – we never drink it, neither of us is partial. But damn, do we look classy eating.

I go home that night, feeling something nervy and burning in the pit of my stomach. I assume it's a mixture of eating hot spicy food quickly and my nausea at my dad's singledom. I'm glad he has someone he can talk to freely and easily. I wish it wasn't me.

A bus goes past. My head turns when I think I see someone I know on the top deck. Except it's just some Indian guy and I'm not sure where I recognise him from.

I walk into the flat. Music starts up and Aziz is on the kitchen table bellowing at me, using a banana as a microphone.

'I'm giving you a looooooong look,

Everyday, everyday, everyday I write the book.'

I wake up the next day and check my emails – only notifications. I tweet: '2 nights ago we found my bro's doppelganger online. I'm still creeped out.'

I get no interactions. I click onto a Tumblr. Someone I follow on Twitter is taking a photo of the nape of her neck for 365 days, documenting it from normal to love-bitten and so on. The photos, all fleshy white nondescript stretches of skin, are hypnotic and the day-by-day nature of the Tumblr gives me a forward-thrust in my own inertia. She gets a lot of love-bites.

I'm making breakfast and staring out of the window at the bathroom of the house at the bottom of our garden, hoping to glance someone, anyone in the shower, opaque pixels of pink flesh, and listlessly stirring porridge when Aziz comes bounding in. He fills the room with his energy and he moves around the kitchen in loaded silence. He smirks audibly. He hovers over me. He leans back against the counter. He reaches over me for things, breathing quickly.

I unenthusiastically ask him what's up, knowing that whatever he tells me won't wake me from my hangover – Aziz and I finished off my Budvars when I came back in last night, and then moved on to rum, and my head's pounding. He and I have mutually exclusive moods this morning. But thankfully he has work to go to and I have an inheritance to burn through while pretending to work on my second, all-important novel. I'll probably go back to bed with my laptop and a pre-downloaded cache of illegally acquired American sitcoms and dramas to keep me company till I fall asleep for my mid-morning thinking nap. Or look at videos of American college girl parties and feel sad about male pack mentality whilst tugging at myself.

'How was Dad?' he asks.

'Fine,' I reply. 'Same. Exactly the same.'

'He ask about me?'

'He's only interested in his own life,' I say, and Aziz nods. He looks around the room for something to distract us. He sticks his finger up.

'I wanted to tell you last night but you fucked off to bed. I've found him. His name's Teddy Baker, like the suit makers and he

31

lives in Brooklyn, and I need to get out of the flat more, man. I've babysat you enough. Time for Aziz to get back on the adventure train. So, guess what? I booked a trip out to go find him. I'm going to surprise him. I'm going to New York. The dream, Kit. The dream is happening. I'm going to bloody New York.'

'What are you talking about, Aziz?' I ask, my mouth full of cereal.

'The bow tie tattoo man. I did some Googling when I got in last night. I found another copy of the same photo, but this time with his name as the file name and that led me to his Facebook page and his Twitter stream. Sorted. The guy sounds wicked. He likes dubstep, he LOVES *The Wire*. I like dubstep and *The Wire*. Peas in a pod, Kit. Peas in a motherfucking pod.'

'Why are you going to visit him?'

'I need to populate my blog with content. I did that one post and then nothing for months. I'm stagnant before I start. I just need something to write about. A proper adventure. And tracking my doppelganger down might be it. I mean, it's better than what I was thinking of doing … I was considering doing a photoblog of my manscaping everyday for a year.'

'Sounds like a dumb idea. He's just some guy off the internet. He could be a weirdo. He's probably a weirdo,' I say, gripping my temples. My stomach churns at the thought of Aziz leaving.

'This isn't 2001, when only weirdos and perverts and *Dungeons and Dragons* were online. Everyone's online now. Normal people. Secretaries and estate agents. And quantity surveyors. Who's more normal than a quantity surveyor?'

'And people want to read about that?'

'Yeah, but it's about the journey to find him, about tracking him down … that's the entertainment.'

'Google destroyed the journey, man. All you have to do is look him up on Facebook and boom, journey over. Message him – he either says, yeah man, stop by or fuck off weirdo and boom, end of journey … over,' I say, not wanting him to go.

'Kit, man … it's just a laugh. I haven't had a holiday in for ever. I've never been to New York. Mimi lives there now and I've got unfinished business in her pants. Why the why not?' Aziz says, opening the drawer where the painkillers are. 'New York's the dream.'

'I dunno. I'll miss you. You never go away.'

'Bruv, if I'm not around, you can't use me as an excuse to not write. I'm going. It's for both of our goods. I get to bang Mimi and have the most legendary time, and you get silence. No distractions.'

I cover my nose and mouth with my hands so Aziz can't see I'm frowning.

'When you going?' I ask, wondering how I can talk Aziz out of it.

'This week. After I've got my new tat. I'm getting the bow tie.'

I look at Aziz with a mixture of pity and confusion. 'Why? Man, it's not a good look.'

'Buddy, it's the one. It's the one of ones. It's the one most toppermost of the poppermost. I want it. I want to turn up at Teddy Baker's yard with a matching tattoo pulling the same shit-eating grin and I want to film his reaction. Wanna be my camera man?'

'I can't, man. No money,' I say, hoping my financial plight will cause him to stay. I can't afford flights to New York. How else will I be able to afford beers and frozen pizzas?

'Little Lord Fauntleroy starting to feel the pinch?'

'Little Lord Fauntleroy needs to put his CV together today so he could find some B2B journalism soon just to keep steady income coming in.'

'Sorry, man,' Aziz says, rubbing me on the back. I stand up and walk to the open drawer with the painkillers. I take 2 out and dry-swallow them, hoping they'll kick in with immediate effect.

'It's alright. I should have written something better.'

Aziz claps his hands to signal the moving on of the conversation.

'Well, remember to finalise your tattoo designs. I booked you in.'

'I don't think I want a tattoo.'

'I hate your hangovers, they're always so full of regret. You're so boring. This is why I need to get away. This funk. This funky stench. This funkington manor.'

I'm walking down our local high street staring at the gentrified ghetto of vintage shops, hipster bars and pound shops, marvelling at the busyness and bustle of 10 a.m. on an unseasonably chilly early autumn morning. Who are all these people and why aren't they at work? Part of me realises that the innate nature of the hipster *is* not being in gainful employment but running about sorting out installations, video shoots and drinking coffee and talking about meta-collaborations. None of these have any place in a conventional office.

I tweet: 'If the innate nature of the hipster is to avoid jobs, what do they do for money when there's no installations to be done?'

@kitab: 'They all suck each other off and roll around in piles of their parents money'

@kitab: 'burn socks'

@kitab: 'Develop Eating Disorders ;)'

I record constructions of a series of nothings in either chronological or flashback order. I string together a few similes like a hack and I send it to my agent and they will either 'like' it and 'share' it or unfollow me. Either way, I'm stuck in a rut of nothing. I don't really appreciate what I do, why should anyone else? I used to read so much. I used to sit in cafés and read. I'd struggle to eat with a knife and fork or with my hands as I navigated sentences on a page. Now that's all been replaced with thinking of arch things to tweet, twitpic'ing my lunch or making up overheard conversations that might make people laugh.

I tweet: 'Im in a café & this girls like to her boyfriend "Jamie, I wish you hadn't fucked me in the arse so hard. I cant stop shitting myself." ZOMG.'

@kitab: 'LOLZ'

I get 13 retweets and it didn't even happen. It gets 4 favourites. Even Hayley tweets me to say: 'We're reading together this week! Haven't seen you in ages, blud. See you at @welovebooksbitches!'

I think I see someone I know sitting in an internet café. I realise it's just another Indian guy with an oily side-parting.

It's inevitable I will get 'Everyday I write the book' tattooed on my forearm. Maybe drunk me knows me better than real me.

I got a tattoo of a bow tie on my neck today.

My brother, Kitab. He got a job description on his forearm. He's a writer so 'Everyday I write the book'. It's so analogue. It's so meatspace, innit.

Anyways, I woke up my man Kit with some Buck's Fizz. Got the guy proper high so he don't back out. Then I did some push-ups to really tone up my neck and chest, because if man has a neck tattoo, man needs to rep it proper, seen. So anyways, anyways, anyways, I passed out. Don't mix alcohol and weightlifting, my friends. It's a dangerous business. I'm finally getting rid of this ugly stupid thing on my neck. This scar from when I was a kid.

We headed to Sick Charlie's for the tattoos. This guy is a proper swagatha. I argued with Kit all the way cos the dickhead wanted to pay with a cheque. He's got some royalties due but still, act like you know, you know? Wear this process with pride.

'Chequebook?' I scoffed.

'Yeah, I need it to clear in 5 days. I get some money in about 5 days.'

'What money?'

'I get that 80 quid from the Guardian for the best Asians in fiction article.'

'Sell-out.'

'Yeah, I know.'

'Still? A cheque? You're so 1997 about things.'

'1997? That's the advent of the cheque in your brain?'

'No, well ... you know ... chequebooks. It just looks a bit lame. Charlie, the tattoo artist'll think you're a mug.'

'Oh right, so you're worried about me looking uncool in front of a tattoo artist.'

'Hey, the cooler you are, the more likely they are to do a good job.' That right, right? Tattoo artists have to do a lot of work. Imagine if they think you're cool, they'll put in the extra 10% to make it 120%.

Sick Charlie's tattoo parlour is too cool for school, my friends. Picture a tattoo parlour in your head. What you're imagining resembles the outhouse of a biker gang's gang hut. Where all the crystal meth and bukkake happens. This place was like a hipster design studio, innit. Everything was angular. There were so many angles, you'd think it was an isosceles triangle. There were iPads to read or watch the iPlayer on while you wait. The magazines in the iPad newsstand were Playboy and GQ. The music playing was loud, up-tempo high-pitched hipster indie ... you know the song ... nee-nee-nee-nee-nee-noo-noo-noo-noo riffs, thumping kick drums. White boy tunes. There was one chair for the one tattoo artist and the mirror was lit by a floating orb, suspended from the ceiling on a transparent string. The chair itself looked straight off the set of Sweeney Todd. Meat. Meat. Meat. Branding meat.

Sick Charlie, he was malnourished thin, no arse to speak of, no visible tattoos, a pointed floppy fringe and dead eyes that told you whatever you're thinking, he was 'already over it'. Every time I see a white boy like this, I always wonder how he balances on a toilet with no bot-bot. What do the girls have to stare at when he walks away?

I Instagrammed the place and added 'Double virgin skin with @kitab'.

I went first into the chair and I watched as the bow tie was sketched onto my neck. It itched on my scar. Sick Charlie kept telling me it was going to be fine but there was one bit, the bottom of the gullet that might hurt a bit. I was like, bruv, I don't care, I'm really drunk, and Sick Charlie laughed because you're not supposed to get tattoos when you've had booze because your decision-making might be impaired and because they tend to bleed more. I told him I'm joking. But the reality was, Aziz had been drinking – we necked 3 bottles of beer from the fridge before leaving – and I'd had 2 Lockets and one packet of Monster Munch to disguise the smell, because Sick Charlie takes himself and his work very seriously. And some onion chutney. There is a lot of onion chutney in our fridge. But that's another story for another time told by another person, innit.

When Sick Charlie started the actual inking, I looked at poor lost little Kitab, sat there watching me like his master's voice and I was like, 'This is gonna be an hour, why don't you step out for a bit?'

38

Kit stared at me and I shrugged and close my eyes. Miraculously, 3 pints in, I fell asleep in the chair.

But when I woke up, I looked like a champion. It hurt like a motherfucker, the red of the bow tie and the red where I was bleeding didn't really mix well together but fuck it, I stood up a champion. I gave Sick Charlie a cuddle and told him he had done fine work. I look like a baller, a pimp, a motherfucking amazing Spider-man or some shit. I look like Teddy Baker. I look the best.

Looked like the wait was too much for little Kit too, so I woke him up. And then I fucked off into the night because there is nothing that can contain this guy right now.

Comments are disabled for this blog.

History:

Should I banter with my tattoo artist? – Google
Girls tattoos nude – Google

When it's my turn, I stand up and walk over to the chair on autopilot, as if this whole lark isn't my decision anymore. Sitting in the chair, I feel like I'm halfway between barbershop and dentist's office. So, somewhere between tensed up and relaxed down. Sick Charlie asks to see the design again so I show him the printout. I found a font online I like, it's called Bell Gothic, and typed up 'Everyday I write the book' in it, printed it out, and now that's in Sick Charlie's hands. He inspects it. I'm not sure I like this guy. He does not give 2 shits about me. I wonder what he's thinking. He's seen a lot of tattoos in his time. He has an opinion on each one, hot or not. Will he put extra special effort into the ones he likes and just emptily, by the numbers, do the ones he thinks are so-so, okay, and pretty shit? Does he just rush through the really bad ones?

'What do you think?'

'Yeah, man. All good.'

'Do you get it?' I say. Everyday, I write the book, I think to myself. It's a political statement. I could pitch this to the *Independent* or the *Guardian*. 'In a world of digital interactions, endless tweets, Facebook haikus, ebooks, I'm taking a stand for the analogue world. I'm feeling the writing on my arm, my writing arm and that's how I will write, with the knowledge that I have etched out my statement of intent on my own skin. What's more meatspace than having something tattooed on the meat of you? Everyday, I write the book. It's there for ever, it's permanent. You can't throw it away. You can't dispose of it. You can't delete it. You can't cache it. It exists. When every word typed on Google is recorded on a server somewhere, this is the most important statement of them all, the physical manifestation.' I take a breath. 'Plus my dead mum was a really big fan.'

I stop talking and Charlie stares at me.

'Right, okay.'

He returns to ghosting out the tattoo on my forearm in marker pen. He's doing a great job of copying what's on the paper. I chose the font because it looks futuristic, like some signage from Tron.

'So,' I ask. 'Seriously, what do you think?'

Sick Charlie looks up at me and grimaces. 'Look, do you want this or not? Because we're about to be at the point where it's too late.'

He looks at the clock. It's nearly office closing time. Maybe he has a hot date tonight.

'Hot date?' I ask.

'You don't even know the half of it,' he says, not looking up from the copy job he is mimicking on my forearm.

Great, I think. I'm a rush job before he goes to get his end away. He doesn't care about this tattoo, whether its kerning looks good or whether its execution is considered and thought out. I'm in the punter zone. I am to shut up and be inked. I look around the room. Aziz is nowhere to be seen.

'Did you see where my brother went?' I ask Sick Charlie.

'What?' He just looks at me and shakes his head.

Then I see Aziz at the door. He's outside, looking for a light for a cigarette. A girl walks past and he mimes to me that he's going to get a light off her. He winks as if the light is just starters for what he has in mind. He throws me a thumbs up and disappears.

'Ready?' Sick Charlie says to me. He holds up his machine and suddenly it occurs to me – I can't do needles. They freak me out. They make me pass out. They make me sweat. They

41

make my skin slick with worry and anxiety. How did I not remember that needles were part of this whole thing? What was I thinking? I'm an idiot. I turn to the other side of the room and nod furiously, tensing my arms. Sick Charlie pats the area he's working on, strokes it and pulls at it. Which might be comforting but he's wearing rubber gloves. So the whole thing feels like a medical procedure. And the drill-drill buzz of the machine is whirring away, banging and banging and I can feel it, without looking at it, approach my skin. I can feel it hone in on the spot it's to attack and reconfigure for ever. I can feel it approach me quickly. Heat all up and down my arm. I can hear it pound and pound in its grooves and then connection – impulse, pow. It scratches furiously from side to side and I hazard a look. I take a peek, just a quick peek. I see it happening, all in reddening, dampening close-up. So I close my eyes. This only focuses the scratching. I open my eyes and I see the apex of Sick Charlie's head as he squints and bends over my arm, working away. I'm nearly straddling him. I try to make my arm as loose and goose-like as I can. But all I can feel is the scratch-scratch-pinch of the gun and it's hard to concentrate.

Do we talk? I'm not sure of the etiquette. My dentist is monologue-happy, meaning he'll natter away with his fingers in my face. My barber, the sexy Swedish girl or her colleague, who is very tactile with the backs of other customers' necks, they can't shut up with their other clients, but me, I don't know what it is. As soon as I get in the chair, they clam up. They ask me a few awkward questions about how my week has been and I answer them amiably and ask about their weeks and they monosyllable me. Why don't they want to talk to me? Maybe they can sense that I just want them to ask me what I do for a living, so I can say 'Oh, I'm an author' coyly and await their being impressed. Because that's part of the whole doing something creatively full-time and semi-successfully, you get to tell people that's what you do, and never qualify it with 'Oh, and I have a day job at the council, reconciling council tax receipts'. Nope, you're the creative thing and that's all. Barbers don't seem to care about that. God, it vexes me. I just want to show off. Why won't they let me show off?

I look down at my arm. He's not even finished the first 'E'. We're in it for the long haul.

There's not much you can do to inspire banter in a tattoo artist's chair, because you don't want to break their concentration. Eventually, the scratching becomes an uncomfortable irritant, rather than a painful blat-blat of needles. The thumping indie's more irritating than the irritating scratching on my arm. It's jolly. It's up-tempo. They sound young and happy. What the hell am I doing? Who gets their first tattoo at age 30? A guy who thinks he's younger than he is. That's who. It's okay for Aziz because it's just the sort of behaviour you'd expect from him. But squeaky ol' me? Nope. I barely stay up past 2 a.m. I've never done drugs except for the odd doobie toke that didn't take. I worry that this is a slip towards something more serious. I'll end up trying crystal meth. I'll buy skinny jeans. I'll start taking my fashionable self seriously, ditching my uniform of jeans and t-shirt for something more transient, like espadrilles. This is all wrong and it's too late. Because if I back out now, I've got the start etching of an unfinished tattoo and if there is one thing I'm consistent at, it's seeing shit through to the bitter end, even if I've decided it's a stupid idea since. What a complete tool. The scratching on the arm is constant until he has to move to a new area, which hurts because these new parts of skin have to get used to the procedure that's taking place. He never looks up at me. It seems like he's rushing. Is he rushing? I don't think he's rushing. Probably. How do you know? What is an appropriate amount of time to spend on a lowercase 'v'?

When Sick Charlie finishes, he gives me some saline solution to use to keep the tattoo clean. He wraps it in cling film and says to me, 'Leave that on overnight, while the skin is still inflamed.'

'Okay, thanks, man. Good job, etc,' I mumble, trying not to focus on the irritated burn on my arm.

'Does it hurt?'

'Yes.'

'That'll pass. You slept through the worst of it.'

'This isn't the worst of it?'

'I could have done anything while you were asleep.'

I can see the letters exactly as I printed them out and I think, yes. Okay, that's dope. I like that a lot. I think I look amazing. I shake his hand, rather limply, because my newly tattooed arm is attached to the hand that shakes. And I say my goodbyes, struggle with getting my coat on, which is a shame because I'm hypnotised by the ink. All I want to do is look at it and get drunk. I open the door and I feel it coming. This is it now. My life is about to change. Oh yes. Tomorrow I will show strangers and loved ones and I will say, oh yes, it's because I write. It's an aide memoire to always be thinking about literature. It's a kick in the teeth reminder that I am a writer. And it's a good tune, I will say. People will inevitably ask, do you like that song by Elvis Costello and I will say it's one of my favourites. It's not. I like it. But it's not one of my favourites. Depending who they are, I'll say it was my mum's favourite.

I leave the tattoo studio and phone Aziz. It goes straight to voicemail. The same stupid message he's had since we were kids. I leave him a breathless message saying how amazing my arm looks. I feel bloody alive, I think to myself. I was sceptical at first but now it's here and it's done and it's indelible, I feel like a fucking rock star, and I'm already a writer. What more could I want? This is definitely going to make my life change, I think to myself. There's no way it cannot.

aZiZWILLKILLYOU episode 4
Aziz vs Teddy
[posted 10 September, 14:02]

Tomorrow I leave for New York, people. I leave to go find
the man who inspired this image here.

You know? My last holiday was never, right? When does a
man like Aziz have time for a holiday? Answer: everyday
should be a holiday. So ... time to hit the road, innit. Time
for adventure.

I got a bow tie tattooed on my neck and now I'm off to go
find the boy with the bow tie tattoo. Know why? If I think
I'm an individual and the internet thinks we're all alike, I'm
going to go find my doppelgangers. All of them. I've found
one and I need to see exactly how he fits the Aziz profile.

- Does he like sandwiches?
- Does he think life is for the living?
- Does he eat everything with his hands?
- Has he had a threesome?
- Will he have a threesome with me and some girl, so we
  can create some sort of infinity pool effect on a spitroast?
- Is that disgusting?
- If it is, is that okay, because we all know why you visit
  this blog, right?
- Will the world implode if 2 doppelgangers have a threesome?

All these things need answering. I'm off to find my doppelganger with the cool-ass tattoo, find out exactly how that

45

tattoo came to pass and I am going to show you the world, shining, shimmering, shameless.

Stick with me kid. We'll go far.

Comments are disabled for this blog.

History:

Meeting strangers off the internet – Google
Hayley Bankcroft – Twitter
Hayley Bankcroft – Google images
Kitab Balasubramanyam – Facebook

I wake up from a dream where Aziz follows me around a shopping centre with a toothbrush and toothpaste, telling me it's time to brush my teeth because my breath smells of chutney.

I listen to Aziz singing to himself from bedroom to shower to kitchen to bedroom. I walk into the kitchen and switch the kettle on. I open the fridge. There's no milk.

I sneak a look at the communal iPad, left on the kitchen table. He's left his browser open on Teddy Baker's Facebook profile.

Teddy Baker's profile avatar is a close-up of his face, which, sans shit-eating grin and sunglasses doesn't look so much like Aziz. There's no obvious reason for why this brown guy has a white name. Bow tie aside, he looks ordinary, solid, just like one of the guys.

He lists his likes as 'vigilante justice, weapons, Megadeth, PVC, abattoir politics' but that's it. The rest of his profile is sparse to the public. He has 'liked' Taylor Swift and the NRA. I hope ironically.

Aziz catches me from the doorway peering at his laptop. 'You fraping me, bro?' he asks.

'Frape ... what a lovely reappropriation of the word "rape". Because outside of Facebook, making it look as if your friend is saying weird stuff is pretty much exactly what rape is.'

'Mate, it's just LOLZ.'

Aziz started off saying LOLZ in conversation because he thought it was funny – I had told him about Cara once Skyping me, me making a joke and her saying wearily, 'Oh … LOL, etc.' Aziz said she was a linguistics genius. Now it's become a grating habit. I've long since given up trying to get him to stop.

'Yeah … tell that to a rape victim,' I say and leave the room to brush my teeth.

'If I blog about the trip, do you promise to read it?' Aziz asks me over breakfast. 'So you can follow my adventures?'

'You're still going away then?'

'I've called the tag "The Boy with the Bow Tie Tattoo". You know I have to go.'

'Catchy,' I say dismissively. If he goes, who'll look after me?

'Will you tweet about it?'

'You hate Twitter.'

'I don't hate Twitter. I've just got too much game for Twitter. Who cares about breakfasts and live-tweeting reality television. I just want people to read my blog. This is a writing thing. I want your respected followers, the writers and editors and whatnot, to know what I'm up to.'

'Why would those ponces care?'

'What? Don't all your illustrious boring literati peeps like laughing?'

'Not if it's over some tattooed hooligan stalking a stranger off the internet. I'm a serious novelist now. Only serious novelist tweets.'

'You're right. I'll use lots of metaphors,' Aziz says, thumping the table.

'Who cares what they think?' I say, knowing in my heart of hearts that I care and thus wouldn't want to associate myself with a bro/lad challenge for fear of loss of credibility points from the spurious few who bestow them.

Aziz's bow tie tattoo is cartoonish. It's huge. It covers the whole of his neck. He has chosen a thick red, like it's the filling of a Jammy Dodger, like it's jam, in fact. It covers up the scar, which probably makes it look darker and richer. His skin is smoother and newer in that part of his neck. It's a proper dinner party bow tie. He looks like a clown on his day off.

Aziz grabs my arm and stares at my tattoo nodding furiously. He's done this 3 or 4 times this morning. He tells me repeatedly to Facebook it, tweet it, Instagram it. I say no. I don't want any of my family to see it. Or Rach.

Rach would have hated me getting a tattoo. Her and my dad. I feel like I'm 14 again, a rebel, a maverick on the edge with nothing left to lose. She has a tattoo of a rose on her foot. She got it when she was a student and regrets it. She avoids wearing flip-flops to ensure no one can see it. I once joked about getting a matching one and she punched me on the arm, hard. She's not the boss of me anymore. And I always thought the tattoo was cute. I'd trace it when she was asleep. The game was to not wake her up by tickling her.

Meanwhile my family rule Facebook. It's become their standard method of communication. When I first joined up, I was indiscriminate about adding people on sites like Facebook and Twitter. You never knew who you might stumble across: girls you liked, people you went to school with, possible networking opportunities. Also, I liked the idea of amassing numbers of people. It was addictive. Like heroin. A numbers game heroin. I got more discerning when the influx of my family arrived. When Dad joined up, and started adding middle-aged females and tagging me in his posts to them as his 'son', and I got a glimpse of who he was dating beyond abstract retold stories, I actively started looking at other sites my family hadn't adopted. I love Vine.

There's no way they'd let this tattoo slide. They interact with my every status update. Even with them on a family list, with restricted viewing, I know them – they're too good, they'd find me and my tattoo and tell my dad. Even on the internet, you can still feel like an 11-year-old naughty boy.

Aziz puts his bowl in the sink. 'Right,' he declares. 'I need to get ready for New Yoik. What happened to you last night anyway?' I look at his back. I have minutes to make him stay. I have a reading tonight. I need him there. I haven't done anything except go to the pub and the shop and the toilet. This is actual 'outside' business. I can't breathe. I look at him.

'Nothing, man. Absolutely nothing. I left the tattoo studio with the express intention of showing people my ink. I tweeted a picture of my arm wrapped in cling film.'

'You didn't Facebook it though?'

'Nope. In case Dad saw it.'

Twitter was a safer haven in that my family was far from the zeitgeist, even though, counting all extended Indian relatives, I was related to enough people to stage an invasion of a small country. I deleted all the emails I'd received in the last few hours and prepared for my new life. I saw a Facebook message from my namesake asking 'Add?!', which I ignored and prepared myself for a night out I'd never forget. I ignored it because I felt guilty about not accepting his request. Dad called. I sent it to voicemail. Listening back to the message, he sounded drunk, saying something about 'life being a journey' – a misquote from what his brother had posted on my Facebook wall. Maybe they crib their Vedic quotes from the same website.

Going out with cling film on your arm doesn't have the same impact as having a living, breathing tattoo to show. So, last night when I left the tattoo studio, instead of going to bars with my sleeves rolled up, I went to try to find Aziz and ran into my friend Mitch, who was always at the same pub every night, sitting at the bar, reading paperback fiction written by great middle-aged American men. Mitch admonished me for getting a tattoo.

'Aren't you a sight for sore eyes?' he said. I smiled.

'Good to see you, Mitch.'

I met Mitch at a book reading I didn't know anyone at. I was going out most nights and reading the same passage that would form the opening chapter of my book. I was anxious and hungry then. Mitch approached me afterwards and offered to buy me a drink. He gave me some editorial advice on my book, which I thought was pushy, but he did have a drink for me in his hand. Since then, he's always been around, very supportive. Mitch thinks the end is nigh and the backs of his ilk will be the first against the wall.

'But' – he likes to remind me – 'I'm the last generation of actual fighters. Any nerd tries to replace me, I'll box his ears.'

'It's been a while,' Mitch said, blowing hair out of his eyes. 'Where have you been? Post-break-up solitude?'

'Something like that,' I replied, shrugging. As my arm lifted up, Mitch saw the contour of my tattoo.

'What have you done? Is this your post-break-up statement? A tattoo? You cliché. You're an idiot,' he said. 'Nay, a blithering wannabe-trendy idiot.'

'Yeah, well … my brother made me do it.'

'Brother? It is all go, isn't it?' he said. He paused. 'Did you see the Samuel Beckett YouTube thing I put on your wall? It's hilarious.'

'I was busy dude, sorry.'

'That's you all over, Kit … you have a book out and you think you're Samuel Beckett. You've changed.'

Mitch believed in only maintaining real relationships online. His Facebook friends were family and friends he knew. He was nothing like Aziz, who encouraged me to be a numbers whore to help spread the word about my work.

'Bruv, truss in an Aziz,' Aziz would tell me. 'The more friends and followers you have, the more interactions you create. It's all about interactions.'

Mitch was just offended I would let people in on my private life.

'Sorry, Mitch,' I said. 'I very rarely go on Facebook. It's become a quagmire of familial oppression.'

'Why have an account?'

'Because my family might be the only people who ever buy my book,' I said, laughing. I looked around the pub. It was loud. There were quite a few drinkers. It felt okay being out. Just fine. I laid out the statistics for Mitch. 'I have 843 Facebook friends, I am related to 207 of them, am good friends with another 234 of them, leaving 402 people I am acquainted with. The numbers don't add up. That's a lot of interactions, a lot of posts, a lot of Mafia invitations. So sorry I missed your Ginsberg thing.'

'Beckett,' Mitch corrected me. 'Wait. You have 234 close friends? I don't think I even know 234 people in the entire world.'

Mitch is my favourite person to hang out with apart from Aziz because they represent opposite ends of a spectrum. I'm either destined to be an over-confident buffoon like Aziz or a curmudgeon like Mitch. He is balding but still carries a comb in his blazer pocket. That vintage attitude is why I like him. I may find the concept of hankies revolting, but I'm glad for him having one. He's Friendster in a Twitter universe, dial-up in a web 2.0 second life. He is my meatspace. Mitch likes to talk about the good ol' days. I've missed him these last few months.

'That's cos you're a barfly.'

'Very true. But 234 people?'

'Maybe I need to cull some people,' I admitted.

'You definitely do,' Mitch said and shook his head. He went outside for a cigarette.

I could easily get rid of 400-odd people, I thought. I could reclaim my space. I could hide the 'add' button too. Make it harder to approach me. The only 3 requests in my 'add' folder were 3 people I didn't know or have mutual friends with. And the only 2 people in my folder labelled 'pending requests' were

Kitab 2 and new-to-Facebook Rach. *Now* she wanted to be friends. I'd left her hanging.

Mitch came back, stinking of fresh cigarette to add to the dull ache of old nicotine ingrained in his sports coat. 'The reason I hate modern life,' he declared, loud enough for those around us to hear, sermonising, 'why I love books, is all this bullshit you're saying ... that's what we're reduced to, isn't it? Etchings and imprints ... Connections used to be important. Now it's all selfies and sandwiches on Twitter. Now the very meaning of the word, it doesn't mean shit. Associations have some weird cultural capital now.'

'Innit,' I said, to purposely undercut him.

'Did you get a friend request from Rach?' I nodded. 'You know she has a new boyfriend?'

'You're Facebook friends with Rach?'

'Oh, yes. Dunno why you don't go out anymore.'

'She dumped me. She said because I was a self-obsessed depressive.'

'She does have a *joie de vivre* you don't really do ...' he said, downing the rest of his pint and signalling for another 2.

'I'm going through a lot of stuff, man.'

'No need to act like a bore about it.'

'Anyway, what's your problem with Twitter?'

'I don't "do" Twitter. It's all pictures of sandwiches and misspelled signs, no?'

'Only for those who don't use it properly.'

'That's what your feed is full of ... Anyways, I hate how we're all diminishing circles of actual friendship.'

'What?'

'All your followers and all your Facebook friends know your every movement. Your real friends know what you're like. Where's someone who knows both?'

'That used to be Rach. But then she hated it when I was always online.'

'Look at her now. She can't get enough of the stuff.'

'She's a social animal,' I mumbled. 'Just another content queen.'

When I got home, I Googled Mitch to verify how off-radar he was. It didn't take many search results to discover Mitch had a secret blog that no one knew about, called 'The Weird Shit People Say to Me'. Of the entries, 3 could be attributed to me. I don't mind.

'I'm really excited about this trip,' Aziz tells me as we're sitting in his room. 'I packed your camera, for the posterity.'

'It is effectively yours. You use it all the time.'

'How else can I document my lifestyle? No one would believe me otherwise.'

'Just keep it,' I said of the unwanted present Dad bought me Duty Free when he returned from a singles holiday to Prague last year.

'Yeah, you can't frame a decent shot.'

'Decent framed pictures do rule the world.'

'If only I could Instagram some of those sexcapades. The world isn't ready.'

Aziz has packed enough underwear for a week, but only 3 t-shirts, because they're his coolest. He bought a black vest that resembles the one Teddy Baker's wearing in his photograph. He and I debate the word wife-beater. He ends it by telling me to man up, which irks me into a sulk. I then ask whereabouts in New York Teddy Baker lives.

'Well, it says Brooklyn on his account,' Aziz says, lifting his suitcase up and down like he's weight training with it.

'Wait, you didn't message him?'

'Nah, man, that's part of the surprise.'

'You're going to just turn up? He'll think you're weird.'

'Part of the challenge is getting through the awkwardness and getting to be best friends,' Aziz says, downing his tea.

'How do you know how to find him? You know New York's pretty massive, right?'

'Dude, give me some motherfrickin' credit. I Googled him. I found his Facebook, his Twitter, his Foursquare and his Linkedin. I know where he works right now. I can see where he checks in on Foursquare or just follow his Twitter. Mate, I'll find the guy. All I have to do is turn my wi-fi on.'

'And your data roaming off. I ain't helping you with another mobile phone bill.'

'That was different. That was phone chat lines.'

'Yeah, I'm not helping you pay another mobile phone bill because you're too much of a dick to use your phone wisely.'

'Fine, anyway, stop making this awkward for me. I was excited till I spoke to you. You know, Kit, you're such a hangover depressive. You just gotta smiley face up. Smiley face up.'

Aziz points at me. I force a smile.

'Yeah. Sorry, man.'

'What's your 5-point plan for your new tattoo? It's new tattoo day. Today your life will change, just a little bit. And it'll be fucking awesome.'

'I dunno, get some breakfast, do some writing. I got a reading later. Whatever.'

'Okay, so have you made a list of fit and female acquaintances you can impress with your tattoo? Have you made a list of places people might approach you and say, wow, that looks cool. Is that Hayley going to the reading?' Aziz raises his eyebrows at me, waving air glasses up and down.

'It's not just for pulling girls. Is it?' I say. 'And yes she is.'

'And now you're finally single.'

I panic. I show him my arm. 'Should it be so red?'

I show Aziz my arm. There are some inflamed red rings around the tattoo. He dismisses it. 'Just put some moisturiser on it. It'll be fine.'

Sick Charlie has given me nappy rash cream to quell the burn so I put that on. I've expressly been told that moisturiser isn't great and petroleum jelly is worse. Aloe vera or baby rash cream is best for soothing 2 hours of skin rubbing. It burns a little. Just like an inflammation. It's fine.

We hear a car horn beep twice outside, signalling the arrival of Aziz's cab I called for him. I don't want him to go. Last night was the first night I've not hung out with him in 6 months. Who's going to keep me entertained? He wants to go. I don't want him to go. I could ask him to stay. He probably won't stay. He's doing this for my good. Stop distracting me. Give me time to write. He clutches me and gives me a long slow cuddle. We have this thing where you hug and the first one to feel awkward or break the cuddle for the sake of practicality loses. Currently I'm losing 172–4 to Aziz. But I hold on because he's my brother and I feel protective over him and he's an impulsive funny man and he's off to do something slightly stupid but I respect his desire to see things through.

And hell, at least he doesn't sit there and over-analyse for an inordinate amount of time. Except he's still holding on and I'm worried the cab will leave without him and we'll have to wait for another one and he'll miss his flight and it'll be because I didn't let go in time. I pull away.

'You better get your cab, dude.'

Aziz smiles, crosses over to the chalkboard next to our fridge and changes 172 to 173. Damnit. I've been hustled.

'See you man,' he says.

'Please take care and don't do anything stupid with a bunch of strangers you found off the internet,' I say, grimacing.

'Read my blog,' he says, throwing his hands out and waving them jazzily at me. 'I'll be back soon.'

'Come back with both your kidneys.'

'Promote my progress on Twitter.'

The cab beeps again.

'Keep your passport in your pocket at all times.'

'Blog comments are always welcome too.'

'Just go.'

'I'm going.'

'I love you very much, Aziz.'

'I know.'

The cab beeps its horn again and Aziz picks up his Eastpak and my suitcase and heads to the door. Instead of watching his cab pull away like a proper surrogate dad would, I go to the toilet and stare at myself topless in the mirror, trying to ingrain the new 'me' into my mind's eye. I spend the next hour with my phone trying to take the best casual selfie of my tattoo for Instagram. Outside a car keeps sounding its horn before eventually leaving.

aZiZWILLKILLYOU episode 5
Aziz vs Stalking Prey
[posted 11 September, 16:10]

Word up homeys, it's your boy Aziz. Welcome to my new blog challenge – meet The Boy with the Bow Tie Tattoo – my doppelganger. So pay attention closely to the breakneck speed with which I do questionable things with questionable people. Because that's what life's about. Living questionably.

I am revitalised, blaaads, like a bottle of mineral water or whatever. Revitalised. Revitalising.

There I was, on the hunt for the Boy with the Bow Tie Tattoo. Just like that Swedish guy in that book where he's looking for some stripper with a dragon tattoo or something. I don't know. I never read. Well, I do – and my main man, Kitab has sent me off with some books, but I haven't got time to read them. I am on one tip only. One mission. The Boy with the Bow Tie Tattoo.

I'm gonna skip the part about the flight because who wants to know about what films I watched (Limitless aka Shittyless, and Rango aka No, Mate, Just Go – thanks for asking), what the food was like (I'm Indian, I grew up on thalis and plates with compartments, what can I say?) and how much I slept (not at all, man's buzzin'!). But I will tell you one thing about aeroplanes … if you spend the departure lounge time eyeing up buff girls and hoping you get to sit next to them so you can be all like, 'hey hey hey' and they'll be all like, 'wanna meet me in the bathroom', IT WON'T HAPPEN PEOPLE.

You will end up next to some fat dude who is mister elbows and he's borrowing your window, leaning over you and dipping his tits in your complimentary white wine, or some old lady who'll take her shoes off and put her stinky feet up on the seat under her like it's her manor. You gotta put that out of your mind and you will end up next to a horny travelling goddess. Trust Aziz. It's foolproof. I know. Cos I ended up sandwiched next to some fat dude all elbows and wouldn't let me borrow his window and some old lady who took her shoes off and tucked her stinky feet under her on the seat. Every now and then. I'd feel her big toenail catch on my jeans. My jeans! What the hell? Or WTF as you kids like saying.

Acronymns. MIAWFOA. Man, it's a world FULL of acronyms.

So, I landed in New York, and I got through customs after having some LOLs with the customs guy. Because I like to put my terrorist face on, get all screwface and serious and see what he asks me. And the dude was like, Aziz, is that a Muslim name? And I was like, hell naw, man ... Just because I appear to be from the Indian sub-continent that immediately makes me a Muslim? COME ON. Asia's got more countries than America's got states, check yo'self, racist fool – what? That is a geographic fact. And eventually he let me through.

I could not wait to get to a wi-fi signal, so I could check in with Teddy Baker and see what was going off in this dude's life. It was cold, man. Like cold-cold. And I was braving it with my jacket unzipped and my shirt opened just a little to show my badass bow tie. I can only wear shirts now cos they go with my fly-fly bow tie. Anyway, I keep getting away from it. I was bussing to get to a wi-fi. Plus I was ti-ti.

59

And then, it kinda just opened its legs and ejaculated all over me from a distance. There it was – New York, New York. And I was like, dude, this city is majestic. I love this place. It's full of everything – tall buildings, vulnerable girls trying to make it in show business, Spider-man. I was on the subway next to some dude who was writing battle raps on a yellow legal pad and 2 girls talking about some guy's choad and I got all excited so I grabbed my phone out and did a data dump. Eff you roaming charges, I am a man on a mission. Roaming this world, looking for the best adventures only your boy Aziz can have.

So I did a data dump, and seriously, all my emails are about stupid fucking bullshit on Facebook – I have one Facebook mission, get my friend Steve's mum to unfriend me. GET. THE. MUMS. OFF. FACEBOOK. Steve's mum just likes everything I do and adds all these stupid applications to my wall about flowers and she has asked me a question about 'my secret love' and that's all she does on Facebook. I met her once, at Steve's engagement party and now she thinks we're BFFs so she just adds an endless stream of bullshit to my Facebook. Anyway, so I checked into Twitter after my disappointing email scan-through and I see Teddy Baker's account. I'm wondering whether I should start @-replying him stuff just so he can see me and get prepared for Aziz-ma-geddon. I might go to the Statue of Liberty and pose for the same photo as his now infamous avatar, but you know, Instagram it with the Earlybird filter, just to make it classy, and make it my avatar. Cos Teddy's avatar on Facebook and Twitter is now just a picture of his face, and without the sunglasses and world-beating grin he doesn't look as much like me, which is a bit disappointing. But it's all about the tattoo, guys. You know? I'm all about that tattoo.

His Twitter said that Teddy was at work but I followed through a conversation he was having with a Twitter user called @justiceforpigs and they were going to meet up at 7 p.m. at a bar in the East Village, and both had to bring things for the other, like Teddy owed @justiceforpigs a book and @justiceforpigs wanted Teddy to see this new outfit he'd bought. Who knows? Maybe they're lovers. I will find out, blog fans. You know why? I'm going to some bar in the East Village at 7 p.m. Tonight. This is happening.

There are 9 comments for this blog:

Anonymous user: LOL

Geraint365: SRSLY? You're a stalker. WTF.

AZIZWILLKILLYOU: Yo, Geraint, if that is your real name, fuck off my blog if you don't like it.

Geraint365: Duuuude, I was joking, innit. Calm down.

AZIZWILLKILLYOU: Safe, blud. Strap in.

Milky_Sorez: This is exactly the problem with the internet. Over-enthusiastic fuckwits like you who can't write. Get over yourself hombre. This is shit. Who gives a fuck? Like, 2 people? And I've listened to your Mixcloud sets. Heard of dubstep? No, I didn't think so. Seriously, this is worse than the worst thing on the internet.

Anonymous user: LOLZ, AZIZ YOU LEGEND.

Gustave_the_First: This point seriously puts human rights into question. Aziz, I've only just come to your site because

61

I was alerted to it on Twitter. Legal issues aside (I'm a lawyer), you are a despicable human being and I hope you get arrested for harassment.

AZIZWILLKILLYOU: WTF, CTFO, MIAWFOA.

History:

We Love Books Bitches – Google
How to do public speaking – Google
[291] – Twitter
[12] – Facebook

I'm walking down my high street and I allow myself to feel good. I never feel good. I never allow myself to enjoy anything. If something feels good, I worry about it going wrong or the next thing to go wrong. The worst thing I can do is feel optimistic, because that's akin to arrogance.

But today, I allow myself to feel good.

Everything about this day smells of possibility and chance. A smell of breakfast takes me to a new café I've not noticed before.

The newsagent stocks one vagrant copy of the *New Yorker* seemingly just for me. A girl smiles at me as she gets off the bus. I get a tax rebate. For the exact amount of the cost of a new pair of Nikes I saw on the internet. It's going my way today. I catch myself in the mirror because once I get back to the flat, despite the autumnal chill outside, I wear a t-shirt and stick the heating on so I can see my tattoo.

I'm doing a book reading later that night at a bar in Shoreditch. We've been asked to read our favourite party anecdote, so I've prepared something about a night I spent out walking the canals with Aziz where we planned to find freaky sex parties on boats and failed.

I pack up what I need to read and some books to sell. I walk outside. It's freezing. I am braving the cold so there's more chance people can see my new ink, so no need to layer up. But it's freezing. I crave hoodie. I crave thermals. I crave warmth.

I walk down the high street, against the contraflow of returning commuters, victorious in their ability to survive another day at work. I wonder if they've achieved the same amount of work as me, except with shielded screens and covert clicking back onto spreadsheets: watched YouTube videos, snacked, clicked through every single social network available; replied to emails as promptly as possible to indicate work efficiency and manage a total concentrated work effort of 55 minutes or so. We all spend our working days looking forward to our next meal.

My phone rings. It's Rach's number. I ignore it. She calls again. I let it ring in my pocket. Undeterred, she calls me again. This time, my impulses can't let a ringing phone go unanswered. Must connect. I answer.

'Can't you speak to me now?' She sounds pissed off for being ignored. The first time I hear her voice in 6 months and she sounds angry with me. Nothing has changed.

'No, I'm out. I'll call you tomorrow,' I say.

'Out, well, that's good at least.'

'Glad you approve.'

'No, I just think that's a really good thing, you really needed to …'

'Is that why you called, Rach? To have a go?'

'No,' she says. 'I was just thinking about you. I wanted to check you're okay. I worry about you. And nobody's seen you. I worry about you being on your own.'

'Well, I'm not on my own.'

'Oh. Good. Who …'

'Look. I'm fine,' I reply. 'I don't need your worry. I'm a fully functioning adult.' I hang up the phone.

I have an @-reply on Twitter. It's from Hayley. It says: 'See you in a bit. I'm running late. Looking forward to it whisky buddy.'

I tweet her back: 'Pre-pub-dutch courage. Join me if you can?'

I reach the pub. Mitch is at the bar on his stool and nods at me. I salute him with 2 fingers to my temple. Mitch, reliably, is always finishing a drink when you arrive, meaning the first round is always on him.

Mitch asks how my day has been. I tell him that my brother has gone on holiday and apart from that and the internet, I've achieved nothing. Mitch knows better than to ask about my second book's progress and the first one's fate. Both are constant sore subjects. I say nothing. Mitch can sense I'm not feeling talkative. I wait for my pint in silence.

I have the jitters for my reading later. No matter how many times I stand up in front of a group of various strangers, I still get nervous. Which is good because complacency is the public speaker's end game. Mitch asks me my thoughts on a few new novels he's read recently. I give answers that would indicate I'd bothered to read them. Truth be told though, since Rach broke up with me, all I can stomach is bad American sitcoms and Tumblrs of arty shots of naked females. Being dumped has brought out the lazy reductive sexist in me. Nothing else registers. I can't be bothered to read. It was out of the blue. I wasn't expecting it. I expected routine from her. I expected us to hang out and eat food and watch movies and make fun of people we knew. I expected us to cuddle and talk about our days and make hot drinks for each other. But now she's gone and it kills me.

'I like it,' I reply to a query about one such book. 'The middle's a bit long.'

'You are so wrong,' Mitch bellows. 'The whole thing is a lazy hack's version of metaphorism.'

'Is that a word?' I ask.

'Well, your tattoo's still shit,' he says, smiling at me.

'Thanks.'

'And you're still an idiot …'

'Why do you hang out with me, Mitch? You hate everything I say or do or tweet.'

65

'I hang out at this pub. You join me. I'd say you're hanging out with me. And I don't know why you do that. Other than for the abuse.'

Mitch walks with me to the Book Doctor, a hipster bar near the pub that has nothing to do with books despite its name. Their official Twitter handle is @welovebooksbitches. I walk down the steps into the exposed-brick basement, wave my way past the pretty middle-class white girl handling the door and I enter the venue. I get a Twitter notification. Someone called @HannahBananaMonana has just tweeted: '@kitab is in the house. Spicy.'

Because all Asian guys are spicy. We all smell of curry.

There are about 20 people in the room, mostly writers and the odd publishing person, an agent or a publicist. The rest are girlfriends and boyfriends and the odd actual fan of people standing up in front of rooms full of people and telling stories in that slow soporific voice.

I greet the people I know with a mixture of pleasantry and aloofness so I can work my way to the organiser, May, and keep the supply of beer flowing. I'm being paid in beer, which is fine because what else would I be spending my money on. I kiss May hello. She says I look different. I amiably ask what's changed. She smiles. I smile back. There's something between us. Definitely. I sit with the other readers, a couple of people I've met before and one I haven't. One of them is the beautiful Hayley Bankcroft.

Today she shows me more attention than ever before and I think, Hmmm, this is interesting – what's different about today? There is something. There is a new energy in her greeting. I haven't seen her since I broke up with Rach. Whenever I was with her at events, I would get the jittery stomach, fluttery sentences and the inflamed skin of a man with a crush on someone other than his girlfriend and a girlfriend called Rach. Now I'm single. And I'm pretty sure she's still single. There is pressure now.

Once we got drunk after I'd done a reading and I asked her why she was single. 'Because I'm in mourning that you're not,' she replied, looking pretend-serious, though I could tell she was serious. We didn't mention it afterwards, probably consigning it to drunkenness in our heads. My memories of interactions with her, real life ones too, are stacked with little moments like that, that could have gone too far, that didn't because I was with Rach. Like the other time when we were walking through the park near my flat. Rach was at work. I had the day to myself so I suggested to her that we go for coffee, and as we walked, she linked her arm in mine and we walked with her head on my shoulder. A casual observer would have assumed we were together. The way my heart was pounding, it's like we were a new couple. And then, there's the time we kissed goodbye, again drunk, because all my stories with Hayley involve boozing, when a cheek-kiss was misfired and our lips definitely touched. I ran home with the energy and fizziness of a schoolboy that night.

Now I'm single, these are now moments to take advantage of. Although, now, there's a pressure to make moments like that happen on purpose.

'You're a beautiful man,' she'd said last time we were together. She was joking about my vanity, because I was wearing a new shirt Rach didn't like and needed compliments, stat. I'm pretty sure she was joking.

'I know you're placating me, but I'll take it,' I replied, watching her face for any sign of truth behind the sarcasm.

We take our seats. Hayley sits with her cross-leg pointing towards me and her naked arm touching mine. She leans in.

'Alright chico,' she says, using our usual names for each other.

'Chiquita, it's good to see you,' I reply, with more bluster than I've achieved before. Confidence towards women. This is a new side effect. 'It's been tiiiime ...'

'I heard about you and ...'

'Rach …'

'That's the one. A real shame. She was so … organised.' She sips on her drink and widens her eyes. She smiles into her glass.

'So where have you been hiding yourself? Have you been writing something new?'

I grimace.

'Well, you look good,' she says, knowing that it's bad luck to ask a writer what they're working on, especially between first and second novel. It's like yelling 'Macbeth' in an actor's face.

'Thanks, same ol' jeans and shirt combo.'

'There's something different. I dunno what. Anyway, sorry about the *Telegraph* thing.'

'What *Telegraph* thing?' I say. Hayley pauses.

I'm only pretending I don't know what she's talking about because that's the aloof thing to do. No one needs to know about my thorough Google Alerts. I know the *Telegraph* refer to me as 'One of those new writers with nothing to say but the pretence of all the style in the world. A fleeting blip in litera-ture's great history of ethnic authors.'

'I suppose it's a humblebrag of sorts,' I say.

'Oh, who cares?' she replies, diplomatically after a careful pause to consider her options. 'What have you been up to?'

'Dodging questions about my second novel. You?'

'I just signed mine to my publisher. It's out next spring. And,' she pauses conspiratorially. 'My mother has signed up for Facebook. Now that's a delight.'

'Awesome,' I say, as if I don't know, as if my Google Alerts don't carry information about my peers and their big deals with publishers bigger than my own. I'm not jealous. 'Get the families off Facebook.'

'There should be a family setting, right?'

'Yeah, I mean, my dad writes LOL on every status I do.'

'I know, I see. He's cute. My mum wrote on my profile picture that I had jowls. JOWLS, Kit.' Hayley grabs my hand and gestures for me to pinch her cheek and neck. I do. Her skin is soft. It smells of berries.

'It feels jowly,' I say, Hayley hits my forearm. I wince because it's on my sore tattoo.

Hayley is wearing brown peep-toe shoes and I'm transfixed by her big toe. It's painted orange. She wiggles it up and down when she talks. She has a very friendly big toe. I look at her and catch her look at my arms and my neck. She smiles and closes her eyes. She grabs my hand.

'I'm nervous,' she says.

'You're always great.'

'I'm not funny like you, though.'

'That's why you're great. You've got stuff to say. I'm just an idiot.'

'Oh shush, you're sweet.'

'Oh ... you,' I say, not knowing how to reply to a compliment.

I get all my funniest lines from the things Aziz says. I reappropriate them and give them a proper narrative arc. He's not here though. 'I'm always nervous too,' I say, and she smiles at me. I hate talking in public. I don't ever dare look out at the audience. That would make me realise they were there. I can't let myself know they're there.

I check Twitter.

'Here for the The Book Doctor Trials. Excited about @Hayleyspen reading. @kitab will bust out his Buddha of Suburbia bullshit for sure.'

'The Book Doctor Trials @welovebooksbitches! @Hayleyspen @kitab @wself #lovereading #literature'

'The Book Doctor Trials are starting. Who is Kitab Balasubramanyam?'

Hayley taps my hand twice to shush me as May, the organiser, takes to the stage to start proceedings. Her attempts to rally a crowd comprised mostly of writers who feel they should be the ones performing mean the evening flatlines before the first reader takes to the stage.

My mind wanders to Aziz and how he's getting on just before I go on stage and so when I'm introduced, my first words are muted as I try to adjust to being in front of an audience.

'His exotic words, his spicy references, his search for identity … please welcome Kitab Balasubramanyam!'

I've removed my coat on the way to the stage and people can see the hint of tattoo coming out of my sleeve and I feel like dynamite.

'Thanks for the introduction,' I say. 'I don't know if you all guessed … I'm Indian. What's up, white people?' I see Mitch in the audience. My heart is pounding. I wish I hadn't looked up. I want to run away. He shakes his head. He tells me I play the race card too much.

No one laughs. I close my eyes and open them again staring at the page, tuning out the 20 people listening to me.

I'm telling them a story about a sex party gone wrong and instead of bawdy laughter and claps, I'm getting stony looks as if I'm a sexist, just because I'm a bloke reading about sex. I'm reading this because I wrote it and put it in a drawer. Aziz found it and read it and said it was too funny not to read out, and by reading it out, maybe I'll become less repressed. I never wanted it to be aired in public. Talking about sex in front of people, it feels too intimate. There's too much focus on the meat and the flesh. I don't like it. As soon as I start reading the story, I realise I've made a mistake. I second-guess how funny I think my anecdote is and rush the set-ups to jokes meaning the punch lines don't make any sense. It feels like I'm up there for 20 minutes longer than I am and the lights are burning hotter as I mosey on down the cul-de-sac of my words. I finish and have to say 'thanks very much, good night' to elicit any reaction from the audience. They applaud politely.

I consign this story back to the desk drawer for eternity. I feel embarrassed. The worst thing will be, because people automatically think you're the subject of anything you write, I'm the priapic guy at a sex party in my story. They won't get that it's about vulnerability.

'At The Book Doctor Trials. Not sure about this Kitab guy. Why do all Asian writers go on about being Asian.'

'@kitab just rocked The Book Doctor Trials about a bawdy Indian sex story.'

'Dude, it says book on @kitab's arm. Check out the pic.'

As I walk off to constipated applause mixed with Hayley's charitable laughter towards the killer punch line I deliver, I wonder why she's finding it so funny. She's so far from jowly it hurts. She's beautiful. Real beautiful. Like unreal and real at the same time.

I'm presented with another beer as I walk offstage. May and Hayley both accost me at the side of the stage and Hayley grabs my free arm. May pulls up my sleeve to look at the whole tattoo.

'Everyday I write the book.'

They both nod in appreciation and Hayley rubs my wrist, 'You were great,' she says, and kisses my cheek. 'Funny story.'

'Was it?'

'Funnier than these douchebags appreciated. What was that line? "The only thing sadder than a sex party on a canal boat on a motherfucking Tuesday is live-tweeting it while getting a hand job."'

'Something like that,' I say, not used to nice things being said about my writing. May takes a photo of my arm and tweets it. Hayley takes a photo of me with it outstretched across her chest. She tweets it. I look around, feeling exposed. I don't like this. I stuff the pages with my story on it into the pocket of my jeans.

'me and @kitab getting freaky at The Book Doctor. Where were you?!'

I can see that whoever is on stage has about 50% of the audience's attention because the majority of the audience is looking at Hayley and May taking photos with me. Mitch walks over and nods. He taps me on the shoulder, 'Well, at least you only mentioned you're Asian once.' He disappears to the bar.

Hayley links her arm in mine and we turn to the stage.

Hayley whispers, 'That's so analogue.'

'Cheers.'

'Hey, did you get invited to Joe's launch?'

'No.'

'Ah shame, man. We should hang out more. Come with me.'

'Always the plus one, never the name on the list.'

'Joe's always saying nice things about you.'

'No, he's not. You know he unfollowed me on Twitter.'

'He said the other day you were a great writer ... what was it? Kitab is a great writer ... no, he said Kitab is great.'

'Great,' I say.

'You know what I mean. Come ...'

'Email me the details.'

'I'll diarise and shit,' Hayley says, laughing.

The satisfaction at the attention is the most I've felt of anything since Rach left. I break into a natural happy smile. I leave May and Hayley by the side of the stage and walk towards the toilet, hoping a hot girl will follow me.

I enter the toilet alone, am doing my business when I hear a voice behind me.

'Ummm, Kitab?' A very Indian, young voice says nervously.

'Yes, mate,' I say without turning round.

'You're him. Kitab ...' he says. 'B-B-Balasubramanyam.'

'That be me.'

I zip up and turn around. I know this man. I've seen him before. He stretches his hand out to shake mine.

'I'm Kitab ...' he says. 'Balasubramanyam too.'

72

Without the white turtleneck sweater, he looks less sinister, more slight, more nervous. Without the laminated passport photo effect, he looks clearer, more real, more like me. My tattoo is itching. My brain is fizzing. My hands are still on my fly. I have to hold on to a urinal to steady myself.

'I know. Bloody fucking hell,' I say, in high-pitched surprise. 'What the fuck are you doing here?' I'm between weirded out and amazed.

Kitab 2 has become analogue. I realise I'm holding my fly and he is still stretching out his hand. Is he real? I shake my head and he's still here, staring at me, grinning wildly, like he's so happy to have found me.

'We meet in meatspace, dude,' he says and thrusts his hand out.

I shake his hand in wonderment. We share a moment next to the urinal while a man farts audibly in the cubicle.

aZiZWILLKILLYOU episode 6
Aziz vs hipster girls in thrift stores (even if they're buff)
[posted 12 September, 14:42]

No one said it was going to be easy. But it bloody was. It was that bloody easy. I saw him. I saw Teddy Baker and I saw the tattoo. And it was bloody glorious.

#bloodygoodshow

Let me back up a bit cos I know you like all the details. I was on my way to check out these 2 dudes Teddy Baker and @justiceforpigs meeting up, from afar, from like the table in the corner, so I headed to a thrift store to get a hat and a raincoat. Why? I was on a spy mission. I needed to look like a spy. I bought a newspaper and cut 2 holes out of the cover for my eyes to peer through mysteriously. All I needed now was the mystery man spy outfit.

So I entered the thrift store. They were playing Kenny G at full blast. It was so motherfucking ironic. And amongst all the 50s Mad Men dresses and astronaut outfits, there was a row of raincoats. Like they must be just coming back into fashion or something. So I tried a few on and this girl comes over to me and she said, with her index finger pointed to the sky like it's an antenna directly to her leader or her god, 'Definitely. Pulling. It. Off.' Like each word was its own sentence. So I went, 'Cheers, mate,' and continued checking myself out in the mirror.

She was stupidly hot, people. Obviously. We were in the hipster enclave of the coolest fucking city in the world, of

74

course she was going to be stupidly hot. But this man is on a timetable, you get me? So much as Little Big Aziz wants to throw his tuppence into her ring, Big Little Aziz is sticking to the timetable.

She ruined my timetable cos she went, 'Are you from London?' like London's the only city on our fair isle. I mean, I love the regions and the peoples. The Scottish are my peoples-dem. The Bristolians get their bass bin music. Manchester, forgeddabadit. But yeah I'm from fuckin' Laaaahndaaahn taaaahn so I fackin tell her, diiint I?

'Yeah, I am,' I told the girl and she smiled at me and bit her bottom lip. Oh hello, NOW we're interested. She turned to her mate, an Indian-looking girl who was browsing through Hawaiian shirts. She looked up.

'Hey Poo-rur-nar [I think she meant Poorna], you're right, Indians with British accents do sound weird. So British Empire, right?' And they walked off laughing.

Now what is up with that racism, New York? I thought we were cool. I thought we were the best of best bloody friends and now you got my own kind, NYC regiment, racialising and brutalising me in hipster-ville. Was that a set-up? Did she know I was English somehow? And why does she think I'm from London but my accent is British? It's not that generic, love. I doubt the Welsh or the Scottish or the Northern Irish or even a Scouser would be too happy to learn that in America, a British accent means sounding like a London rudeboy. All your regional inflections, that's not very quaint is it?

#badboysinnalondon
#rudeboysinnabrixton

But I digress (purposefully, cos I thought that little cultural exchange was worth noting). I bought the raincoat and a trilby and I got on the tube, sorry the subway, and started acting the spy. I look proper gangsta. Well, proper spy-sta. People were taking pictures of me with their camera phones. Like I was a spectacle. No one dared ask what the fuck I thought I was doing but they took photos. Probably tweet them or Facebook them – look, another NYC nutjob. But they didn't talk to me. I started wondering to myself ... how many photos are we in the background of? Look at all those photos tagged of you on Facebook – there's about 700-1000 of them, right? Because you love the look of your face. Look at all the people in the crowd. Imagine they were tagged. Imagine you knew all their names. Imagine some of them had mutual friends with you. That would be a true world wide web. Think of all those photos of Aziz online right now that I don't even know about. Now think about your own image. Weird innit. And I don't even want to think about how many photos of my wang there are out there. #dickpics is a trending topic I never want to revisit. I saw a lot of shaft out there.

I arrived at the bar, like 15 minutes after Teddy arranged to meet his mate. It was one of these dive bars you got in the basement of the red brick apartment buildings – the famous New York brownstone, home to every sitcom actually made in California ever. There were like 400 beer lamps on the wall. Polaroids of drunk girls. The same 2 miscellaneous drunks you always saw, and miscellaneous rock guitars thrashing away (which is better than the miscellaneous house music of wine bars filled with shirts and shoes and secretaries) so I was like cool, sitting in the corner, waiting. Just waiting.

There was one guy on his own who might be @justiceforpigs. The problem was his stupid avatar is a pig on a weighing scale. What the hell is that? It doesn't mean anything. It's not even a literal visualisation of the man's stupid Twitter name. So yeah, it could be @justiceforpigs. I bet his name's something like Justin Oinkman, and he took a politics class once. 10 years ago. Cos he fancied some girl in it who was destined to become an environmental lobbyist. And he followed her there and found there was nothing he loved more than having an opinion. So he learned about politics. Because it was either that or film-blogging to get him off with his opinion-high. He looks the sort, this guy on this table. The sort of post-political guy who wears a t-shirt with an unverified slogan like 'Cultural Revolutionary' or 'Drop Beats Not Bombs' and fills his Twitter stream with worthy left-leaning retweeting of articles from the Huffington Post and anarchist bloggers. Yawn whoopty do, you are changing the world @justiceforpigs .... with your stupid fucking name and your RTs of comment blogs. I bet your ringtone is the Stars and Stripes because, oh the irony.

@justiceforpigs made a phone call that didn't get answered. But immediately after that, the door opened and in walked ... the 3 dimensions of Teddy Baker. He looked like me. But with a more drawn nose and lighter eyes. And his hair was definitely thinning. I know it's a dive bar, I know it's dark but man, dude needed some plugs. And I don't mean the butt variety.

He wore a t-shirt that said: 'FINE – You can take me to bed tonight.'

He was wearing flip-flops.

HE WAS WEARING FLIP-FLOPS AND THE WORST T-SHIRT IN THE FUCKING WORLD.

He went to the bar and got his mate, @justiceforpigs, Justin Oinkman, a beer and himself – a white wine. This man was too cool for school. A white wine with one ice cube. He knew what game he was playing. 'Yeah, and what? I don't mind the taste of beer in certain situations but I'm not bound by the laddish needs of others, so if I want a motherfucking pinot grigio with one motherfucking cube in it, that's my business, you douchebag.'

When I got back to my hotel, I saw that Teddy Baker had tweeted that he just got home. And with the geo-positioning of his synced Twitter account, I saw that the street he lives in was 2 blocks from the bar we were just in. I lay down in my bed and start planning how to meet him tomorrow morning. I'm doing it.

Get ready my people.

There are 9 comments for this blog:

AZIZWILLKILLYOU: I forgot to add, people ... I need food advice. I want good meatballs, I want the best pizza and I want a good Samantha Fox ... that's Aziz for sandwich. Peace out.

Anonymous wrote: Lame.

Kitab: Aziz, email me. Weirdness. Remember Kitab 2? Shit got real. Send help!

GustaveGeronimo: You can block my IP all you want, dick-head, but know this ... you are everything wrong with the internet. Who the fuck wants this vacuous bollocks? I hope the guy turns out to be a rapist and butt fucks your Paki arse till you bleed.

DF23: LOL, is Aziz single?

AZIZWILLKILLYOU: Gustave, I thought you were a lawyer. Does the law let you get away with racism?

GustaveGeronimo: I've read back through your blogs. You are a lawsuit waiting to happen. I can't wait till it happens and someone wipes that smug shit-eating grin off your face.

AZIZWILLKILLYOU: You know I can see your IP address, don't you? XOXO

DF23: Have you tried The Meatball Shoppe in Williamsburg? Best meatballs ever.

History:

Why do Indian men always wiggle their heads? – Google
Why do Indian men stare? – Google
Why do Indian men like white white women? – Google

I tell Kitab 2 to grab a seat while I stand at the bar and try to work out what to do. I'm thrown. I feel fizzy. I look round at the second Kitab, at Kitab 2. He's sitting at a table staring intently at someone across the room. I follow his eyeline. It's Hayley he's looking at. I don't know what to do. I'm freaked out. I call Aziz, but I don't have any reception down here. I send him an email through wi-fi saying, 'Call me!! Something weird's happened.' He'll know what to do. What does this guy want?

While the readings continue, I find a corner table and sit with Kitab 2 against a backdrop of exposed brickwork I wish I could crawl into. I'm still perturbed he's here. Right here in front of me. I almost have to do one of those cartoon eye-rub-blink-blink gestures.

Mitch stands near Will Self, waiting for his attention. Will Self rolls a cigarette. Mitch pulls one out of his pocket, ready-made and follows him outside. I imagine it's to berate him for *The Book of Dave.* Mitch really hated that book. He thought it was lazy. Mitch hates every writer until he's in a room with them. He becomes a sycophant. He told me once that meeting authors was the only thing that excited him now. His day job as a lawyer, his burgeoning functional alcoholism, literary fiction – they were all muted constants. I used to think he only hung around me so much because I let him talk my ear off.

Kitab 2 is very stereotypically Indian. Like all the semi-racist questions that pop up when you Google 'why are Indian men …' Indian. He's wearing leather sandals and has the bum fluff spray of a moustache on his top lip. A film of hair oil has collected in his side parting. If he's a mirror of me in an alternate universe, then I need to remain firmly in this one. I need to establish a fine balance between him and me, one that dictates that I do not know this white tiger at all.

My eyes flick enviously from Kitab 2, nervously telling me about his tube journey, to Will Self, returned with Mitch 3 steps behind him, across the room, holding court with Hayley and May and a few others and I think, if I go over there, he'll ask who I am and I'll say I'm an author and he'll think I'm one of those 'aspiring types' from the internet and from creative writing classes and I'll feel like a shit-bird. I'm stuck with Kitab 2, out of shame and embarrassment.

Kitab 2 is wearing a t-shirt that says 'Fruity and Juicy' with linen trousers. His toenails are white and cracked. He has a permanent toothy smile even when he's not smiling and there is a thick film of saliva daubed on his front 2 teeth. His skin is pockmarked with the ghosts of acne. He looks like me when I was a teenager, albeit darker, skinnier and with greasier hair. My hair was always washed but thick with gel.

Kitab 2 cocks his head to one side as the next reader is introduced and as he grinds his jaw the saliva on his teeth works its way onto his lips. We sit in silence because neither of us knows where to start. To break the tension, I scroll through my @-replies on Twitter.

@thebookdoctor: '@kitab 2 coloureds in the audience. A world record?'

@kitab: 'seriously? Is this 1853? RT @thebookdoctor @kitab 2 coloureds in the audience. A world record?'

@thebookdoctor: '@kitab Oh sweetie, it's not racist if it's ironic.'

I look up at Kitab 2 and he's still staring at me. He smiles. I smile back.

'So,' I say quietly. 'What are you doing here, man? Were you just passing through this part of the city and thought you'd say hi? I mean, how? How did you find me?'

'I messaged you and asked where you were a whole lot of times, dude,' he says anxiously, nodding his head with worry. 'You didn't accept my add request.'

'I didn't understand why you kept doing that. We've never met. Why would I tell you where I was?'

'So I could come and find you. Never mind, I'm here.' Kitab 2 pauses as if a bad memory has invaded his brain. He straightens his smile. 'You didn't accept my friend request on Facebook.'

'No, but seriously, Kitab. Were you just passing through? What are you doing here, man?' My brain is scrolling, I have itchy feet, I want to get up and leave.

'No, but your website and Twitter said you would be here tonight. So I wanted to say hello. Why didn't you accept my add request?'

'Right, okay.' I make a mental note to never say anything about my whereabouts online ever again.

'You did not accept my friend request on Facebook,' he says again. This time, more firmly. 'Why not?'

'I didn't see it. Sorry. I've been busy,' I lie.

'Really? I sent it this week. Your events tab on your website was empty.'

'Sorry, I must have missed it.'

'But, Facebook,' he stutters and his face falls. He remembers himself, smiles again. Another social media conversation, I think. That's the tie that binds strangers now.

'Sorry, bro,' I say. 'I've been really busy. I didn't not accept your add request. Anyway, who uses Facebook anymore? It's all about Twitter. Am I right?'

'I use Facebook. I wanted to interact with you. We have the same name.'

'Yes, we do,' I say.

'Do you think we're alike?' he asks. I can see Hayley looking in my direction from across the room, shooting me a quizzical look followed by a stupid 'hey, I'm stood with Will Self' grin. I smile back and mouth 'Smug'. Except she doesn't understand me. I wave her off.

'I don't know,' I say.

'Do you like computer games?'

'They're okay,' I reply. Kitab 2 looks sad.

'Do you like *Friends*?'

'The sitcom?' He nods. 'Everyone likes *Friends*.'

Kitab 2 nods. 'What about pizza? What's your favourite topping?'

'I don't know. Pepperoni?'

'Oh,' he says. 'You eat meat.'

Kitab 2 looks crestfallen. He stares at the coke I've bought him and then notices my arm. He pulls it towards him and stares at the tattoo, rubbing it. It stings. I'm too weirded out by his touching me to even consider its inappropriate impact on my personal space.

'Dude, you have a tattoo?'

'Yes, mate,' I say, briskly, looking around the room, hoping Hayley hasn't left yet.

'You didn't tell me you had a tattoo.' Kitab 2 looks dejected. Then annoyed. He drops my arm to the table. It lies in the slug trail of someone else's beer condensation. The occasional hygiene obsessive in me recoils. 'When did you get this tattoo?'

'Yesterday.' I'm starting to feel agoraphobic. I want to get back to the comforting whirr of my laptop.

'Oh. This isn't good. You have ruined your body. I thought we were alike.'

'Mate, you've never met me. How would you know?'

'I have read your book and I have watched your tweets and YouTubes and everything. I think you are like me. Except this …' He points to the tattoo with the whole of his outstretched hand. 'This changes what I think about us both.'

'Listen, Kitab, it was nice meeting you but I need to talk to some people before they go,' I say. 'I've had enough. I start to stand up. Kitab 2 grabs my hand.

'No, please. Stay here. Talk to me. Please.'

'Seriously, Kitab, let go of me. I need to go and sort out some stuff, okay?' I say with my eyes on the door, the ultimate prize. 'It was nice meeting you. Maybe I'll run into you again? How long are you in London for?'

Kitab 2's lips are moving but he's not saying anything. I assume he's translating what I'm saying in his head.

'We're alike,' he says. 'I am you. You are me. I want to see your life. Show me London, Kitab. Please. I've travelled so far.' He looks at his hands. 'I don't know anybody and I'm scared. I have never been on a plane before. I like computer games. My daddy is very strict. I … have never worn jeans. I want to kiss a girl. Have you kissed a girl? I don't drink alcohol but I drank bhang lassi once. I was sick on my cleaner. Please.'

'Sorry, man,' I say, unsure what to do with the onslaught of information. 'I need to go.'

I grab my bag and finish my drink, bang it down on the table emphatically and stretch out my 'no hard feelings' hand for a 'no hard feelings' handshake.

'Hey man, lovely reading. Maybe you should try something from a woman's perspective,' a man in non-prescription glasses says to me as he passes.

I nod at him intensely, burning the feedback deep in my soul. I nod at Kitab 2 in the same way and begin my extraction from the situation.

'But …' Kitab 2 stammers. 'I need a place to stay. I don't know anybody in the UK. Please Kitab. I need to stay with you.'

'What?' I say to him.

Kitab 2 has launched a surprise attack on me. I look at him with a mixture of pity and bemusement and wonder what is expected of me. Pity because he might have backed the wrong namesake to expect a display of helpfulness. Bemusement because he has definitely backed the wrong namesake to expect a display of helpfulness. I'm not helpful and I do not like telling people where I live.

My dad, though not religious, believes in seva. Which is Gujarati for selfless work, voluntary service, a way of giving back to the community when you have something to give. Disregarding the last bit, where I feel like I have something to give, maybe I have the capacity for a selfless act. Maybe I have the capacity for something other than my own sense of worth. My dad used to donate 15% of his paycheque to an orphanage in the place he and my mum both grew up in.

'You only care about the injustices prevalent in the Indian world,' I said to my dad at a fundraiser for Hindu street children he threw, hoping it would attract some single ladies. 'What about Africa, South America, other parts of Asia, maybe even parts populated by Muslims? What about kids on estates in South East London?'

'At least I'm doing something, Kitab-san,' he replied quickly. 'What are you doing? Working in a job you hate. Writing a book mocking where you grew up? What good is that doing in the world? The community leaders of the place where you grew up, the place you mock, they raised thousands of pounds for my charity. What have you done that's charitable?'

'I'm here.'

'Only because I bought your ticket.'

Maybe this is my own personal seva. Their preferred charity found shelter for street children in India. Maybe I can do the same for Kitab 2. That way I'm honouring all the good work my family did.

'Please can I stay?' Kitab 2 says.

'I don't know you, man. You're a stranger,' I reply and I stand up. He stands up too.

'We're the same. We have the same name. We both like *Friends*. Please, look, I only have one suitcase and my laptop. I have nowhere to go. We are brothers. Brothers by name. Come on.'

'Kitab, do you watch films?' I say. 'This is the start of a film that ends badly. I'm going to have to say no.'

'I read that review,' he says. 'That says you have no heart. I think they're right.'

Stung by my nightmare review, the one that haunts, the one that hurts, the one that sears, I look at Kitab 2 and for a second feel a quiver of upset.

Kitab 2 is looking beyond me, probably at the curly redhead in Converse and a summer dress who has just walked past us, and he looks so sweet with his never-been-kissed smile, and I think, fair enough, and I think, what's the worst that will happen, and I think, he can stay in Aziz's room.

'Yeah, no worries, man. Come and stay with me. For one night only. Then we find you a hotel. Or something.'

Kitab 2 looks at me with a mixture of validation and confirmation that 1) I respect him and 2) he knew I'd eventually say yes and he pushes his chair away from the table. He knocks his coke over the table. I step back and unwittingly into the path of his cuddle, which is thick and spindly as he throws his spiderweb arms around me.

I repeat, 'Yeah, for *one* night only. Then we find you a hotel.' I leave out the 'or something' because that's too wishy-washy for someone who needs to remain firm in such situations.

As we leave, Hayley grabs me. Kitab 2 stands awkwardly next to us. 'Sorry we didn't get to hang out much,' she says. 'In fact, I'd say you completely ignored me.'

'You were busy … with Will Self.'

'Oh, him … he was busy talking about himself. I made a mental to-do list.'

'He *is* very Self-interested.'

She rolled her eyes. 'Soon, though, yes?'

'Yes,' I say, loudly. People look at me.

'I suppose,' she says, feigning disinterest. 'Yes, soon! Don't disappear on me. I miss hanging out. We haven't even done the whisky challenge we said we were going to.'

'Yeah. We haven't. Listen, soon,' I say. 'Oh yeah … Good story.'

'You too.'

'You're too kind.'

'No, seriously, Kitab … it was really funny.'

'You are too kind.'

'Oh, anytime, sweetie pie. It was busy tonight, eh?' Hayley has placed herself between me and Kitab 2.

'Right,' I say, starting to feel awkward, like I want to stay but I have to leave but I don't know how long this conversation is going on for. 'Take care.'

'We should get a coffee sometime. You were always so "in a couple". You forget what it's like making new friends properly when you're doing readings every night.'

'Yeah, definitely, DM me.'

'Or, we could phone each other like it's 1995.'

'You're so retro.'

'What's your number?' Hayley says, holding out her phone. I type it in. 'I'll one-ring you,' she says and I feel my phone vibrate in my pocket. 'It's official. Twitter, Facebook, now text message, I'd say we're properly acquainted.'

'What's your address, so I can send you a congratulations card?' I say. She smiles.

Hayley kisses me on the cheek and says, 'You know, it really is good to see you, chico.' I smile and shuffle Kitab 2 towards the exit of The Book Doctor.

I dream about Elvis Costello. He's sitting in a bar with Kurt Vonnegut and JG Ballard. They are telling him off for never mentioning their names in any of his songs. He throws his drink over JG Ballard, and Kurt Vonnegut gets a cigarette flicked in his eye. Elvis Costello stands up in this bar, one that looks suspiciously like Cocktails and Dreams, Tom Cruise's dream pub in the film *Cocktail*. I realise this because Tom Cruise is standing on the bar delivering his Last Barman poem from the film *Cocktail*.

'The Alabama slammer …' he says, gyrating his hips.

My dreams are never this pop culture-related and they're usually about people I like. I mean, I love that Elvis Costello song and a few others but I don't think he's all that, really. I mean, he's funny and political, but whatever, I'd rather listen to something more miserable and emotive.

So, Elvis Costello crosses over to me at the bar. I'm writing 'NEVER REFERENCE YOUR DREAMS IN FICTION' on a napkin over and again, going over the same letters till my pencil nib breaks off. Elvis Costello slams his freshly refreshed drink down on the table and says, 'How can you not like me? I did one of your mum's favourite songs.'

'She didn't know it was about Thatcher. She just thought it was a nice song. She voted for Thatcher. Twice.'

Elvis Costello points to my arm. 'Why have you done that?' He's referring to the tattoo, which I know in my dream, if you scratch it, it plays the Elvis Costello song it references.

'I thought it'd be cool.'

'Getting a red starling on your neck, that's cool. This is just a poser being a poser.'

'Nope. It's my carpe diem. Everyday I must write. And own that writing. I permanently ink whilst being permanently inked.'

'You're about to get a drink thrown in your face,' Elvis

Costello says. He stands up and throws a drink in my face. 'Be the best you that you can muster. PS, tell your mum I said hi.'

'She's dead,' I tell Elvis Costello.

'I know,' he grins. 'Tell her anyway.'

I wake up to find I've knocked a pint of water over my face in the night. My pillow soaked, I move over to Quiltina and fall asleep.

Next door, in Aziz's room, I can hear canned laughter on the television.

As soon as I wake up, I check my phone. No reply from Aziz. An email from Susan telling me that after careful consideration, she won't be offering me a job. She has reservations about my attention to the productivity of social interactions in a synergetic way. I delete the email. A few tweets about last night. None mention me except one from Hayley that says:

@hayleyspen: 'Great reading with @kitab last night. He's possibly the nicest guy I've met.'

I don't feel very nice.

I tweet: 'I met myself last night.'

I delete it. It doesn't make any sense. I try: 'I met my only namesake last night. Now I know how Dave Gorman feels.'

I delete that. It's a pretty English reference. I need to be international in my tone. I try: 'I met my only namesake last night. He's the most Indian person I know. He's brown Kitab. I am coconut Kitab. #50shadesofkitab'

I'm happy with that.

I scroll down through my tweets. I go back as far as the days my book came out and I was on it, tweeting bloggers, reviewers, readers, anyone who might be interested. That was my heyday of excitement. I'd been waiting my entire life for that book to come out and then it did and it felt exactly the same as before. Now what? I thought. So I tweeted everyone I could, trying to get their attention. I replied to anyone who said they were reading. I told book bloggers they'd love it. Hardly anyone tweeted me back. No one likes a showboat.

The first thing I'd tweeted that day was 'Suddenly, everything has changed' with a link to a Flaming Lips song.

Kitab 2 is unpacking his suitcase when I walk past his opened door the next morning, in just my boxer shorts, a pup tent of morning glory dangerously, perilously close to a wide reveal. I can see Aziz's wardrobe open. I knock on the door and he looks out at me.

'Hey dude,' he says in an accent that sounds like he's trying his hardest not to sound like he's from Bangalore.

'What you doing there, buddy?'

'Just unpacking, dude. I hate being in a suitcase. What is all these things? Your t-shirts? They look too small for you.'

'No. My brother. Aziz. He's back in a week. Seriously. What are you doing there, buddy?'

'You have lots of photographs of him as a kid. Hey man, where are your family from?'

'Gujarat.'

'I knew it! Me too! My dad only moved to Bangalore for a job. Where in Gujarat?'

'Ahmedabad. Seriously, man … what are you doing?'

'Come on, man … let's get a bacon sausage fry. I'm from Ahmedabad too!'

'Kitab, I said one night. Last night was one night. You can't stay here again.'

Kitab 2 stops refolding a pink dress shirt and looks at me with a quivering bottom lip. I use this opportunity to go to the toilet.

I spend more time than I need to in the toilet, sitting on the bowl, trying to work out the nicest way to tell him I have things to do so he should leave. But then I start to wonder, if I just sit still and not move and not make any sound in here, maybe he will just get the message and go.

Kitab 2 says 'sh' when it should be an 's' and vice versa. Sushi is pronounced Shu-see. He starts every sentence with 'But-aaaaa', and he calls me 'Kithaaaabuh'.

I try to find the most comfortable way to sit still with bare butt cheeks on toilet seat but the squeaky floorboard underneath my foot lets out a wood fart and I freeze.

'Kitab!' I hear Kitab 2 shout from somewhere within my flat. I don't answer. I will not answer. 'What's the wi-fi password?'

Wi-fi password? Why does he need the wi-fi password? Maybe to find a hotel or somewhere to stay. Last night, as we walked home, I'd asked what he was doing in the UK.

'I moved here to study.'

'Ahhh cool, where are you studying?'

'Over at Queen Mary University. In East London.'

'Nice. What are you doing?'

'Just carrying on my degree.'

'Cool, what was that in?'

'I want to design computer games one day,' he said firmly, and we walked in silence. He was being evasive.

'You play a lot of computer games?'

'All the time, man. I'm a master at *Call of Duty*.'

'I don't really like them.'

'What? You seem like you would love them. I mean, they're so cool. How you pretend to be other people and go and explore universes and see from other people's points of view ...'

'... kinda like books,' I said.

'And kill zombies and Muslims and time jump onto other planets ...'

'So where are you meant to be staying?'

'In the dormitories but they are closed till next week. We booked the wrong flight. Silly Dad.'

'And you don't have any relatives here?'

'No. All in India. Or Canada. I have an uncle in Australia but he's a horse trainer.'

'No family in England? You're a Gujarati with no family in England?' Kitab 2 shook his head. 'That sounds impossible. Every Gujarati has a distant uncle in Harrow, Wembley, Birmingham or Leicester. That's why they still exist as places.'

We arrived at my flat and I showed him in. When he entered, he dropped his suitcase and spun around, arms outstretched, like there was a camera above him, filming in slow motion, his ecstatic joy at having attained nirvana.

'This is the coolest place, dude,' he said before setting about touching everything, from my stack of articles I'll most likely never re-read on the kitchen table, to Aziz's gun controller for his Wii – the one he pestered me to buy for us both and the one he hasn't played since the end of his first month of owning it – to my books. He kept pulling out my books and not replacing them properly, wearing the wide-eyed grin of a vacant child. I followed him around, watching him be stunned by the simple household life of 2 bachelors who understood basic hygiene and the need to provide for oneself but also liked to drink and watch television in the most luxurious way possible.

Kitab 2 looked at me and said, 'Dude, you're like my idol.'

'Are you drunk?'

'I don't drink, dude. No way. Look at you. All this freedom. All these things. What's this about?' He pulled out an erotica photography book of Aziz's, pushing some postcards to the floor. I ignored him.

All this is flooding back to me now, piecemeal reminders of how the rest of my night unfolded. I remember him asking me to buy him cigarettes, which I refused, because he didn't have any money and I didn't want to waste my own. I remember him asking for different sheets as Aziz's hadn't been cleaned that week. I remember him clearing his sinuses of phlegm and mucus so loudly, you could hear the neighbours retching. We were all in the back of his throat and in the outer perimeters of his nose with him as he hack-hack-hack HAKKKKKKT up something disgusting and fully formed into my sink. I'd checked my email for word from Aziz, nothing. I checked his blog. Nothing. He was probably fine.

And then I'd put Kitab 2 to bed, leaving the door half open so he would feel too embarrassed to wank himself to sleep. Then I went to bed.

'Why do you need the wi-fi? Need to look up a hotel to stay in?' I shout back.

'No, dude. Just checking my email. I found it. "69duuuude" you are so funny. Bill and Ted. Excellent.'

I remembered – Aziz put a sticker with the wi-fi password on his headboard one night, so girls staying over could treat themselves to a Facebook status update if they woke up before him.

I flush the toilet and boxer up. I tie a towel around my bottom half and leave the bathroom with my aggressive arms folded and a pursed brow.

'Kitab,' I say and he looks up from his computer where he is either looking up porn or a medical condition. The skin contours are unmistakable. The actual shapes aren't. 'Kitab, I'm really sorry but I have a busy day today so I can't hang out, so you need to get going to your next place you're staying, if you don't mind, mate. Sorry – deadlines.' I punch my hip in frustration that I am not being firm. I'm being 'nice'. Since when were nice guys able to extract strangers from their house without a conflagration?

Deadline – what a joke. Empty pages await.

'What? Dude, I thought I was staying here …'

'No, you didn't. Kitab, I told you, like, 400 times, one night only.'

'I know. But then I thought you'd get to know me and it would be fine. One week. Only one week. Till halls. Please?'

'Mate, we've been asleep for 8 hours. When would I get a chance to get to know you?'

'I haven't got anywhere to go, dude.'

'It doesn't matter anyway …' I say, hoping he gets the message, that I'm not interested.

'How similar do you think we are, dude?' Kitab 2 stretches himself out on Aziz's bed.

'What?'

'I mean, I don't like bread, or jazz. I like video games. I hate my dad. He's a *pudu* …' When Kitab 2 says *pudu*, his neck oscillates so violently, it looks like it might snap.

'What's a *pudu*?'

'It's a word I made up, dude. It means arsehole.'

'Why not just say arsehole?'

'It's a disgusting word … So, dude … I love girls. I love the blonde ones, I love the black ones, I love the brown-haired ones. I kinda like the Indian ones … but the ones I love the most are the redheaded ones … What about you?'

I don't know if Kitab 2 knows this but redheads are the elixir of the Indian male. We're drawn to the fieriness. Maybe it's because old men stain their hair red with henna when they go grey to appear more youthful, and these girls remind us of that. Maybe it's the freckles and alabaster skin, the ginger of the hair – the exact opposite end of the spectrum to us. Maybe it's because it's the whitest you can get, and secretly, we all want to date white girls … but redheads are our lifeblood of crushes. We have no success with them though.

'I like a redhead.'

'I knew it, dude. Peas in a pod. Have you ever had sex with a redhead?'

'Look, Kitab, let's not … okay?'

'Please, tell me … I mean, you're my doppelganger. If you can, maybe I can.'

'I think we should find you a hotel, my friend.'

Kitab 2 looks sad and horny all at once. It's as confusing to watch as it probably is to feel.

'Sorry, Kitab, listen … I have a really busy day. Let's … go, okay?'

There's a look in his eyes that makes me hesitate. Like the final cute-but-pathetic doe-eyed stare into the oblivion of death of a puppy that's been shot point blank. But with some coaxing and the directions to a budget hotel, 50 pounds taken from Aziz's 'cash in hand' stash and an endless stream of apologies, I get Kitab 2 to leave. I watch from my window and he must linger in the hallway for 20 minutes hoping I'll let him back in because it takes about that long for him to appear outside.

I sit down on the sofa and think, I am such an arsehole. Hayley's a fool. I'm not nice. I'm a *pudu*.

I scratch my tattoo to see if it'll hum me a song to cheer me up. Instead I get the coarse burn of a rash flaring up.

The rest of my day is a write-off.

Mission accomplished, my friends.

I was like James Bond.

This morning after waking up and going to get a really early coffee and bagel from the bodega next door to my hotel, I came back to my room and dressed myself up to look like the one of Teddy Baker in his avi. I put on the same tank top, some dark blue jeans and my aviators. It wasn't even warm out, family. It was freezing. But I did this for you. Now, the guy's a freelance graphic designer or something so I assumed he'd be working from home all day BUT, everyone in New York goes out for every meal, of this much we can be sure, isn't that what Seinfeld and Friends and Sex and the Motherfucking City have told us? They have fridges to chill bottles of mineral water and the odd condiment.

I walked down the street towards Teddy Baker's apartment building and I waited outside. Just leaning against a lamp post. Nonchalant. Nothing going on. Just hanging. Just waiting.

Teddy Baker walked out of his building onto his stoop and stood there, lingering in the day trying to work out what was awaiting him or what he wanted for breakfast or whether he should go for a shit first? I dunno, either way, the man paused and looked around. I skipped into action and struck the pose: hands on hips, shit-eating grin, sunglasses on. I was still bothered by how much this guy looks like me. And another thing, what's a brown brother doing with a milk bottle name? Comedy racism, you love it, white people. I love you. You're the only ones who get me. Why is this obvious desi called Teddy Baker? He sounds like a suit.

So, I stood there for a good 10 seconds or something, which felt like a long time to be stood out in the street with your hands on your hips modelling an amazing tattoo in a wife-beater in early autumn, sorry, The Fall. But I did it. I did it for you. Finally Teddy Baker walked down the steps and at the same eye level, he noticed me. He circled me. He walked around me slowly and placed his fingers on his chin, like that would help him work out exactly what was going on. I was a human statue. Of you, Teddy Baker. Of you.

'Holy shit, is this a 3-D painting?' he asked. I don't know who he's asking, it's just him and me.

'Nah, mate. It's me, Aziz. I believe you're my doppelganger.'

Teddy Baker, into it, smiled. 'Wait, doesn't that make you my doppelganger?'

'Why can't you be my doppelganger?'

'Cos you're my doppelganger.'

'And you're mine.'

'Teddy Baker.'

'I know. I'm Aziz. Pleased to meet you.'

97

I held out my hand to the brother. He grabbed me and gave me the biggest bear hug in the fucking world, like we were twins or some shit.

Wait, what if we're twins? Long lost twins. Kitab would be freaked if there were 2 of us.

'Wanna come to breakfast?' he asked me.

You KNOW what I thought? Double breakfast day. I said yes. But first, I asked him to pull down his t-shirt and show me the tattoo. We bow tie tatt-bumped, innit.

He started walking me down the street and wanted to know what's going on, why I'd turned up on his doorstep with his tattoo. I told him the whole story, about discussing new tattoo ideas with my bro Kitab, about Googling for bow tie tattoos, about finding him on the image search and about being so amazed that I just had to come and meet him as soon as possible to see how similar we were. It's not often you get to meet your doppelganger. I was well chuffed. He talks with that very clear and booming American voice that you can pinpoint in any bustling room and hear every single word. He talks very clear, never stutters or anything. It's amazing. It's like an episode of Law and Order. He's like John Barrowman. But actually American.

So, we got to the breakfast place and he turned to me and said, 'So you saw I looked like you and you got a matching tattoo?'

'Yeah, fuck it, innit,' I said to him.

'I get that. It's pretty amazing. How did you track me down to my apartment block?'

'Bruv, you need to invest time and effort into not tweeting your location every few hours and leaving the Twitter Location turned on. I knew where you were at all times, bro.'

Then he took out a pen and paper and wrote down everything I'd said. He looked at me and I was thinking, damn, either he's falling in love or he's just marvelling at my intuition. So then he said, 'Wanna party with me?' and I was like, 'Yes, mate, that's what I came here for.' He said, 'Right, tonight, meet me here.' He pushed the paper he's just written on across the table to me, and said, '8 o'clock.'

And then he left, just like that. And I thought, wicked, that guy was super safe. Except then, the bill for all the food he'd just eaten arrived and mug here is stuck with the bill. You can all PayPal me some money cos I think this guy might be a chief tonight and leave me with a bar bill.

Now that's what I call an interaction.

There are 2 comments for this blog:

df345: OH EM GEE. This is too funny.

Gustave Geronimo: I've just blogged about everything I hate on the internet. People like you are number 3. Check it out: www.gustavegeronimo.biz. I look forward to the comments. If you can pry yourself away from your stupid self-obsessed life.

History:

The perfect CV – Google
Kitab Balasubramanyam – Facebook
Hayley Bankcroft – Google images
[104] – Twitter

The flat feels empty and still so I pay a surprise visit to Dad in my childhood home. I spend the journey catching up on Aziz's online antics. I check his blog – he's sporadically updating his adventure. He's met the boy with the bow tie tattoo, Teddy Baker. Something big's gone down. I laugh at his writing diction – it's like he's in the centre of the room bellowing at you like Brian Blessed, hitting you over and over with a wet mackerel of anecdote. Without him around, I feel weak and impulsive. Weak because any decision I make doesn't come with the weight of my enforcer and impulsive because that then means I could go on to do anything.

At Dad's house the heating's cranked up to tropical conditions. Sad Bollywood songs are shrill and loud. He's holding a tumbler of vodka. He's surprised to see me. I've let myself in and snuck up on him. He's never jumpy when I do this, just annoyed at the surprise visit.

'Kitab-san, what are you doing here?'

'Just wanted to see my dad.'

He closes his eyes and returns to sprawling out in his favourite armchair, the one opposite the sideboard with his iPod dock on top of a stack of old stocks and shares magazines. I can see the door to my old bedroom at the top of the stairs, closed. The rest of the house looks like a museum of how things were and what they used to be. In the kitchen, as I fix myself a glass of water, I notice films of dust over the cooking implements. I open the fridge out of curiosity as I walk past it. There are 6 takeaway containers, a bottle of ketchup and 3 2-pint bottles of semi-skimmed milk. The oldest carton, the milk went off 6 weeks ago. I don't mention it as I walk into the living room, where Dad sits staring at large photos of my mum and smaller ones of dead family members, his feet up on a pouffe, the pouffe covered in one of Mum's old shawls. Her old shawl – it used to smell of olbas and hair oil, the 2 smells I associate with her, because, much as I don't remember her physical form, every trace of her existence in the house, from her clothes still hanging in the wardrobe to her scarves and shawls in the coat cupboard, they smell of olbas oil and hair oil. Just like this shawl he rests his feet on. Now it smells of my dad's feet.

'How are you, Kitab-san?'

'Fine,' I say. 'Weird, actually. There's this guy, another Kitab Balasubramanyam, I found another me. Weird, eh? Another one. I thought I was, you know, special or something.'

Dad looks at me. 'What do you mean, found another me?'

'Never mind,' I say.

'I don't know where my life is going,' my dad says. Whenever he's home, he's low, talking about ending it all. When he's out, he's the life of the party. This is the opposite of who he is when he visits. This is the him I avoid.

'What about your girlfriends?' I ask, sitting down.

'What's the point?'

'Dad,' I say. 'I was just thinking about things. We should … you know … What are you doing on Saturday?' He looks at me. I came home because I wanted to feel the comfort of being home. It feels like a shrine. I feel nothing. I've made a mistake. I need to leave.

I'm wearing a long-sleeve top because I don't want Dad to see my tattoo. He may think, socially, he's living out the last days of the libertine, but morally, he's still a parent who thinks that their child smoking and getting tattoos is a mark of the devil. Luckily I've given up smoking. He used to ask why I listened to guitar music when growing up, because he said it sounded like they were attacking you until you started worshipping the devil. Which, he added, was difficult for us, because we were Hindu.

I stand up to go.

'You know,' he says. 'That girl who I said was fat?' I nod. 'Look what she did to me.' He stands up slowly and unwraps his arm. There's a light shade of bruising on his wrist. 'Can you believe it?'

'Why did she do that?' I ask. 'Did she hurt you?'

Dad laughs. 'No,' he says. 'She was pretending to try to hurt me. And she actually did.'

He bursts out laughing and grabs my arm to demonstrate the Chinese burn. As he pulls at my right arm, my shirt sleeve tugs up towards the edge of the tattoo I am hiding. But he sees the corner of ink that is the 'ok' of 'book' and pulls at my arm.

'Unwrap your arm,' my dad says and I do because he's my dad and his steely glare still holds me in its gaze. I show him the tattoo and squint at the situation. Can he still send me to bed without dessert or pocket money? Does he still have that power? 'Elvis Costello – he does good songs. To make you dance. Your mother's and my favourite song was "Chipbuilding",' Dad says through a sniffle. I can forecast the crying shakes approaching.

'"Shipbuilding",' I correct him. I instantly regret doing that.

'That's what I said,' he says. 'Remember when she used to sing it in the kitchen?' I nod. It sounds like something she did. Dad hums the melody, badly. 'Why have you done this?' Dad says, looking into his now-empty tumbler of vodka.

'I wanted to make a statement about myself to myself.'

'And you want to live with that for ever? That statement? It's not even a good song. You can't dance to it. How do you dance to this song?' he says and shakes his head. 'It's too slow.' He sits down. I follow him.

After that, any attempt I make to kick-start a conversation is met by a shrug and a shake of the head. I ask if he wants me to cook for him. He shrugs his head. There's nothing in the kitchen I can do anything with anyway. I ask him about his social engagements and he grunts. I stand up to leave so I can get home and out from this oppressive regime of father-hood. I can feel the disappointment seeping from his pores and it smells like onion and garlic.

But he's disappointed in me, and that feels comforting as much as it feels humiliating. I can sense he is desperate to get away from me from the way he avoids looking at me. It's almost nice to be reminded that in a whirlwind of dates and drinking he still spares a thought for all the things I do wrong.

I announce I'm leaving. He turns to me and says, 'Son, I have worried that you were too passive in this world, just letting it let you live. Then you wrote a book and I thought, this is the guy who understands how the world works. Now you have a tattoo, like a sailor and I don't know who you are anymore. Passive, writer or sailor?'

I think, I'm probably all 3 in some way, or none at all, but that's a passive writer's way of dealing with things, endless scenarios and eventualities. What does he mean by sailor?

He shakes his head. 'You will look at that stupid thing when you're my age and think, I'm a fool.'

I nod. 'Good night, Dad.'

'What is wrong, son?' he asks.

'I don't know, Dad.'

He shakes his head. 'You need to move on, kiddo,' he says. 'If I can, so can you. It's been so long now.'

I try to give Dad a hug but he offers no arms. I disengage and leave the house, walking through the same streets, past the same shops, the same everything of my childhood. It feels alien to me now. Like a biopic that approximates a version of my life.

On the train, I line up tweets.

@kitab: 'I've literally had enough of the misuse of the word literally.'

@kitab: 'Without Instagram, I wouldn't know what nail polish you all have and you wouldn't know how well I eat.'

@kitab: 'People call it brownnosing. Brown people just call it nosing.'

Perfecting those 3 tweets takes me a 45-minute journey and I'm still not happy with them when I release them into the world in a flurry as I leave the train station and dial my landline repeatedly till my phone catches a 3G signal.

I look down my high street, considering hitting up the local where Mitch might be, or a short story night where literary fans of the female persuasion might be, or home where a television and Aziz's spiced dark rum is.

This is the busiest day of the week because it's Sunday and on Sunday the most ironic nights happen around here. Like Shit Film Club, Twatfunk (a made-up genre from Twitter turned real with its own club night and tribute bands), *Keeping Up With the Kardashians* marathons, Tweet Dating (which is exactly how it sounds). The bars are full. I don't want to be near people. I head home, stopping off to buy some limes and ginger beer to help Aziz's spiced dark rum go down.

My head is down at the pavement and my mind is processing what my dad said, the look of disappointment in his eyes. My neighbours are having a party. I can hear it before I get past their front garden. They're always playing loud thumping break-neck indie – the nee-nee-nee-noo-noo-noo kind – when they have a party, because the speed of the song dictates the speed of their dance and they need to dance Sunday night off. Usually, I'd be annoyed.

Today, I am only disappointed. But mostly in myself.

As I get to our front garden, I notice some black Clarks shoes on my front step and look up. Kitab 2 is standing there, facing the door, peering in through the frosted glass, his suitcase next to him. I sigh, watching the trail of exhausted fumes leave my mouth. Then he points towards the hour and he made in study.

'Yo, Kitab,' I call out. He turns to face me, looking the happiest a man could possibly be. 'What the fuck are you doing, man?'

'Help me please, brother Kitab. I've run out of money and nowhere to go. Please help me.'

Maybe it's because I'm feeling selfless in the face of disappointing my dad, but I think, what would Dad do in this situation? I invite him in to drink some of Aziz's spiced dark rum and warm up.

Kitab 2 scrolls through his story. He spent the night in a hotel I recommended to him but skipped out when it came to the morning of paying as he only has enough money to see him through the first term at university and nothing more.

'I am on a strict budget. I have to collect receipts too. I can only spend money on books and essential food. And travel.'

'Maybe you could get a job,' I tell him.

'When will I have time, dude?'

'Why did you arrive in the UK a week early if you didn't have anywhere to stay or any money to pay for somewhere to stay?'

He shrugs. 'It was the cheapest option,' he mumbles. 'Cheap ticket. Plus, I got the start date for term wrong in my G-Cal.'

'I thought your dad booked the wrong flights.'

'He did. I gave him the dates.' He pauses and thinks. 'Do you have a job?'

'Not currently. Well, yeah, writer,' I say, proud.

'How much money do you make, dude?'

'That's personal,' I say, pouring myself a drink.

'So ... not much then? How do you survive, dude?'

105

'Kitab, that's personal. I'm not comfortable discussing it.'

Kitab 2 looks at his shoes, something he does a lot, then back up at me. 'I've never had a job. I never needed to. My dad made me study. Then he bought me computer and made me study. Then he got internet in the house and he made me study. All the time, I was playing computer games.'

'I can help you find a job, if you need a job. Do you have the right visa to work?' In my head, I think, by helping you find a job all I really mean is, I can give you 3 or 4 websites to check for job listings.

'I shouldn't work,' Kitab 2 says. 'I don't know how to take orders, dude.'

I sigh and point back towards Aziz's room and he wheels his suitcase in there like a small child trailing a blanket behind him.

I don't have a plan to get rid of him. He is my other and I pity him. I look at everything he is and everything I'm not and wonder if we're yin and yang. Maybe we've been brought together to become the perfect human. He is incapable and wet. And I am depressed and able to utilise Google to solve any problem. He's so cheerful and enthusiastic. It's a welcome counterpoint to my usual misery. Having seen Dad earlier, how lost he looks on his own, I feel the need for company. With Aziz gone, maybe I do feel lonely, maybe that's why this crushing wave of depression is over me. Maybe it is loneliness. Much as I don't want to admit it, it's nice having another body in this house, this mausoleum of static and failure. Hell, I might even apply for another job tomorrow.

'Oi, Kitab,' I call after him.

He emerges from his room in a formerly-white vest and small penis. He is naked from the waist down. I don't want to look but I do. It's comparable to mine – i.e., more average-looking when it's erect, probably.

'Dude, put some pants on.'

'Oh, sorry, roomie,' he says, smiling, and runs back into Aziz's bedroom. He re-emerges with pants on and a toothy grin, all top row and overbite. 'What's up, dude?'

'Which university are you at, again?'

'Queen Mary University. You're not far from it, are you?'

'Okay, so I'll go with you tomorrow and see if we can get you some accommodation for the rest of the week, say there's been a mix-up or something.'

Kitab 2 nods. 'I'm hungry, dude. Got any pizza?'

'Nah, mate. I've eaten. There's some bread over there. Make some toast or something. Help yourself.' I point him to the open plan kitchen, overlooking the lounge in the way only a place where 2 boys live could. Kitab 2 looks dejected, like only pizza would do. I find a frozen pizza in the freezer and put it in the oven for him. That dejected look. It's the worst. The way his eyes become wider and browner, his eyebrows quiver like they can't quite hold the line over his brow and the upturned pursed lips, pinched together in an X of disappointment. Oh god. This is what parenting is like. Aziz has been a relatively easy child to deal with up until now because, regardless of his impulsive chaos, you can calm him down with a stern word or just release him into the ether, fully cocked. This guy – oh my god – it's like being stabbed with sadness. I never want children of my own.

Kitab 2 sits at our dining table, one foot on the chair, head on knee, and tears into the pizza packaging. He picks off the pepperoni and looks at me, shaking his head. 'You are non-veg,' he says.

I know the lingo. I went to India once with my dad as a teenager. I hated the whole trip. It was hot. My family was stressful and I didn't speak any of the languages – Hindi, Gujarati or the Victorian English everyone spoke. I was struck by the non-veg thing in restaurants. Non-veg is what they refer to meat-eaters as, because veg is the norm, which is cool. In the menus, all the non-veg stuff is at the back because most people turn to the veg things.

'I eat meat,' I say. I won't say 'non-veg'. I won't make fun of his vernacular for the LOLs. It's a lazy way to get laughs – the *Mind Your Language* approach – the bud-bud-ding-ding of it all.

'So you are non-veg.'

'I eat meat.'

'Yes, non-veg,' Kitab 2 says, bending down to peer into the oven.

'No, meat-eater.'

I leave him with that and turn my back to him, face the television. I grab the remote control and switch it on, flicking through channels without any interest, using the whole thing as a prop for conversation avoidance.

'Kitab,' Kitab 2 says. 'Do you have a girlfriend, dude?'

I turn to him without breaking the TV flicking motion. 'What? None of your business.'

'This is a place for boys.'

'So what, man.'

'You should get a girlfriend. I bet she would be nice to you.'

'Okay, man.'

'In fact, we could find some girls now. Have you got an iPhone, dude?'

I turn to him. 'Yes.'

'Cool, download Blendr, dude. It's this app that lets you find girls near you who are DTF. Do you know what DTF means? Definitely To Fuck. We could find 2 girls and have some fun, no? Blendr's free. They might send us photos of their boobies.'

'No, man. I don't want to do that,' I say, getting up to take out Kitab 2's pizza.

'It is late. Yes, you're right. Sorry.'

'Yeah,' I say.

'Maybe tomorrow ...'

'Tomorrow we're going to your university.'

I focus all my energy on the television.

I settle on an episode of a sitcom I've seen before but am happy with the familiarity, and the conversational silence that canned laughter brings to a room. I sit and watch the sitcom, listening to Kitab 2's loud chewing, like I'm inside his mouth, being tossed around with masticated burnt bread and cheese. When he laughs, I can hear the squelch of food against the back of his tongue and teeth so I turn the volume up and hope to drown him out.

A couple of episodes of the sitcom and an entire eaten pizza later, he's still awake but has joined me on the sofa. He shifts up and down in his seat, plays with his toenails, clears his sinuses in that AKAKAKAKAKUGH way and generally informs me of his presence with every single tic and move, every second I am with him, so I tell him I'm going to bed and to be ready to leave for the university at 8 a.m. I assume we'll get there for 9 a.m. when it opens. I go to bed and can't concentrate on the internet porn I choose to soothe me to sleep because the volume is off in case Kitab 2 hears my shame, and I want to hear the noises. I've gone amateur tonight and there's sometimes nothing sexier than hearing real people film themselves orgasm, even if it is a simulated amateur orgasm. I try to sleep, unfulfilled, then hunt around for headphones, watch the clip again, realise it's lost its impact and search for another, by which time my bedtime ardour has subsided and I switch my lamp on, doing the one thing I haven't done since Rach left. I pick a book off the stack of freebies publishers have sent me, if to just endorse on Twitter, and scan the first line. I put it back down on the pile. I load up a website that streams illegal television and find myself something with canned laughter to tune out the sound and feel of another human in my flat. It has started to feel suffocating.

*

'Write drunk; edit sober LOL' is the text message I receive from Hayley. I ignore it. How do you react to a non-sequitur like that? She follows it up with another text: 'I'm adding LOL to the end of all my texts now. What do you think LOL?'

'What's happening, babes? You cool?' I reply an hour later.

She replies: 'Yeah, just wondering when we can hang out LOL Also, babes? LOL.'

'Soon,' I reply.

'Specific. Almost too specific LOL.'

'Sorry, got a weird day. I'll tell you about it.'

'I've got secrets too,' she replies. 'Stuff that'd melt the nose off your nose. See you soon LOL xx.'

Out of courtesy, I reply with 'x'. Just one. Not 2. To keep her on her toes.

'LOL x' is how she leaves it.

Sitting on the train with Kitab 2, you'd think he'd never been on a train before. His eyes are everywhere: reading over people's shoulders, watching hushed commuter conversations, down the tops of poor unsuspecting females.

'Have you never been on a train before?' I ask him.

'I've never seen so many hotties, dude. They are everywhere!'

I look around at the scorched scowls of commuting faces, each one steeled with the need for space to read or zone out or check Facebook repeatedly. Everyone looks ordinary at this time in the morning. They're all dressed in grey or black with matching nail polish, their lips downturned in disappointment. And they don't wait for passengers to get off the train before pushing on.

I ask Kitab 2 for more background details. He is very good at avoiding telling me anything specific. Other than strategies for winning *Halo 4*.

He smiles at me and shakes his head. 'I dunno, man. Look,

she's reading *Fifty Shades*, dude. *Fifty Shades*!' He nods his head. He nods away my question. I persist. 'It's got sex in it,' he adds as a stage whisper. 'I bet she loves it. Sex. It.' He gyrates in his seat, biting his bottom lip with bunny teeth.

'Seriously, Kitab. Tell me about your family,' I say, persisting. 'What did your parents do?'

Kitab doesn't break his stare at the woman reading *Fifty Shades of Grey*. 'My mother was a housewife. My father was a hard worker. Very hard worker,' he says, like an automaton.

He turns to face the commuters, his eyes away from my mouth, which is in an O of confusion. He spots a girl, a pretty, blonde girl in a naval jumper and skinny jeans, reading my book opposite us and down the aisle. He thumps me on the side and points.

But I'm cool. I clocked her when we got on and tried to remain calm because this was the dream – seeing someone organically reading your stuff – it's never happened before. Well, that would require someone actually buying the fucking thing. I don't want to lose my shit in front of Kitab 2 so I keep quiet, bursting into the vaguest of smiles whenever the cover catches the corner of my eye. Kitab 2 can barely contain himself. He thumps my arm and says, 'Dude, dude, look. Dude.'

The commuters in earshot try to subtly look around to what he's pointing at.

'I know, man. It's all good,' I say dismissively, and wish I had something to stare at, other than the crotch of a man in jeans skinnier than the skinniest of my fingers.

'But, dude. It's your book.'

'I know, man. It's cool. It happens.'

'This is exciting, dude.'

'Bro, I know.' Be cool, I think. Let me enjoy the moment. This is a first. This is a legendary moment. Please just shush and let it sink in, awash on top of us. Stop talking. 'Shut up. It happens all the time.'

'Hey,' Kitab 2 calls out. 'Hey!' he says, louder. Everyone is looking at us. I look down at my hands. *Wow, I should cut my nails*, is the look I hope I'm giving. Kitab 2 calls out the name of my book. The girl reading my stupid coming-of-age book looks up. He points at it and then at me before realising I'm not playing. 'That's my book!' he shouts. 'I wrote that.'

The girl holds an ironic thumb up. 'Wow. Cool,' she says flatly. I project my embarrassment onto her. Kitab 2 claiming credit for writing my book is one thing but acknowledging it to a stranger doing the morning commute – that is an urban no-no. The other commuters are looking at him like he's a smug a-hole. The girl has ignored him and returned to his/my book, silently judging a living breathing writer now. She'll probably hate it more than she already does.

At the next stop, we get off the train and so does the girl with the book.

We leave the station and walk in the direction of Kitab 2's future university, hemmed in amongst council blocks and chicken shops. I can sense the girl with the book walking behind us. My ears flush the reddest brown ears can get. My eyes are down at the ground. I am half-listening to Kitab 2's running inventory of his soon-to-be new surroundings.

Chicken shop.

Light fittings.

News vendor.

Supermarket.

Indian supermarket.

Caribbean supermarket.

Chicken shop.

Pub.

Indian supermarket.

African supermarket.

News vendor.

Chicken shop.

It's like a song and this is the repeated chorus. I pull out my phone and type into Twitter: *'Inventory of East London: chicken shops, multi-ethnic supermarkets, a light fittings shop and my target demographic of readers.'* I click send and wait for the ether to respond. I refresh. I refresh. No responses. No interactions. I get a favourite from @partyorifices. A favourite? What's the point? It's not even a retweet. It's a collection of things you might revisit when you're reviewing Twitter's greatest hits. I check to see what @partyorifices is. It claims to be a sex party. Probably a bot. I report them as spam.

'What's up, dude? Tweeting?'

'Yeah.'

'What did you write, dude?'

'Oh, just something funny about this area.'

'Get any RTs, dude?'

'No. Not yet. A few favourites.'

'Who cares about favourites, dude?'

'Yeah.'

'Maybe it wasn't as funny as you thought.'

I don't reply. Kitab 2 breaks the silence by live-tweeting In Real Life what he sees around him. 'Look at this place, dude. It is so real. It is the London I was promised. My dad was worried there would be no Indians. But look at all these shops. And look at you, my best friend in London, another Indian. I am home away from home but here I can do whatever I want. I can eat in that chicken shop all day if I want to. Maybe in London, I will become non-veg like you. Maybe in London, I can write books and have a flat with alcohol in the fridge and a big television. This is it, this is my future. I can feel it. I love it here. I don't ever want to go back.' He pauses and looks at me, waiting for me to look up from my phone. 'Don't ever make me go back.'

'That's up to immigration,' I say.

'This place, dude ... this PLACE!' He goes silent and stares around him. I look back at my phone.

Kitab 2 is happy to note that the university is opposite a phone shop that sells phone cards at discounted rates. He writes down the price per minute of the India card in a notebook he keeps in his trouser pocket.

I look at him. He smiles at me.

'Excuse me.'

We both turn around. It's the girl from the train who was reading my book. She's smiling now. She's not looking confused. 'Hey,' she says, to Kitab 2. 'Sorry, I was just in the zone on the train.' She is Australian and outside in broad daylight, with her blonde frizzy hair waving about in the breeze, looks attractive. She has a hostile reading face, compared to the gummy smile she's flashing my namesake. 'Love the book. Will you sign it for me?'

I look at Kitab 2, as if to say, *What now, dickhead?* He looks at me for visual permission and I give him the slightest tilt of my head. I am in control of this situation, I think. This is the first time this has ever happened to me – talking to someone who has organically read my stupid coming-of-age book and I wish I was the one getting the kudos instead of my namesake, but with that tilt of the head, I confirm that I am the big dog in this situation.

'I didn't love it at first. I thought it was really immature and puerile, and just banging on and on and on about being Asian. But now ...' she looks at us both. 'I get it. I really get it. I mean, who would have thought growing up, for you was so different from how I grew up ... and the same. I mean, I liked the stuff with the dad. He was funny. He was a bit whiny though.'

The girl fumbles in her bag for a pen but Kitab 2 has one in his trouser pocket, tucked into his notebook. He pulls it out, drops the notebook, picks it up and holds out the pen at the same time the girl offers him one. They do the dance of your pen or mine.

The first time I signed a book, I wrote a long and thoughtful message: 'Thank you for being my first, my last, my everything. Don't eBay this. It won't get you any money. Love, Kitab.'

Now I just sign my initials and put a X.

I try to visualise how many physical kisses I might have promised by doing that. I mentally line up all the men and women and imagine kissing them all. On the cheek for lower case x and on the mouth for upper case X. They have mostly been upper case Xs. If x's were actual kisses, I'd have glandular fever.

Kitab 2 takes my book and signs the wrong page. He signs the blank end leaf at the front, and not the title page. This is not author industry standard. Hayley taught me this. You're supposed to cross out your name and write underneath it. He does it all wrong but she doesn't seem to know the difference.

'How long did it take you to write the book?' she asks. Kitab 2 looks up at her and then me.

'Years,' he says. 'Lots of years. But it was worth every word.' He smiles and hands the book back to her.

'I want to write a book,' she says.

'Good. You should.'

'Any advice?'

Watching this all from my side of the fence makes me realise what a phoney I sound like whenever I do 'advice'. Sometimes I co-opt Amis and say 'Get it finished.' If someone asks me for advice, I've been known to say, 'Don't ask for permission.' If anyone asks me where I get my ideas from, I say, 'Life gives us nuggets everyday. Whether we choose to make them chicken or gold is up to us.'

I'm not very good at talking about writing. I'm not that well-read. I've never read Joyce and I've never finished anything by Dickens. My favourite book was turned into a film starring Brad Pitt. Kitab 2 can have all this. Maybe *he* can not squander it. All he has to do is earnestly enjoy the attention, instead of wondering all the time why his peers are doing better than him, like me. He can just enjoy the ride.

'No,' he says. 'I don't need the competition.' He is smooth, I think to myself. I tap him on the shoulder as she bites her lip in appreciation of the sound bite, and gesture him on. He says his goodbyes. I nod at the girl and we walk on. I make us cross the street so we can avoid an awkward same side of the street goodbye. I'm a little gutted that the first time I see someone reading my book in public I don't have the guts to take credit for it, but it's still amazing. My heart does a little extra pound from pride that makes me sweat. I smile as she walks away. I am somebody, I think. Go me.

'Does that happen to you a lot, dude? Wow,' Kitab 2 says, hitting me on my arm.

'Hardly ever, man.'

'It's like electricity.'

'Yeah, it can make your head swell.'

'I know. I like it. Kitab the writer. I like that too. I really liked that. I liked that a lot.'

'You should write a book then,' I say.

'Write a book? I like that.'

Kitab 2 says 'I like that' a lot. But he makes it sound like someone's said a zinger and he appreciates it. Like, 'I ... like ... thaaaaaaaaaat.' He has said it about my shower, about Aziz's mint shower gel, about the tea I made for him and about an email he received this morning, the contents of which were never revealed.

The university is anonymously located in and amongst some estate buildings. It overlooks the river and once you're on campus, it feels like a calm enclave, miles away from the through-road to the east of the city and the rows of chicken shops.

We follow signs for the administration office. Despite the lack of term being in session, students on their theses and dissertations amble about smoking, talking on phones, dressed down for the off-season. I spot 3 pairs of tracksuit bottoms

116

and a questionable pyjama ensemble as we pass the library. In the hub of buildings where teachings happen, there is a zombie apocalypse of quiet. The reception building has its doors open and we walk up the steps into it. There's a statue of an old queen, overseeing administration for the campus. Inside, there are 2 members of staff looking perplexed at computer screens. Everything is quiet. I feel self-conscious breaking the atmosphere of concentration so 'ahem' my arrival. Both of the perplexed receptionists look up. One smiles. The other notes us and returns to his computer screen. The smiling one has the pulse and fizz of someone who is doing something tedious and is happy for the interruption.

'Hi,' she says.

'Hey there,' I reply.

'And how can I help you today?'

'Hey, so this guy here, he's enrolled in your university. He's starting next week. But he hasn't got anywhere to stay yet. When is the earliest he can move into his halls?'

Once the receptionist has realised this is someone else's department she points us in the direction of the housing office. I walk and Kitab 2 follows, looking around at his new place of education.

'Dude,' he says, in a reverential hushed tone. 'We shouldn't bother them. Maybe I just stay with you? Yes?' Kitab 2's body language has changed. He's hunched, his constant fidgets are more nervous.

'Look, Kitab,' I say. 'I'm not being funny but I don't open my house to strangers. I've done it twice for you already. You're not my problem, man. You need to get on with your own stuff.'

'Kitab, I ask only for your kindness. You see, I saw in your eyes, your kindness. You are a kind man who can help me. I have nowhere to go for one week and I don't want to make a fuss. I want only to stay somewhere I can call home. I miss home so much. Please can you help me miss home less. I am no trouble. No problem. Please. I am scared. This is a strange country. You are like me, no? Same-same? Parents from the same place. Please? I ask you.'

'No. I'm really sorry, man.'

'I can make bad trouble for you.'

'Excuse me?'

Kitab 2 touches his finger to his nose and finds blood oozing out slowly. He looks at it and then at me and before we can process what's happening to him, his eyes roll up and back and he falls to the floor. A trickle of blood slithers from his nose.

aZiZWILLKILLYOU episode 8
Aziz vs the Bad Guys
[posted 14 September, 13:06]

My children, I am one of the 1% of people who has kicked someone's ass in the name of righteousness. Take that in your face and smoke it like a crack pipe, bankers.

You are now the 99%.

Look, politics – whatever. Be nice to everyone and everyone will be nice back and if you ever do a fuckery, you will find yourself at the wrong end of an Aziz ass-kicking one day, truss.

Aziz Will Kill You. Get that tattooed on your arm and look at it everyday. Because it is the truest thing that's ever been said. Except 'We were on a break' by Ross to Rachel.

#teamdrgeller

What's all this politics got to do with my special status as kicker of asses? Well, I'll tell you, man. I am ALIVE right now. I went to visit Teddy Baker at his house last night. He met me outside and he was acting weird. He was flinchy and nervy. Like he had a bomb strapped to his chest. You know ... flinchy. Like a flinch. He had a gym bag with him and a long raincoat, like he was going to go and expose himself to a bus stop full of girls and the bag was full of whips, chains and dildos in case shit went off. Nothing says perv like a long raincoat and gym bag. Take that with you on your morning commute tomorrow. Oh, how wrong I was, and you know I hate to be wrong, but in this case, I was more than happy to get it so wrong.

We rode out on the subway to Brooklyn, to an undisclosed location somewhere in this 1 of the 5 boroughs. Let's call it Sector 4. On the way, Teddy Baker told me that he's been Googling me and he was into my blog and all the cray-cray shit I did and maybe I was a cool dude after all, and I was like, Teddy Baker, bruv, you have no idea. Would just anyone in the world come out here on this crazy whim just to share tattoos with each other? I asked the guy if he has a missus or a mister or whatever, I was cool with whatever. He smiled and says he didn't have time for loving, he was on a path of righteousness. This was when alarm bells start ringing in my brain because, to me, a path of righteousness translated as 'I love Jesus, wanna love Jesus with me?' So I started asking him more questions to try and establish his religious beliefs, like, did he believe in an afterlife or whether he believed in heaven and he looked at me, like 'Dickhead, why you asking me about God?' So I shut up. I was rumbled. Then he told me where we were going – I couldn't reveal to no one. It was our secret. I winked at him. I am not telling you where we went. No way. It's a secret.

Okay, so not an exact address, but you know … a thereabouts to set the scene, because we were in New York and it is the coolest city in the world. Sector 4 of the Brooklyn Quadrant in New York.

Somewhere in deepest darkest Brooklyn, he took me to this bar that wasn't too far from the subway; it was underneath one of those flatpack houses that looked like a big bad wolf could huff and puff and blow it down. It was all PVC white panels on the outside, and inside, it was all square boxes and American drama series clean kitchen counters and hardwood floors. There was one that was kinda leaning against its neighbour. Underneath it in the basement, there was a bar called Micky McGinty's (truth serum aside: this is not the real name of the bar, but instead the coolest name for a bar ever – I'm gonna open a bar. It's gonna be called Micky McGinty's. We'll only serve rum and play sea shanties. And you'll have to piss in the street if you need the toilet. That is how we do).

Inside, he ordered us shots of Jameson's and they came with free cans of this thing called Pabst-Blue Ribbon that tasted cheap and disgusting and 7 parts water to half a hop; it's the best beer I've ever had. We shotgunned the beers and he said, let's play darts. So I said, yeah, cool, let's play darts.

Now we were playing darts for a good hour or so, and I'm a good darts player. I kept thrashing him at '301'. And we were knocking back shots of Jameson's and shotgunning Pabst-Blue Ribbon. We had like 6 of them in the hour and I beat him 3 times and we didn't really talk while we were playing but that's cool. I just watched him. He occasionally looked at the door or at the bar and smiled at people walking in, but it was pretty dead. They didn't even play music in this place. The girl at the counter was reading David Foster Wallace like a fucking ponce (yo, Kit – they love that Foster Wallace shit out here. Shame you're too much of a dumb fuck to understand it. Sorry peoples, that's my bro. Carry on). We started practising throwing our darts backwards and we missed the board by miles. Teddy Baker kept doing his unhinged throat giggle – a real 'tee-hee-hee'. He threw his darts backwards as hard as he could while I was styling out

121

attempts at overhead throws. We were pissed and we were breaking all health and safety conventions in safe darts playing. We were throwing them blind, over our heads, through our legs, we were laughing like goons. At some point, I nearly threw the dart through the side of the face of this guy in a baseball cap and turquoise basketball vest as he walked past. He turned to me and was like, what the fuck you doing cuz? So I went ragu sauce on him, like, 'Bruv, don't worry about it. I get you. I didn't do nothing, naaaaaah'mean. Leave it. Leeeeeave it,' like I was Lethal Bizzle defending the Tulisa sex tape on YouTube. He pushed at me and I pushed back at him. Suddenly, I couldn't breathe and I was being pulled back by a pool cue against my neck, like tightly against my neck, choking Aziz, proper choke-hold. The blue baseball cap guy put his drinks down on a table and walked up to me smiling. I was trying to figure out where Teddy Baker was and then I clocked, the boy holding me was him. Teddy Baker had taken me hostage and the guy who I nearly darted was squaring up to punch me. And Teddy Baker was whispering in my ear, 'Dude, just let it happen. Don't fear it. Don't be an asshole. Just let it happen' and I was spluttering cos I couldn't breathe but my splutters were like spitballs of W.T.F. And I remembered the gym bag and the long raincoat and I thought, 'What's in the gym bag? What's in the gym bag?' The guy went to hit me and I tensed my stomach muscles and Teddy Baker pulled me close and the guy stopped his fist at my solar plexus ... just hanging there and he looked up at me and Teddy Baker released me and they laughed.

They were pissing themselves.

'Bob, this is that crazy cat Aziz I was telling you about. Aziz, this is Bob.'

'Who's Bob?'

'I'm Bob.'

'Yeah, Bob. I get that, Bob,' I said, rubbing my stomach and my neck. 'But who the fuck are you, Bob?'

He laughed and said, 'The dude who's going to change your life'.

Bob has not met me. Obviously.

There are no comments for this blog.

History:

Lose weight in 30 days – pop-up
Flights to New York – Expedia

I'm not proud of it but I ran. I left Kitab 2 there between the administration office and the housing office on the floor, curled up, hyperventilating and bleeding from his nose and I ran. I ran towards the library and then out of the university, which was filling up now with out of season students working on their coursework.

A day later and I'm racked with guilt. I check my interactions. Today's motivational Vedic message from my uncle is: 'If you have never eaten rice with your hands, how can you know the taste of the earth on your lips?'

I delete it from my Facebook wall. I check Rach's Facebook account. She is now friends with 263 people, 16 of whom are mutual friends. There are a few new photographs of her, all with that impish half smile of hers. She looks good. I want to call her. That impish half smile is what attracted me to her in the first place. And the Pippi Longstocking-like plaits in her hair. I check through Aziz's blog and email him some corrections. I listen out for his sounds in the flat. Nothing. Not even the squeak of a mattress or the whirring of an electric blanket. I look over my computer at a picture of him and me pinned to my noticeboard. We're riding bikes. He's flexing his bicep. I'm laughing. Always laughing with Aziz.

I refresh my Facebook feed. The Vedic message has reappeared. Even though I deleted it, it refuses to go away.

'If you have never eaten rice with your hands, how can you know the taste of the earth on your lips?'

I tweet: 'Oh to be truly anonymous online. Says a nobody.'

It gets retweeted 17 times and favourited 4 times. I delete my uncle from my Facebook account. If he notices, I'll blame a bug. I don't want him in my space anymore. I want to reclaim myself online.

An hour after deleting my uncle from my Facebook, he calls me up and leaves a message asking why I've done this.

I didn't feel any guilt about running away at the time. It was only when I got to the train station and took stock of my flight that I felt a morsel of remorse for leaving him on the floor, unable to fend for himself.

I got on a train and returned home. At home, I threw myself into writing, which meant I promptly checked my email and got lost in a slurry of job alerts, press releases of books and songs I'd never bother with, and Facebook and Twitter notifications, which I deleted to keep me at inbox zero. I thought about setting up a Tumblr called Vincent Van Gok Wan, where I would superimpose Gok Wan glasses onto Van Gogh self-portraits. I'd have to learn how to use Photoshop.

No one else had contacted me. I didn't dare visit any social networking sites in case Kitab 2 was following me – certainly nothing that betrayed my movements or my feelings at my abandonment of another human being in their time of need.

The flat feels empty without Aziz, and dealing with Kitab 2 makes me feel like I've lost the day. I send Aziz an email he'll probably not bother replying to. Sitting here with my own space returned to me, with the coffee pot still wringing juice from its beans, with the slow caress of Smog playing on the speakers, I feel nothing.

By the time the evening comes, I realise I haven't spoken to anyone since leaving Kitab 2 at the university. I have forgotten how to communicate. I log into Facebook and look up my name.

Guilt has made me think I will add Kitab 2 on Facebook after all. We can be electronic friends and when he has his own life here with his own space and his own friends we can moot a drink that will never happen. My way of apologising for abandoning him when he passed out is to add him on Facebook so we can be electronic friends. This is the barest minimum of friendships now. It's a peace offering though.

I find something bizarre when I look him up.

The search results display 3 results. One is me – I recognise it because I have recently taken off the option to see my list of friends or add me as a friend. Also, the photograph is a picture I took of a window display involving my novel amongst 3 of my heroes that someone sent me from their local bookshop. There's a fan page my publisher set up, that has a pathetic 40 'likes', pretty much all of them being my family apart from someone I met at a wedding, who 'liked' the page in front of me, during the speeches to show how impressed he was that I was a writer. And there's Kitab 2. Except I can't see Kitab 2. Only another profile that has my picture as its avatar. It's the 'official' me photograph that Aziz took outside a restaurant, against the ubiquitous brick wall of creatives who want to appear urban and edgy. Which is how I would define myself.

Why is there another me on Facebook? How is that? I click on it. Have I been cloned?

The information listed is bare. It has a name only. No age, no likes or dislikes. Just the name. My name. And a map, which shows London and Bangalore as the last places this account has been.

Kitab 2.

The cock-end.

He has taken down his photo, the one that looks like a scan of a driver's licence photographed on a camera phone, and put my photo up, a press shot he must have got off Google.

I pace the flat weighing up the facts. I play Flappy Bird

violently. Is identity theft worse than abandonment? I left him in a corridor passed out when I could have helped him or at least checked if he was okay. What he's done, well, if I was actually famous, like Kanye-famous, would be de rigueur for a namesake. If I was called Brad Pitt, I'd probably have a photo of Brad Pitt as my avatar. Standard operating procedure.

But this, this isn't right. I'm an individual. I'm myself. I'm the only me. So for him to do this, it counts as identity theft. People could be searching for me and finding him. He could be putting up all kinds of rubbish on his timeline, in my name. I'm the only me there is.

Angry, I write a message to him, not knowing how else to confront him but when I read it back, it feels garbled and silly, an overreaction. How dare you use a photo of me instead of a photo of you online? What kind of person are you? You arsehole, you dick. All the insults. On re-reading, I feel silly for even being annoyed about it. It's not like he's stolen my passport or anything. I don't send the message.

I stand up and walk around the flat, working out my best appropriate response because this shouldn't go unnoted.

When I've finished pacing the study, I come back to my computer and stare at Kitab 2 masquerading as me. I click onto my news feed. There's nothing else to do. I click on the private messages and decide to plough through them as a distraction. I have 17. 10 of them are invitations to events, reminders of birthday parties and announcements of news. 5 of them are the remnants of Facebook chats I got bored of and checked out of, meaning the messages ended up in my inbox. It's a mixture of 'see you later' and 'xxx' and so can be ignored.

But, there, second to top, is a message from Kitab 2. I look at the time it's been sent. It was sent 2 hours ago.

2 hours ago when I was staring blankly at a Word document, at where I left off some work a few days ago, trying my hardest to summon up the impetus to write what was in my brain.

Kitab 2 is fine! I think while my computer thinks and loads up the message.

It says:

Dude,

Uncool. I thought we were going to be friends. I only wanted to be like my namesake, dude. You are the coolest, dude. But today, that was uncool, dude.

Xoxo The Real Kitab

What does he mean, The Real Kitab? The rest of it is understandable, a semi-peace offering but understandably annoyed given how I abandoned him up at his university. But The Real Kitab? The Real Kitab wouldn't hide behind an avatar of someone else. I want to message him and ask about the photo calmly now. Instead of angrily. Inside though, I feel rage, an unmitigating fiery burn of desperate need to unload on the internet. I look at the clock. I have been on my computer for hours. I have achieved nothing.

My brain is wrapped in circles. I can't think. I miss Aziz. This is a time when I need his unwanted unburdened-by-self-consciousness advice. The best I can do is log off and pull my laptop shut. I look at the time. My chest is tight and burning, with nerves. I don't know why I feel nervous. I crouch down in a squat to help me breathe.

I check Twitter. Nothing is happening. My last tweet: 'Dudes, I'm alive' – I don't even remember writing it.

I look up at the time. I head to the pub.

Mitch's take on the whole situation is clear: 'If you sign up for one of those social networking sites, you deserve everything you get. You know he's probably a spy. For Google. Or the CIA. Either/or. It's all the same. It all sounds a bit much for you at the moment, doesn't it?'

Mitch doesn't know what he's talking about. I tell him. 'Mitch, you don't know what you're talking about.'

'Don't I? Looks to me like you've got yourself into a pickle of shit. A shit pickle. A shit pickle of your own doing. People are always tweeting their breakfasts or telling the world they're mildly annoyed about something. What about books, Kit? What about phone calls? Whatever happened to watching the flicks at the pictures and not the telly on the phone? I tell you something, I like things. I like books and I like vinyl and I love privacy.' There's a spot on Mitch's head that he always rubs, up and to the right of his crown. I asked him once if that was why he was going bald and he shook me by my lapels angrily.

'You're a dinosaur.'

'And Google is my asteroid, my friend.'

I go on Twitter but I'm kicked out of the app. I reload it and it signs me back in. Mitch sighs. I check my follower count. I check my interactions – none. I check my last tweet, 'Girls like writers. Where are my groupies, dudes?' I don't remember writing that. Mitch grabs my phone from me and puts it on the bar.

'Be in the room, Kit,' he growls.

'Sorry,' I say. I'm confused. I saw the screen so quickly maybe it didn't say what I thought it did. 'What you reading at the moment?'

'Oh, man,' Mitch says. 'What am I not reading? If I'm not eating, I'm reading. Sometimes both at the same time.' I want to look at my phone. 'A collection of Don DeLillo short stories.'

I've never read Don DeLillo, which goes against every single interview I've ever done, all of which cite him as a hero. The books are too long. I don't have the patience. What's wrong with blogs documenting canapés and Tumblrs about the career of my childhood crush, Gillian Anderson? While Mitch orders our next round, I pick my phone up off the bar and check Twitter. I find myself with an influx of followers and new @-replies.

'LOLZ – your cock's tiny.'

'Hahahahahaha – your books are cock and bull stories. Shame your cock isn't.'

'Bro, y r u so prverted.'

'SEX PEST AUTHOR. SEX PEST AUTHOR. SEX PEST AUTHOR.'

Mitch looks at me and notices my frown of confusion.

'Checking your phone again. God, what now? Someone telling you what they had for dinner?'

Why are all my followers calling me a sex pest or commenting on my penis? I check my @-replies all the way down to someone I know. It's Hayley (@Hayleyspen on Twitter). It was 20 minutes and 40 @-replies ago.

'Oh, chico … WTF?!'

I view the entire conversation. According to my timeline, I tweeted 20 minutes ago (while I was being berated for all of modern life's sins by Mitch) saying, 'My penis is bigger and better than my books' with a link to a twitpic.

I know what it is. I can't bear to confirm what it is. I know what it is.

I have to see what it is.

I click on the picture. Mitch is harrumphing, opening up an old paperback he's brought with him. The picture loads. I wait. The minutes build up, we're all slowly dying waiting for things to load on our phones.

It's a close-up of a flaccid brown penis. More ball than shaft. More curve than straight. And hairy, like a Jimi Hendrix picture, wild, thick and unkempt. Like a yeti with a long nose.

I pinch in till it blurs then out again.

Is this me? Did I do this?

It's definitely not mine. I keep a trim perimeter. My stomach burns. I feel a cold sweat.

I pull my fingers apart on the screen to zoom in and examine all the contours of the penis. It is very brown, browner than

130

the thighs at the fringes of the photo. The hair is thick and wild. The Jimi Hendrix comparison still stands. The penis droops to the left and into a point, like the end of an elephant's trunk, except the foreskin has been pulled up over the end. It looks vacuum-sealed.

It hits me. I get a flash of a waddling bottomless brown man.

I flash back to Kitab 2's penis, adding a 'Toaster' filter from Instagram to the memory. I saw his penis this morning when he was waddling about like Donald Duck. He must have tweeted this picture of his penis on my timeline. But why? I immediately start worrying about silly things like my reputation, my standing with females, my friends, anyone who might see this and think I did it.

An online reputation can last for ever. Ask the Star Wars lightsabre kid.

I delete the tweet from my timeline but it's too late. The damage has been done. He's inflicted maximum carnage. I can see it's been shared about 50 times. I excuse myself to the loo and sit on a rancid former toilet seat, trying to log into the Twitpic website. I find the incriminating photo and delete it. I change the password to my Twitter account and tweet that I've been hacked.

@kitab: 'apologies for any damage done to retinas with previous tweet but I've been hacked by a tiny-cocked exhibitionist. at least he's indian.'

But it's too little too late.

The books editor of a major broadsheet has retweeted the photo. She followed me after I tweeted something funny to her so I've been holding on to her patronage for dear life. But she has retweeted the photo with an added 'The things authors do for attention eh?' So have a lot of people I know IRL. People are calling me all manner of names, like sex pest, rapey Kitab, pervert, idiot, cunt, douchebag – any rude word said about anyone is being levelled at me by friends, strangers and users of the internet. A couple of publicist girls are tweeting anecdotes about times I was drunk and sleazy towards them. Backlash to my book, seemingly well received at the time, is turning vitriolic. Someone calls me the 'most unimportant writer of his generation'. Another says that my cock is more impressive than my writing, and my cock is tiny. Somewhere in the world, Kitab 2's penis is tingling with all this attention.

I check the photo against my own penis just to make sure it wasn't taken candidly or secretly. Definitely not mine. It's too wild and unkempt to be mine. I'm caught looking at the phone screen and my own penis by a man wanting to use the cubicle. I've forgotten to lock the door. I nod at him as I leave hastily.

He arches his eyebrow at me.

'Cancer app. Checking for testicle cancer.'

He nods and pulls out his phone.

'Cool, what's the name of the app?' he says.

'Nuts to Cancer,' I say quickly, and leave before he can ask for clarification.

Back at the bar, Mitch has disappeared out the back for a cigarette. He's left his paperback on top of his pint. I down half of my beer, dry-heave a burp out of the depths of my stomach and realise I need to leave. I've got a film of cold sweat on my top lip. Mitch is still out at the back of the pub, smoking, but won't mind being left to his own devices. Often, I think he enjoys it. This is his local. He's used to bringing paperbacks here on dates.

I hurry home to press refresh on Twitter, waiting for the fuss to die down and for people to tweet about reality television again. Of this much, you can be sure. Twitter is the water cooler of the evening. Imagine all those conversations with loved ones lost to quipping on the internet with comedians for lolz. I don't respond to anything, least of all to people I know. I don't have anything to say. The phone, the connection – the thing between Rach and me. Eyes on 2 screens, phone in hand, ready to be the first to tweet the most obvious joke about what's on screen at any given time. The minor fuss eventually peters out. I don't have that many followers. A few thousand. And now ... most of them and their friends have seen my penis. I notice an auto-tweet from Amazon on my keyword search for my own fucking name saying that Kindle sales of my novel have hit the top 10 in fiction bestsellers. Maybe I should have done this myself months ago.

That night, I don't sleep.

I stare at the wall above my laptop, which lies on the bed next to me. The screen eventually goes to sleep and I'm left in a cocoon of semi-darkness. I have no plan. I don't know how to deal with this. This is certainly new. This is not where I expected my week in a fortress of solitude to lead me.

My room feels like a cage. I can hear the opening chords of a Jimi Hendrix song. In my head, Kitab 2's penis is the head of the axeman, thrashing away at Foxy Lady. I open my eyes and turn all the lights on. I feel unnerved.

When I can't sleep, I scan through unopened emails. I find a job advert for a freelance journalist required to write blogs for a waste management site. To distract myself, I pull together a covering letter to go with my one page CV, the one that basically says I'm unhireable because all I've done is write a book.

I send the application off, thinking good karma thoughts to myself about getting something constructive done.

I check my interactions.

The final word on my Twitter scandal comes from Mitch, who has signed up for an account and so far only follows me and @guardianbooks.

'Saw you left me in the pub so thought I'd see what all the fuss was about. Apparently, it was your cock. What a shitpickle.'

My dad phones me 4 hours later. It's 6 a.m. – his usual wake-up time. I answer the phone on the first ring.

133

'Kitab, beta,' he says. 'Is this what it takes to sell books? Nude media? Why can't you just be an accountant like your good old Dad?'

'Thanks, Dad.'

'No, thank you. You made me laugh more than anyone in the last year.'

'Well, I'm glad you got a kick out of it. How did you see it? Are you on Twitter?'

'I have a look now and again to see what my son does. He never calls me. Now … whose willy was that, son?'

Bless you, Dad. For you can tell my penis apart from a stranger on the internet. At least I know you care.

I'm distracted in my search for Kitab 2 the next morning by emails. This is what popularity must feel like. My search has been fruitless. It's been online. I haven't found him. I'm about to contact the university when I notice my broadband hub is flashing that it's down. I reach over to reset it.

My phone rings, shocking me. All my interactions have been online. The number isn't in my contact list but I recognise the last 3 digits from the amount of times I dialled them. It's Rach. It's been 6 months and not a word then 2 phone calls in a week?

I answer wincing, like she's already telling me off, 'Hello?'

'Hey Kitab, how are you? I thought I'd check in on you. Nancy, you remember Nancy?' (Of course I remember your lairy-when-drunk sidekick.) 'Well, Nancy said you've been sending people pictures of your penis on Twitter. Why are you doing that? Is everything okay? I know things are tough …'

I pause. 'Hey Rach, lovely to hear from you. How are you?'

'Are you having a breakdown?'

'Of course I'm having a breakdown. Someone hacked my account and put a picture of their tiny cock on my Twitter feed.'

'I couldn't believe it so I had a look for myself.'

'Rach …'

'I'd recognise your penis anywhere, honey.'

'I don't have time for this right now.'

'Please don't say it's to do with grief. You can't live off that excuse and a ridiculous inheritance for ever.'

'Rachel. Please. I need to go.'

'I'm glad you're proud of yourself. Stuff like that makes it very easy to get over you, Kitab. Which hasn't been easy. Now, though, it suddenly feels like the right decision.'

She hangs up.

She obviously doesn't remember my penis that well, which is darker and less ball-heavy than Kitab 2's. Which begs the question, who takes stock of each phallus they come into contact with? Could you match the boobs and face of everyone you've slept with, Kit? No, probably not.

I'm mentioned in a flurry of comments on the *Guardian*, where commentators mock my tactics for getting noticed for a book that was okay. Nothing special. Not Hollinghurst or Rushdie. Just funny and twee and harmless. They didn't know who I was yesterday. Now they're experts. The commentators discuss the lengths authors go to for attention now they have the channels to take control of their own promotion and be responsible for their own content, bypassing a previously successful vetting process by a publicity team, and is that a good thing? The final comment before discussion peters out wonders whether Dickens himself would have been more famous in his lifetime if he'd printed a picture of his Dick[ens] next to install-ments of *The Pickwick Papers*, which is a stupid comparison. He was famous in his lifetime. And probably had a massive penis.

I wake up to the same number of followers on Twitter as I did last night but 50 new 'is now following' emails. At least I'm gaining at the same rate I'm losing. Which means I'm still losing. Luckily this hasn't really exploded on my Facebook profile yet, so my family is blissfully unaware of my shortcomings as a man.

It's not like I've been punched. It's not like it's been a physical public shaming. These pixels carry weight.

I need to find him. I have to ensure he has no other passwords of mine, work out why he did what he did. I can't access his Facebook. He hasn't accepted my too little too late friend request. He's not obvious on Twitter. I've searched through all my followers hoping to spot him but I can't. He's a digital ghost all of a sudden. Google searches only bring up me and I drill down to the 20th page, and there's nothing about him. The only result that comes up is the search for his Facebook page. He obviously doesn't care about privacy that much, or prospective employees only finding his Facebook during the inevitable Google check.

To the university.

I run to the train station, panting with months and years of inactivity sending my heart rate into conniptions. I flick through a free newspaper, trying to calm myself down, but every word seen burns away on my retina and I take nothing in. I check my phone, knowing there's no signal in these tunnels. I scroll the screen down to refresh, like a tic, knowing that there's no reception. I need to be plugged in. I need to know what's going on. I wonder how our brains function in these short bursts of signal outage. How do the commuting masses cope when their 3G signal drops in and out and they have to either read or listen to music or converse? I'm trembling, desperate to check my Twitter and see if I've been replaced by something of actual worth as a literary news story in my little ghetto of the internet, something bigger than my penis. I can't cope with this black hole of no information.

Arriving at the university, I keep an eye out for Kitab 2. Maybe skulking in doorways, following me, shopping for food. He's Single Brown Male-ing me.

At the administration office, I ask after him and no one has heard of him. Or me. But that's fine. It's not important right now. No one remembers administering medical attention to a passed out single brown male yesterday morning, which makes me wonder whether it happened. I trace our steps back to the stairs leading up to the housing office and look down at the linoleum, hoping for blood traces like I'm a TV detective and this is the crime I need to solve the day before I retire.

I chase the trail up the stairs to the housing office. It's closed for lunch. I allow myself a Twitter break, plug my phone into an unused electrical socket and sit down on the floor.

Twitter has moved on to Prime Minister's Question Time and reality television. I am officially yesterday's news. I break my Twitter silence with a tweet about sitting on linoleum being bad for my piles.

I send it into the ether and click on refresh till I get a reply.

'Send us a picture of your piles next to your massive bollocks, mate. #themostpointlessnovelistinBritain.'

I sigh and ask him not to flirt with me in public, breaking the cardinal rule of the internet: 'Do not feed the internet troll' – whatever sarcastic comment you make they will deconstruct and make you feel stupid within 5 seconds. Don't even think about it, mate.

'Why do you want to see my bollocks so much, "mate"?'

'I don't. I want you to fuck off and die.'

'Why don't you fuck off?'

'With this witty banter, I'm surprised you haven't won a Booker.'

During this back and forth, I leave my own body and watch myself from the outside, laughing at my own brilliant putdowns and snorting at his. After 7 minutes of a back and forth, I come to my senses and stop saying anything. I can feel my heart racing. I feel no better than before. No more vindicated or venerated. I'm still the guy who put a picture of my penis on the internet.

I wish Aziz was here. He'd know what to do.

An hour later, a harassed-looking lady with glasses and middle-aged spread opens the door to the housing office, wolfing down the last 2 bites of a sandwich.

'Yes,' she says with a voice that says I have 30 seconds to catch her attention.

I decide that asking after Kitab 2 is pointless because bureaucracy's favourite policy is hiding behind confidentiality. If I ask for Kitab 2's contact details, I'll be fobbed off before I finish my query. A 29-second shutdown. That's what she wants.

I share his name. I have the bankcard to prove it. I channel his accent, which is Americanised Indianised Queen's English, not too comedy, not too international, and say, 'Hi, I'm Kitab Balasubramanyam. I wanted to look into perhaps enquiring into my accommodation for the term.'

'You know term doesn't start for a week.'

'I know. I want to know where to send my boxes.'

I realise the mistake I've made. If she's already seen Kitab 2, then maybe she'll recognise my name. She doesn't. Not a Twitter follower either then. She's probably definitely not seen my penis picture.

She sits down at her computer and licks the remnants of pickle off her fingers before logging into her desktop. I thank her and she asks me to spell my name, which I do. She searches. I can't see the screen. But a warning 'urrr' stab keeps sounding through the PC speakers every time she hits 'Enter' on the keyboard.

'Is there a problem?' I ask, forgetting my accent. She looks up at me and then back at the screen.

'You're not a student here.'

'I'm what?'

'I don't have you registered as a student.'

'But I am a student here. I've travelled all the way from Bangalore to be a student here.'

'Honestly, I have no record of you on the system. Are you sure you're at the right university?' She pauses. 'It happens a lot with foreign students.'

This goes on for a few more minutes, a circular conversation where I qualify my name and she insists she has no record of it. I say my name louder and slower and she insists louder and firmer. Either way, we don't get anywhere so I thank her for her time and leave the office.

Outside, I retrieve the iPhone I've left charging in the wall by accident and sit back down.

Before processing what I've just learnt, I check my email, Facebook and Twitter ...

I've been asked to no longer contribute a short story to an installation at a gallery, one that required 4 hour-long coffees to discuss, as my inappropriate online behaviour makes me less than family friendly. This is £250 for 4 hours of my time I won't see.

On Twitter, the references to my penis picture have slowed. People are talking about something else now. Which is fine by me. I want to jump in and have my say on what's now the water cooler topic but I don't dare. My fingers try to betray me.

On Facebook, my cousin posts a picture of his baby's first birthday party, a video of her babbling something incomprehensible but cute. I 'like' it. Out of obligation. I 'like' a few more things hoping the goodwill will bestow some karma on me.

There is no reply from Kitab 2.

Kitab 2 who doesn't even go to the university.

I leave the accommodation building and decide to walk along the canal running behind the university buildings back towards the general direction of my flat so I can think.

I remember when Twitter was fun.

*

A couple of weeks after Rach moved out, Aziz took it upon himself to get me to leave the flat. I resisted but he's one big war of attrition. He wore me down and we spent a night walking the length of the canal looking for adventures. Our mission was to live-tweet the journey and drink as many cans of beer as we could find. I was feeling cavalier with Aziz next to me. I didn't care how I came across online. We started at 9 o'clock, having decided to embark on this grand journey at 8.50 p.m. instead of going home. We'd gone to the pub for a quiet drink but had forgotten the pub was having its monthly poetry night and thirsty for good times, we decided to bail and do something stupid instead of listen to autumnal turgid couplets.

Along the walk, we saw 17 different graffiti artists, 24 runners, 2 cyclists, 12 homeless people and an arguing couple. No one wanted to talk to us and no one would take us on an adventure. When we walked past a row of occupied canal boats where couples and singles were settling in for the evening, we fantasised that we might accidentally walk in on orgies. Instead we walked in silence the whole time, complaining about the cold and the lack of people to talk to and needing the loo. We'd been together all day and had nothing to say to each other. In lieu of adventures, we decided to make them up. We made up a story about how we had met a series of costumed and cloaked men and women on their way to a houseboat sex party and somehow, because we had a blue plastic bag full of beer cans, we were allowed to come with them. We tweeted about the weird people we came across, the weird made-up people and their priapic expectations for a sexual healing of an evening. We made up horny housewives, impotent bankers who liked to watch, and Gary – everyone's mate Gary who loved doing everything and thought everything was well funny, in a proper Essex accent, like 'that's well funny' because everything was well funny. And he was going along for some sexy shits and giggles. We had a lot of fun doing it and it probably caught the imagination of 5 people who kept asking us weird things to ask the weird people we'd made up we were with. We soon became the mystique of the evening. Real life didn't matter as much as the claim of a life better than the one everyone else was having, i.e., pressing refresh on Twitter instead of talking or absorbing or having adventures of their own. We had the smugness of being 2 people who were inventing a life more interesting than a life spent on Twitter, on Twitter.

We then tried to live-tweet a bank robbery. But after people started tweeting us stay safe tips, alerting media tweeters and worrying about us, the game was up. It had lost its thrill.

Walking back home along the canal today, I get a pang of homesickness. I'm alone. I have to come up with solutions myself. I don't have Aziz around to advise me, tell me the wrongest thing to do in order to make the right one seem so clear. The canal looks nothing like our inventions and when I get home, I trawl through his old blogs, emails and texts, hoping there'll be a message from the past telling me what to do and how to do it, and then I'll know what the right thing to do is.

I get distracted by how much trouble he appears to be in. I phone him and it goes to voicemail. He hasn't changed his voicemail since he was 14. I'm doing the backing vocals. 'Yo-yo-yo-yo it's Aziz [one time]. I'm busy killin' em softly [2 time]. Leave a message [one time].'

141

Bob was an intense dude. You'd best describe him as a cop
on the edge, a maverick who played by his own rules, a red-
faced sizzled douchebag. He had terrible pockmarks and dirty
fingernails – the hallmarks of a deviant. He had no swag.
Teddy Baker called him his 'favourite motherfucking city-
dwelling redneck'. I shook his hand and Bob just kinda nodded
at me. Teddy Baker ushered us out of the bar and we went
into the flat above it. Inside it was this empty exposed floorboard crack den chic kinda place where there was no furniture,
only a sofa and a chair and a mattress that all looked like
they'd been at the business end of a stream of piss. 'Right
on,' I said. And they both laughed. Inside the flat – sorry, the
apartment – was cold and empty. No one lived here. But Teddy
Baker walked over to the cupboard by the door and opened
it. Inside there were 3 long costumes hanging up. He grabbed
them and threw one to me.

'Put that on,' he said. I asked what it was. 'You'll see,' he
said and winked.

He stripped down to his meat and stood in front of me, cock
swinging for all to see. Let me tell you homeys, right? If
Aziz is the guy with the ample length to arm himself with
a billy club then this guy has a weapon of mass ejaculation
down his pants. He pulled at it and I was thinking, what the
hell is this place? Some kind of weird swingers doggers
furries bears circle jerk empty flat? Was I about to get

myself killed? Now, peoples, you know I don't mind a bit of stranger danger but this is weird. He started putting on his outfit and it was an all-in-one wetsuit spandex monstrosity. It was black and grey with silver shoulder blades, and ... yes, a cape.

'Are you about to murder me, Teddy Baker?' I asked. Bob and Teddy Baker looked at each other, then towards me and laughed their cocks off, both swinging in my direction.

'No, dude. We're not going to murder you.'

'Coulda did that in the bar,' man of few words, Bob, said.

'Tonight you join us in the fight for justice. We need numbers.'

'You guys crime-fighters or something?' I've read comics. I know the ruckus. They both nodded sheepishly, like they were ashamed of it. Crime-fighter Aziz, I think. Fuck it. I've been fighting crime since I was a youth. Might as well do it properly. I stripped down to my meat.

'You can keep your boxers on if you want,' Bob said. 'Teddy here likes to swing free.'

'Yeah,' Teddy Baker said. 'You haven't lived life if you haven't kicked a purse snatcher in the face with your big balls flying through the air.'

'What if someone whacks you in the nuts?' I asked. They both shrugged.

As I slipped my spandex costume over Big Aziz, I realised there was protective padding around the nuts. I was a bit unhappy cos my suit is mostly gold sequins. I looked like an Egyptian god.

'What's your handles?' I asked.

'Like what?' Bob said. Dude was so aggressive.

'Like your superhero names?'

'This ain't a comic book, buddy,' Bob said. 'I'm Bob. He's Teddy. You're ZZ.'

'Aziz.'

'Whatever.'

'Yeah, dude,' Teddy Baker said, coming back from the mirror in the bathroom. 'We're just fighting on the side of right-eousness so we don't hide behind any names.'

'Oh, okay. Why is my costume so gold?'

'That's for our lady, Mika. She's this Japanese student who studies Egyptology. That's her suit.'

'Where is she tonight? Dead? In the hospital?'

'Nah, dude. Period pains. Women eh?'

For the record, #azizlovesallwomen. I ain't down with all that subjugation talk.

My costume, made for a Japanese student, kinda groaned around the Aziz bulk. It was properly tight. Even with the protective padding, you could make out every vein and contour on Big Aziz, which was cool if purse snatchers were fit. But they were probably just idiots with beanie hats. Not my style.

Once we were suited up, Teddy passed round some camouflage paint to wear on our faces. 'Aren't I brown enough?' I said. They both nodded.

'Where you from?' Bob asked, like it would be a problem whatever I said, unless I said the Good ol' US of A.

'I'm from England,' I said.

'I know where you live,' he said. 'But where you from?'

'Oh. London.'

'Not India. Taliban?'

'Nah, mate. Hindu.'

'So, Muslim.'

'Fucking hell, you really don't know the rest of the world, do you, chief?'

Bob stared at me hoping I'd explain the difference but I let it hang and turned to Teddy Baker.

'You look Indian, Teddy. How come? Swarthy parents?'

Teddy Baker looked up and rushed towards me, trying to grab me by the neck but Aziz knows self-defence so I batted him away and put up my dukes.

145

'No one asks about my parents,' he said. 'No one.'

'Yeah, cool, man. No worries.'

What a strange and mysterious reaction. He's got issues there. In the last 24 hours, though, I'd added him on Facebook and when he accepted me, I went through all his friends and family. He had his whole family listed there. His sisters Rita and Anita, and his mum wrote 'lol x' on every status he made and his dad worked for a hospital. The things you can find out online, eh? His mum's name was Rupa and his dad's name was Tim. I think I get it.

Now we were suited up, we all looked at ourselves in the mirror and despite the stinky atmosphere – not only was it awkward, but it smelt of dead cat faeces in this place – we all looked suitably bad-ass.

We headed out into the night.

And what adventures we had, dear reader. You have no fucking idea. Here's a spoiler though: Bob remains a douchebag throughout.

There are 15 comments for this blog:

df325: Wow, Aziz, you are the coolest.

KJAYSAYYAY: Dude, this is amazing. I knew you were a superhero.

Gogo Girl 322: Aziz, What DId You Guys Do?

AZIZWILLKILLYOU: @Gogo Girl 322: patience my

GerryMander: Fuck you, this is bullshit. I was with you till that superhero bullshit.

GustaveGrime: Exactly. It's just all bullshit. No way this happened. This guy is a fraud.

GerryMander: Why are we reading this?

GustaveGrime: I'm keeping a Tumblr documenting the death of the internet. And this is one of my case studies. Bullshit people write to make their lives sound better. Fake blogs. Constantly updating people on a life you don't lead. The pointlessness of our existence. Fucking hell, Aziz should kill himself.

AZIZWILLKILLYOU: Yo, Gustave, why don't you go troll someone else. You know why? I WILL KILL YOU.

GustaveGrime: If this is an actual threat, I am reporting you to the authorities. Remember: I am a lawyer.

GerryMander: Chill Gustave, it's not that bad.

AZIZWILLKILLYOU: All I know is, you love me too much to ever just let me get on with it. Why don't you fuck off? You don't have to read it.

GustaveGrime: But I do, mate. This is exactly the opposite of why the internet was invented. You are ruining our world. One blog at a time. There's Wikileaks. There's Guardian Comment Is Free. There's NetMums. Then there's you. Right at the bottom of the pile, trying to get everyone's attention with your bullshit. If the world was just, I'd have this blog shut down in a second and you reported to the European Court of Human Rights for crimes against art.

AZIZWILLKILLYOU: aaaaaaand ... blocked.

df325: I love the suspense. When's the next one up?

History:

Kitab Balasubramanyam penis – Twitter
Kitab Balasubramanyam cock – Google
Kitab Balasubramanyam nude – Twitter

I'm having breakfast with Hayley the next day when I start wondering why she'd texted me late last night to request a meet-up over bacon and eggs and freshly cooked hash browns in my local organic café.

Maybe she thinks she's seen my penis. Surely, otherwise she'd never want to hang out. Maybe she saw something she liked. In someone else's penis. Because she'd never just ask me out just to ask me out, would she?

We've only ever seen each other at events. We're each other's go-to emotional crutch when the room is filled with publishing types and 'aspiring' writers.

'I hate other writers,' she'd told me once. 'All they want to do is talk about writing.'

We'd been having a discussion about what roles we would take in the zombie apocalypse. I had decided that based on my skill set, I would be in Comms, tweeting zombie locations, but in reality, in a dystopian at-war society, we would need soldiers more. 'I'd have to gun up and hit the front line, right?'

'See? That's why I love you, Kit,' she'd said. 'Writers are desperate to debate the death of the novel and you're the only one brave enough to acknowledge the threat of zombie apocalypse.'

It had been one of those moments where we could have kissed. I was holding my phone the entire conversation, and a picture of Rach was my background.

149

My phone stays in my pocket this time. I'm so nervous about breakfast I don't dare bring it out. I want to plug in. But I can't. This is the first time we've been alone together. It feels more intense than usual. I have to work hard to be like I usually am with her when there's other people around to be a counterpoint to.

We talk about the trials of being jobbing writers. She sighs. 'Every fucking day I'm contacted to write something, usually for free, about my favourite handbag, or where I get my hair cut. Have these people not heard of the Women's Prize? Do they not follow Caitlin Moran on Twitter?'

'As a feminist, you're above handbags and haircuts?'

'Well, of course not,' she says, cupping her tea in 2 hands. 'I love a handbag and I love a haircut. But does no one want my opinion on the welfare cuts? On how bad the new Mumford album is? It's so boring. You must get it too, being, you know …' she stage-whispers, 'an ethnics. I used the plural on purpose.'

'Yeah, of course. I get asked in online Q&As repeatedly what my parents think of my work. Who gives a shit what they think? Also, if I get one more email from *Esquire* asking me to review my top 5 curry spots in the city, I'll lose my shit.'

'Literally?'

'Literally. I'll be like, "Hayley, I've misplaced my shit. Can you help me find it?"'

'"No, Kitab, that's just disgusting, but where did all that shit come from?"' Hayley throws back her head and laughs.

'"I reviewed all these curry spots and now I can't stop shit-ting …"'

'We're just avatars, Kit,' she says, sipping on her tea to illus-trate a point well made.

'Everything your Twitter bio tells the world about you, that's what people want to know. Gender, ethnicity, likes.'

'I think it's more than that … I think we're at a stage where no one cares what authors think. We used to be spokespeople, opinions for hire,' Hayley says, looking over my shoulder to see if our food is coming. 'When did we get boring? When did people stop caring what we thought and asking footballers instead?'

'When Cantona became a poet …'

'When middle-class people swapped paperbacks for season tickets …'

'Classist.'

'How can I be a classist when I support Leyton Orient … team of the people, Kitab, my lad?'

'If I see one more picture of a footballer leaving a club with a blonde girl …'

'Speaking of pictures,' Hayley says, getting her phone out. 'Is this your cock? Cos if it is, then it's very embarrassing.'

She shows me Kitab 2's penis, its messy manscaping ingrained in my brain for ever more.

'I got hacked.'

'I figured. It seemed a bit too brash for you. I imagine you're the flowers, dinner and a movie type, right? Before anyone gets to see anything.' Hayley leans forward and taps me on the arm. I let her hand rest there.

'You have to really romance me,' I reply. My voice is dry and I cough over my words, nervously. It's rare we're by ourselves, chatting, not surrounded by others. It feels more intimate than I can cope with.

'Who hacked you?'

'It's a bit of a weird long story. Remember that Indian guy I was with at that book event?'

'There were 2 Indian guys, at a book event?'

'Yes, well, the other guy …'

'What was he called?'

'Kitab.'

I let the answer hang there.

Hayley smiles. 'Right.' She laughs to herself.

151

'What?' I ask.

'It's just … I dunno. You spend all this time not wanting to be defined by your ethnicity and then you're saying some Indian guy with your name rolls into town and puts your cock on the internet.'

'His cock.'

'Well, it's weird,' she says, laughing.

We're surrounded by yummy mummies. We've gone for breakfast in the post-school run at the only time you'd see artists eating breakfast. We're the jobless paid. We eat after the rush hour and before daytime television gets going. We eat between the first of the morning coffee and the pre-lunch coffee. Before we take meetings about abstract projects at abstract art venues that want us to channel our inner-douchebag. The yummy mummies coddle their babies and coo to each other about their spawn's achievements, from first steps to first words, from bon mots to hilarious 'kids say the funniest things' anecdotes. They bray and guffaw at each other like seagulls fighting over seaside scraps. I hate this awkwardness. It's the first time Hayley and I have done anything away from other people, just us, not at an event. I don't want it to be awkward.

'How do you live?' Hayley asks me just as our food arrives.

'What do you mean? Like, how do I sleep at night?'

'How *do* you sleep at night, Kitab Balasubramanyam?' Hayley laughs. 'No, I mean, like, we hang out at things and I know I don't know you well enough to ask this, but if you're on your publisher with the amount you sold, how do you live? I only ask because I'm about to need to find a job and all the jobs I can find involve writing about handbags or haircuts. What's your secret?'

'I'm a rich kid,' I say, smiling.

'Oh.' Hayley looks around the room, disappointed.

'I mean, like, my mum died when I was young, from cancer. When my book came out, my dad gave me a chunk of my inheritance to keep me going in case the book didn't set the world alight. The book didn't set the world alight. So here I am, burning through the money and contemplating jobs writing about top 5 curry spots. Because the book didn't set the world alight. Whoops.'

'At least you know where your shit is.'

'True. But yeah, it's not like writing's paying the bills. I might as well write what the people want. News stories about engaging web content or something.'

'And thus, the rich kid becomes a hack.'

'I can't even … I can't even find a job writing for B2B sites. I got rejected from writing for a tourism site because I seemed "ambivalent".'

This is the first time I've felt honest about anything in months. I feel sweaty.

'I like your tattoo,' Hayley says. 'It's like the ultimate state-ment for analogue, for printed books, for objects to touch.'

'Thanks,' I say, hollow.

Hayley places her hand on my wrist, where my arm is resting on the table. My mind flashes between her and Kitab 2, finding him and finding her, this girl I've liked for a while, showing me the 'sign'. It's distracting. Kitab 2 Kitab 2 Kitab 2. But Hayley. But Hayley. But Hayley. I look at her hand on my arm. She has orange nail polish on short cut nails. Like her toes. Instagram has made me obsess over people's nails. Which reminds me, I forgot to take a photo of my food. Her fingers are long and feminine. Rach had small, stubby digits. We'd never hold hands because my meat fists would feel like they were spreading her fingers too far apart.

'So, you're single …' she says.

'Yeah.'

'How's single life?'

'I don't know. I haven't really done much with it, to be honest.'

153

'It's hard to meet people. I mean, how do you set up a dating profile and put your profession as writer? It means people can judge you before they date you.'

'They can judge you anyway. In Google Search, veritas,' I say. 'I set up a dating profile. I didn't really get any responses so I closed it down.'

Hayley pulls my arm over so my forearm is pointed upward and pulls the sleeve up the tattoo.

'Everyday I write the book,' she says. 'Like Elvis Costello.'

'Chapter one, we didn't really get along ...'

'Chapter two ... I fell in love with you.'

She laughs, as if that might be a possibility. I laugh back, because to not would be awkward. I'm not good at these situations. I haven't had to flirt with anyone since before Rach and even then I was never that type of guy. She's beautiful. I'm out of practice. How do I advance this? It's impossible. Ghost protocol. Black ops. Call of duty. It's an impossible mission.

'I don't really like Elvis Costello,' I say, like an automaton, pulling the mood-killer parachute. 'My mum did. So did Aziz. So does Aziz.'

'Me neither,' she replies and smiles. 'Well, not as much as I'm told I would, given the other bands I like. He sounds so 80s.'

'I guess that means something to some people.'

'Not me. But when a band in 20 years' time reminds me of Nirvana and I tell young pups that, I bet they'll hate me as much as I hate the nerds who tell me Elvis Costello "is my jam".'

Our food's getting cold so I get my head down as I arrange eggs on toast with bacon on top, drizzled with beans, before I get ready to tear it apart and devour it. Hayley takes 3 bites of her bacon butty and puts it down. 'I'm full,' she says. Looking up, I see Hayley looking at me like I need to hurry up. Maybe she hates eating. 'Wanna go for a walk?'

We're walking home and I'm telling Hayley about Aziz and Teddy Baker.

'So, he's just packed off to America?'

'Yeah. He lives dangerously.'

'What if he gets hurt? What if he meets this guy and he's such a massive disappointment, he regrets his tattoo?'

'I don't think he really thinks like that. He'd be like, "If you've lived such a cool-ass life, you don't give a fuck anymore." Probably.'

'He sounds fun.'

'He is and he isn't. I mean, he's obsessed with looking as cool as possible. He has this … this inbuilt necessity to read blogs, tweets, Tumblrs and magazines to find out exactly what's the next hype. Aziz's website favourites, his bookmarks and his RSS feeds are filled with images of coats, t-shirts, shoes, bands, comic strips, words of the day and new takes on acronyms so he could imbibe, constantly, absolutely everything, simultaneously. He could be into a band and declare them a sell-out in the same afternoon. He will stop everything to go and hunt the vintage and charity shops around us for a new hat or cut of shirt that harks back to whatever trend is coming back in fashion. Every band he likes is a band you won't have heard of. On purpose.'

'That sounds exhausting. I barely have time to keep up with the news.'

'I dunno. Without him, I wouldn't like half the stuff I like.'

Hayley grabs my hand as we pass my local pub. Her fingers are cold at the tips and clammy and fat at the base. They feel soft and squidgy, like those bendy rubber separators you use to paint your toenails with.

She aligns her shoulder with mine so we're arm to arm. Apart from allowing the hand holding to carry on, I am putting nothing into this situation. And yet my body is betraying me because I am hard and I am flush. I can feel the static sting of embarrassed horniness under the melanin in my skin. I can feel her lean into me.

'How's the new book coming along?' she asks me.

'What new book?' I ask.

'"Everyday I write the book" ...'

'Yeah. I dunno. I don't know what to write. What do you write about once you've done your whole coming-of-age tale and life has been plain-sailing since?'

'You have adventures you want to write about. Or you write something with superheroes and gun battles and gangsters. But in the real world. It could be funny.'

'Those are my only 2 options?'

'Yeah. Well, they say your first book is about everyone you've met till you write it, and your second is about writers and writing because that's all you meet afterwards.'

'I'd rather have a cup of tea.'

'There's always the pan-ethnic novel, set in India, with mangrove swamps and arranged marriages.'

'I'd sell a million.'

'More frangipani literature, that's what the world wants.'

'I hate it.'

'You hate yourself.'

'What about you? Surely there are more middle-class marriage structures to exploit?'

'You mocking me, Balasubramanyam? I'll have you know my parents' divorce was very painful to watch ...' Hayley says, poking me in the side. It tickles. Ripples of a long-forgotten sensation spread across me.

'What's wrong with writing in some non-white characters once in a while?'

'You're cocksure for someone who's shown everyone their cock.'

156

'I didn't,' I say, desperate for someone to believe me. I realise I haven't checked my phone in the last 2 hours, since I've been with Hayley. I have no idea what's happening in the world. And I feel fine about it.

'I know.'

'I don't know how to write non-white characters. Help me. Do ethnics talk funny or different?'

'They talk like me.'

'You talk like a white guy.'

'And just like that … his point was proven.'

We reach the end of my street in an 'oh, how did we end up here' way and something comes over me. It's the potential, the expectation. It's the knowledge that all roads lead home. It's the feeling of power. Mostly, it's because I've thought this woman was so beautiful from the moment I saw her, but it's only now I possess the necessary leverage to pull her towards me. I pull Hayley in tight.

'That's my flat,' I point.

'Show me,' she says, with a slow smile.

At my door, I fumble for my keys, drop them to the floor and we both go for them. As we rise from our crouches, her hands find my face and she pulls my jawline towards hers. We kiss. It's tentative at first. We're sizing up the contours of each other's mouths, not wishing to overstep the welcome of each other's lips. We quickly mould the size of our mouth holes to each other's and we press in harder. I then slowly slither my tongue into her mouth, but she bats it off with her own. Our tongues tussle. I feel a hard, horny stitch in my stomach. She's the first person I've kissed since Rach. It feels good.

My arms clasp around her back and then move down towards the outward curve of her bottom. It's like a video I've seen. When the guy accosts the girl on the street and convinces her to come home with him. Conveniently, she's never wearing underwear.

157

I feel self-conscious about our public display of affection. The whole of my neighbourhood is watching. Metaphorically. Because realistically they're at work. Or doing some hip installation at an underground art gallery. But that mutual coyness leads us inside where we press against the closing door, followed by a fall onto the sofa. It's all tongues and wrapping limbs and awkward exploratory hands and lips. I alternate between her mouth and neck with my lips, and her hair and lower back with my hands. Her focus flits between my face, pulling me almost entirely into her mouth, and the greying shorn bristles of the back of my head hair.

I want to live-tweet this moment so badly. Just so I remember it.

'She kisses me, pulling me almost entirely into her mouth #50shadesofkitab'

It doesn't feel like the videos I spend days watching. There's too much kissing. Everything flows from one act to another. We don't jump-cut from kiss to blowjob to anal to her willing face.

Her mouth feels forceful on mine, leading me. It's a revolving gif in my head stuttering forward into an awkward loop. I imagine her naked flesh till the pixels blur into the beige blocks of her skin.

We are interrupted by a phone call that vibrates in my pocket, which, even though she insists I answer, I try to ignore it, until 3 successive phone calls remind me of my little online warfare with Kitab 2. So, assuming the persistence can mean it's only him or about him, I answer the phone. While I talk, Hayley's hands seek to distract me with gentle strokes in inappropriate places. I bat her off because a very efficient and assertive nurse from a nearby hospital is informing me that I have been noted as the next of kin for a Kitab Balasubramanyam and he has been brought into the hospital as the victim of a brutal beating. I am to come into the hospital and check in on him.

Kitabus interruptus.

I could stay away. He deserves his fate after trying to affect mine. And I hate hospitals. They make me think of sick people. I don't like sick people. I could be a forgiving Christian and go, forgive him and move on with my life. Or I could choose the heathen's path – go and confront him, and find a way to fuck with him while he's whacked on morphine. Maybe that's the coward's path. I do dislike confrontation.

I look at Hayley and at her body, pointing everything towards me. She takes my phone out of my hand, places it on the floor and bites the end of my finger. I palm her cheek delicately.

'That was the hospital,' I say. 'Something's happened.'

'Everything okay?' she says, rising up on to her knees to kiss my neck.

'No, there's been an accident. I'm so sorry. I want … this …'

'Yeah, that's not sexy, dude,' she says, standing up. 'Call me when you're done. Hope it's nothing too serious … Besides,' she winks. 'I've got handbags to review.'

As she turns away, I go in for a cuddle. The cuddle trajectory is mistimed and I bat one of her breasts instead. She swings towards me and pushes me on to the sofa.

'You had me at hello,' Hayley says, laughing. 'Why is it so hard to quit you?'

'Hashtag sorry.'

'Hashtag call me later.'

'Hashtag no really, I'm sorry.'

'Hashtag stop going on about it you foppish doofus and deal with your shit.'

Hayley grabs her coat and bag, doing each action deliberately enough to give me time to intervene, but I feel no imperative to do so.

I'm furious with Kitab 2. He has damaged my public personality on the internet. He has reduced me to a laddish loutish pervert who would do that sort of thing for attention – and there is nothing more precious to preserve than your online persona. Because it's for ever. I deleted all those sex party tweets I did with Aziz the day after; in the cold light of day, realising what a stupid thing it was to put that on the internet. People misread things like that, think they know you. So many people think they have an informal relationship with you, that they can react to your news in the same way as a friend. I used to have a guy comment on my Facebook every time Cara (she of the Skype dinners) and I talked about anything. He would invariably butt in and try to impress her.

E.g.:

Me to Cara: Dinner soon?

Cara to me: Yeah – deffo. lol. aint seen u in ages. Skype?

Me to Cara: NO Real life > Skype.

Cara to me: Fine. When?

Me to Cara: Cool – free next Tuesday. Wanna grab some Thai food in town?

Random man: Dudes, if you're looking for Thai, go to the Sai Thai restaurant. It's dope. I know the owner. Say you're my cousin and he'll give you free drinks. Swear down.

Eventually, I asked this guy why he only ever spoke to me when I was conversing with Cara (he was a guy I went to school with years ago who had added me, and out of a perverse sense of nosiness, I accepted so I could see what his life became). He replied: 'Cos ur m8 is BUFF! m8. shes well fit. she got a boyf?'

Language is dead, I thought. I told him that it was weird he was chirpsing my friend but made no effort to ever talk to me. How did he know she wasn't my girlfriend, I asked?

'Cos it don't say so in ur relationship status bruv.'

He unfriended me and sent me a message saying: 'Jus cos u wrote some book or whatevs … you ain't my boss, get me?'

I left it at that, mostly because I didn't understand his reply. It was a well-established fact that I was not his boss. A day after that exchange I noticed he and Cara were now 'friends'. And so these monoliths of inappropriate exchanges continued to drive a wedge in all our lives while masquerading as the thing that would bring us all together one day.

And last month she announced their engagement party. I'm not going to go. She's going to broadcast it on Skype though.

I reach the hospital and I ask for myself at the reception. Down a corridor and up 2 flights of stairs – my knees are quivering with fear and a lack of fitness. I exercise as much as I do a tax return ... less than once a year. I've only ever had to go to a hospital twice. The first one I visited was to see my mum just before she died. The time after that, Aziz had been in a bicycle collision. Oh death, and bicycle collisions – you keep me in stock for visits to this mausoleum of scalpels and tumours.

The beeps and strip lighting, the disappointing heft of British nurses, the vending machines that sell dog shit pretending to be coffee – it's uniform up and down the country. I find Kitab 2's room and enter. There are 3 people in there, lying on the edge of their beds, with their faces resting on pillows, the band of an eyepatch visible around the back of their heads. They're still, like they've been sent to sleep by a hypnotist.

Kitab 2 is in the bed by the window, which shows off a view of the back of the stairwell. He has one eye closed and the other patched up. He has a downwards arrow hovering above the patched eye. At least someone somewhere is in command of the technology in this hospital to avoid embarrassing eye cock-ups.

The room is a hotbed of industrial, ambient sounds: a slow whirr of neon lights and air conditioning, the Darth Vader-esque rasp of oxygen machines and televisions, and bleeps and machines and bloops. The sounds of chaotic silence.

I sit next to him in as noisy a way as I can, scraping the plastic seat against the linoleum. He stirs but doesn't wake. I wait. He looks weak.

I flick through a discarded newspaper on his bedside table, catching up on the latest antics of celebrities I have no awareness of. I tweet. About the power of hospitals being enough to make you face your mortality. In the last day, I have lost 17 followers. I check through my emails. My publisher has got in touch asking what the hell I'm up to with the whole penis picture thing. I've been invited to speak at an event in India but have to pay my own travel.

My dad has forwarded me a picture of some woman he's chatting up asking me to check out her tattoos. Tattoo is a euphemism for breasts. They're saggy and real and the way she pushes them together can't disguise age's natural gravity. I wish my dad would stop thinking I was his friend instead of his son. I don't reply.

I look at Kitab 2 asleep. The destroyer of worlds. The man with my password is the man who rules the world. I could hit him. I could take a pillow and whack him on the head to wake him up.

I scroll through the internet instead.

All this takes up 10% of my battery, which is a currency in modern life. Without battery, you can't tell anyone where you are or what you're eating. Kitab 2 eventually stirs and wakes and sees me through the stoned haze of painkillers. He smiles.

'Emergency contact,' he slurs.

'That's me.'

'You came.'

'I did indeed.'

'You are me. I am my own emergency contact. No one but me.'

'Kitab, what happened?'

He tells me the story. Slowly. Slurring.

Feeling alone and with no one around to tell him off, he wanted to try some weed so he could be like Kumar from the Harold and Kumar films. 'I love that film,' he slurs. 'That guy gets so high.'

'Yeah, it's funny,' I lie, staring at the arrow above his damaged eye.

162

'I'm in London, dude. I gots to get high,' he says. '*I want to get hi-iiigh*,' he sings, and laughs. 'I'm high now,' he whispers. 'I wanted to get high, dude. Like really high. So I thought I'd buy some druuuuugs. And they give them to me for free. All I had to do was get beaten up, dude.'

He tells me he looked up the best place to buy some drugs online. He couldn't find anything online, but remembered his father warning him away from King's Cross, because in the 60s it had been filled with prostitutes and drugs. He walked around asking various people how to buy weed. Eventually he met a beautiful tall blonde woman who could help him. He followed her up past the station to the canal where there was a man waiting for him. He was a short guy with a hood who offered to sell him weed. He stuck his money out and the guy grabbed it and punched him in the face. His glasses crashed into his eyes and one of the shards of lens pierced his retina. He woke up here, without his shoes or suitcase. His eye, he says, 'is black like the night, not red like the moon'. He points at the window to the big cake in the sky – it's cheese-coloured tonight. I shrug, not knowing what he means.

He pauses after his story, taking stoned stock of having nothing left. All his clothes, paperwork, computer, his bootleg copy of *Assassin's Creed III* – they're all gone. He has nothing.

'But this morphine,' he slurs. 'I bet it is better than weed.' He smiles with all of his teeth.

'What the fuck, Kitab,' I say. 'Why did you put up that picture?'

Tactless of me, but I almost need some consideration from him before I can begin to feel sorry for him. Sympathy is worth an apology for travesties committed before the incident.

He smiles. He giggles. 'You … you … were … mean … to me … I just wanted to be your friend.'

And I immediately feel like the one in the wrong.

'Plus,' he adds. 'It was funny, right dude?'

aZiZWILLKILLYOU episode 10
Aziz vs the bad guys 2: reloaded
[posted 14 September, 15:41]

We hit the streets, brothers and sisters. We suited up and headed out into the night, through the streets of Brooklyn, lined with the sad faces of those coming home from their regular Schmo jobs like chumps. Teddy Baker led us back towards the subway. People were shouting at us, 'YO! Douchebags, it ain't Halloween.' And at first I was shouting back, 'It ain't 1988 neither, wannabes', because with their pink dyed hair and shoulder pads, they were just sending out a message that they weren't there the first time. I don't get you white people and your revisionist fashion statements. But Bob shushed me.

'These are the people we fight for,' he said.

Bob used to be a security guard in a bank. He used to watch bank job films endlessly and wonder why his life resembled nothing like the guard's (usually called Marv or something) who got shot in the leg for trying to be a hero during a heist. He would stand at his job and wait for something to happen and nothing ever did. He got obsessed with the idea of being a hero because so many things on television told him he would eventually be one. Every bank – if you believed CSI, NCIS, NYPD Blue, The Wire, whatever – was prone to a bank robbery. Especially in New York. Life was passing him by, he thought. One day he saw a guy get mugged on the train and he did nothing. He just sat there like a lemon, wondering if this was his time to be a hero. Outside the context of, like, the bank or something, he wasn't sure if this was his moment to shine. But Bob's the kinda brother who lets life pass him by. And when that mugged bloke comes up to him and said, 'Why the fuck did you just sit there like a lemon?' he didn't have a decent answer. He was like, 'I'm not a transport police. I just work in security.' And the guy spat on him and called him a dickhead. Being called a dickhead must have stayed in his brain because all he could think was, 'I'm not a dickhead. I'm ready to be a hero. My moment just hasn't arrived yet.' Bob woke up one day and decided he was a dickhead no more and he was a lemon no more, so called up his old college buddy Teddy Baker and together they decided to put the world to rights by making it a safe, crime-free environment.

Teddy Baker, on getting the call from his old boy Bob to be a superhero, thought the timing was perfect. He'd been fired from a job for streaming Game of Thrones on his computer and the sex scenes constituted inappropriate imagery for the work place. He had nothing going on. He thought, why not? The latest season of Game of Thrones is about to end.

We were coming into a train station 3 stops from where we were getting off; a hotspot for purse snatching, Bob claimed. We were moving to one side to let people get off when the train came to a halt, just outside the station. The lights flickered on and off. And the train announcer boomed on the tannoy something that no one understood. Literally. I mean literally. Not like I literally just wet my pants or he literally threw up everywhere ... I mean literally there wasn't a single person in the carriage who knew what the brother was saying. People started getting worried. They were all texting and tweeting furiously. Only one guy actually makes a call and tells whoever that he was going to be late.

He then said, 'I woulda tweeted you but I didn't want Mandy to see I was coming to see you.' I called affair, quietly, to Teddy. He smiled.

If you're sitting out in a public space, like a train or bar, and noted down everything people said, you would learn a lot of intimate details. Like, the amount of times you hear people dictating their addresses or their card numbers or saying the names of their loved ones on the phone. It's ridiculous. Or they just tweet where they are the whole time. We're all sitting ducks for identity theft.

When Teddy Baker announced 'I'm gonna go see the driver' you could almost hear the trumpet fanfare.

People were peering out of the window to see if they could see what the problem was but all they could see was shadows and silhouettes on the train platform.

Teddy Baker checked Twitter and turned to Bob: 'There's nothing on Twitter.'

Shaking my head, I pushed past him and walked between carriages, feeling the gust of traffic down below gush up my Lycra arse. As I walked through the next carriage, with Teddy Baker and Bob following me, people started applauding us, shouting stuff like 'Here they come to save the day'.

So I bowed to the applauding masses and knocked on the door leading to the driver's cabin. And there was some shuffling but there was no answer. I knocked again. More shuffling. No answer. So I banged harder and I got Teddy Baker and Bob to start shouting 'OPEN ... OPEN ... OPEN', which spread around the carriage, and then down the carriage into the next one and within 30 seconds the entire carriage was shouting 'OPEN, OPEN, OPEN'. The cabin door opened and I was pulled into the cabin with the driver. Everyone clapped and he shut the door behind him.

This was a very sweaty man. This guy was bald and pink, like a pig that's been shaved. I looked at him and he wiped a river of sweat off his forehead. One of the droplets landed on my lip so I pushed him. 'Bro,' I say ... cos when in doubt, go darkside, ya get me? 'Whaa' blow. What's going on?'

'There's ... I ....' He looked at me, confused.

I could hear Teddy Baker and Bob talking and lightly knocking on the other side of the cabin door. Bob was saying to Teddy Baker, 'Dude's stealing our shine. What the fuck, Teddy? Who is this guy?'

'He's my tattoo buddy,' Teddy Baker said. He was defending me. Guy is a top class legend.

I turned back to the train driver. 'Seriously, mate, spit it out. What's going on?'

He pointed out the front window and I could see the platform now.

There were 30 people gathered on the edge of the platform, all looking and pointing to underneath the train. Some were using camera phones to record the event. Others were hysterically pointing and clutching their faces in horror.

'What's under the train, man?' I asked.

'I ...'

'Bro, you have a train full of angry commuters about to rip your piggy face off and eat it in a hotdog. What's under the train?'

'Mother ...'

'A mother. What do you mean? Like, a woman? What's under the train? What's under the train?'

'Mother ...' He shakes his head. 'A mother and her baby. Under the train. They jumped. I hit them. I ... hit them.'

There is one comment for this blog:

dfc232: Jeez, is she okay?

History:

Casual encounters – Craigslist
Flights to New York – Skyscanner

Kitab 2 is trying to eat yoghurt with a big plastic spoon. Depth perception from the lack of one eye leads to yoghurt stabs on his cheek. I help him. I feed Kitab 2 yoghurt. He slurps the yoghurt off my spoon smiling, lowering his head into the downward bowl's trajectory as I keep the spoon stiff, letting him do all the work.

'I need to check my email,' he says. 'Hashtag unplugged. Hashtag matrix.'

'Do you need to let people know you're in the hospital?'

'Maybe. I don't know. I've never been in a hospital. Do you let people know when you're in the hospital? I feel stoned. Did you see that video? When the kid is whacked off drugs in a dentist? Charlie bit my finger.'

'I think that's something else. And yes. You should definitely tell someone you're in the hospital.'

He pauses, then remembers. 'My laptop. It's gone. The guy stole it.' He strains to get angry, but the painkillers have cushioned his rage and directed it straight into a cloud of fuzziness. 'I'm so angry,' he slurs.

'Why were you trying to buy drugs? You said you've never drunk or smoked.'

He shrugs.

'It's London, baby,' he says, smiling, tired.

'Look, Kitab, I'm trying to be calm about this because obviously it's not nice being beaten up and having all your shit stolen, so I'm going to be sensitive to that. But, you have to try

169

to explain to me why you put a picture of your penis on my Twitter account and how exactly you accessed my account.'

Kitab 2 opens his mouth up and shakes his shoulders as if he's laughing paroxysms of delicious victorious guffaws. 'Dude, that was hilarious. I was sitting there thinking, dude. Like, about writers. You're a writer, dude. You write. You have all this cool stuff around you – like girls, guns and guts. Like balls, dude. You're not dangerous, dude. I was reading about all these writers, like Ernest Hemingway and Oscar Wilde, and they fought bears, dude ...'

'I don't think they did.'

'And they fucked so many women. Do you know how many wives Hemingway had? Do you know how many girls Oscar Wilde went to town on, dude?'

'I don't think many.'

He ignores me. 'And I think, look at Kitab ... no one knows who he is. If I show the world a little something, the world will know who we are. Give the world a little D, get a big lot of P. Yes?'

'We?'

'Sex sells, dude.'

'So, you thought you'd try to help my sales by putting your penis on my Twitter stream?'

'Our penis, dude. Your penis. I saw your sales ranking went up. It worked.'

'Why? Why would you do that?'

'I was trying to help. You're sad. You're failing, dude. You're nothing. You can't even sign books in public. I want to help you. Because you're me. I love you.'

He thinks about it.

'Kit ...' I start to say.

'I love you and I want to help you. Like you help me. But you're unhappy, dude. Why else would you have left me like that? That's not what a friend would do. Because you're sad

170

and you're failing, dude, I thought I would help. Everyone thought it was you, too. I love you.'

'How did you get into my account, Kitab?' I ask, changing the subject, deflecting from his misplaced love. He looks at me with attempted cute eyes, like a cat gif, like he wants to kiss me but is showing me he's not a threat first.

'When you were in the toilet, I set it up so all your email would be automatically forwarded to my account. I requested a forgotten password. It gave me your password.'

I automatically filter out any emails from Twitter into a folder I never check. This guy's good. He preyed on my lack of attention to detail.

'Totes LOLz yaar? I'm like Lulz. Hacking, dude. Anonymous.' Kitab 2's head shakes, half-slurring.

'Yeah, but why did you do that? What possessed you? It can't just be because I didn't want to be friends with you?'

'Wait, what? You don't want to be my friend?'

Rach once said, after reading through my Twitter stream, that she couldn't believe I'd had all these thoughts and opinions and never thought to share them with her. Somehow I had more to say online than in person. I was glad for the attention, happy anyone was listening at all.

'The mistake you're making,' I'd whine, 'is just because I'm a prolific tweeter, it's not like I'm giving 100% of my personality out to the world. I think long and hard about those quips and opinions. They're carefully curated.'

'Why can't you put that much effort into a conversation with me? Especially when you're checking your phone every few minutes. Telling people where you are. Talking about the stupid things I say.'

'I never tweet about where we are.'

'But you make fun of me.' I knew the tweet Rach referred to: 'My girlfriend calls tracksuit bottoms trackie bo-bo's. No opinion offered.'

'That's affectionate.'

'No. You're taking the piss out of me. So instead of being in the room with me, you're taking the piss out of me.'

'But I never tweet about where we are …'

This was a conversation we had near the end. She was right though. I never tweeted about the nice things we did. Who would have cared?

As a break from this conversation with Kitab 2, I hover over my phone for 5 minutes at a time, the cursor blinking, willing something to say to occur to me.

Not being able to think of anything, I look at Kitab 2. He's asleep, purring like a lawnmower 4 streets away.

'You're not here to study are you?' I ask him when he wakes. Kitab 2 looks tired and smiles. He shakes his head. He's tired. 'Are you shaking your head to say no you're wrong I am here to study or no I'm not here to study?'

'I'm not here to study. I do not possess a student visa.'

'Then what are you doing here, man?'

'My dad, he bought me the tickets. But he did not know my student visa was not approved. I could not disappoint him.'

'So you came here anyway?'

'Yes.'

'Why?'

'It's a free ticket to the UK. I can find a job while I am here.'

'Doing what?'

'I am a great coder, man. I can do all the codes. I have the facility to work as a coder on database systems. I trained at the best technical college. I thought, I could just come here with my CV and maybe meet you and see if you could help me find a job. I don't want to do electrical engineering like my dad. I want to write computer games, dude.'

'Why don't you study that?'

'You kidding me? I have a very strict father, dude. I have to

172

do what he tells me. Video games? Bitch please, dude. He thinks they are a waste of time with no money. He doesn't realise how much money you get for good games.'

'What happened to your paperwork?'

'I sent it too late.'

Kitab 2 tells me his story.

'I grew up in Bangalore, dude. My dad's from Gujarat, just like you, but he got this job teaching engineering at Bangalore University. It's the 9th best university in the whole of India. He's a respected electrical engineering lecturer ...'

'The 9th most respected engineer ...'

'Huh?'

'Sorry, carry on.'

'He has always been a lecturer. His dream was always to teach in the UK at Imperial College in London. When I showed signs of being good with computers and coding, he made me apply towards a masters in the UK.'

Kitab 2 talks on – he tells me about the degree he got at Bangalore University. He had graduated cum laude and was all but guaranteed a place at a decent university here in the UK. However, it sounded like he got lazy – hubris and an encroaching lethargy that came with having a mother and father who handled all his life administration for him meant that he wasn't very organised.

'Then my mummy died of breast cancer.' Like mine, I think. 'One year ago ... and I got very depressed ...' Oh god, this is so cringeworthy, it's so familiar. Maybe he is my 'other' after all. 'I couldn't concentrate on anything. I deferred my masters. Dad took a year off to write a new textbook for the course he was teaching, but instead, we both just lived in our flat. He in one room and me in another. We lived on campus. I didn't leave my room, dude. I just played video games, talked to sexy girls on Facebook. I'd go online and play *Call of Duty* with all these American college boys and pretend I was some big shot football player from Harvard.

173

They thought I was so cool. They always wanted me on their teams, because I knew where all the rocket launchers were and I knew the best hiding places, which meant I lived longer than all of them and always won by blowing up the other team.'

He demonstrates his best American accent for talking trash online or talking tactics with teammates: 'Dude, you are *so* beyond shit. Dude, you suck.'

His name was Chandler, like on *Friends*, and what he lacked in tactical nous in *Call of Duty*, he made up for in loyalty and falling on his sword for the sake of a team.

He lost friends that year because he only ever left his room for ablutions and refreshments and only ever really left the apartment when he was required to do something functional like get new pieces of kit from the shop for his ever-expanding entertainment centre.

'Dad and I ate separately. We didn't have to do anything, dude. We had a cook and a cleaner who we never saw. The house was always clean. The clothes were washed and folded and left by our doors. The food was cooked and left served on plates with cling film over them. It was awesome, dude. I could play video games for hours and then go to the kitchen and have sandwiches made for me. I was like a prince. But after one year of Dad not talking to me and me feeling depressed and getting fat, things changed, dude.'

Kitab 2's dad announced he was returning to work having finished the textbook he was working on, and he insisted that Kitab 2 snap out of his online world and go do his masters. He paid for the tickets to London and gave Kitab 2 a cheque for accommodation and books. Kitab 2 was to get a job when he was here to supplement his income.

'I forgot to submit my application online in time. I was playing *Call of Duty* on the day and missed the deadline by, like, 15 minutes. Can you believe it, dude? Only 15 minutes! I was so scared because my flight was in the next few days.'

'Wait, your dad booked your flights a month before you came and you still missed the deadline for applications?'

'Listen, man … I'm a busy guy, okay? I can't just drop everything for my dad when he needs it.'

'Fair enough,' I say, grimacing.

'That's why I messaged you. To see if you were around. I knew one person in London.'

He panicked, he told me, about finding a job or having stuff to do. He tried to hack iTunes so he could sell the code online. He failed. He tried to hack PayPal so he could PayPal himself some money. He failed. The departure time loomed. While Googling himself in a panic, he found me. And when he found me, he did what most people with obscure names would do if they found their other online – he added me. Doing a bit more research, he found out I lived in London. 'It was like fate,' he says. 'My other lives where I'm going. I thought, you could show me the world.'

'Why me?' I ask.

'I thought, you're a dude. And you seemed like a nice guy from Twitter, from your book, from your blog – I thought, he'll look after me. We're brothers.'

'I have a brother.'

'London's the best city in the world and it needs coders. I can do so much. All I have to do is find these people and I'll find a job. I don't need university. I can work for a year then apply next year.'

'How's that going for you?'

'I don't know how to find the companies.'

'What about a job agency?'

'You need a CV for that, dude.'

'So write a CV then.'

'I don't have anything to put on it.'

It wasn't the best thought-out plan. It was plain stupid. But he had made his bed. And now he was lying in a hospital bed.

Every now and then Kitab 2 says, 'Money over everything.' I know it's from a rap tune but I ask him about it.

'You know, dude. I need to make money. Over everything. Like Kanye West.'

'He doesn't sing that song.'

'I know, dude, but I could be that guy. From nothing. To something. Hashtag game, recognise game, dude.'

I shake my head. Kitab 2 can't live his life by rap aphorisms. I think back to the longest conversation I've had with anyone before today with Kitab 2 and with Hayley. It's been a while. With Dad it's a one-way street. He's texted me while I've been in the hospital. He wrote: *wot is cheapest condom???* I ignored it. With Aziz, it's relentless piss-taking. I haven't spent this much time talking to anyone in a long time. Even the break-up with Rach didn't take that long, because I got distracted by my phone vibrating halfway through the conversation.

'Do you need to contact your dad and tell him you're in the hospital?'

'No. Because then I have to tell him why I'm in trouble.'

'That's not the worst thing in the world.'

'It is. He does not handle disappointment well. He once set fire to my Xbox, dude. While I was playing it. I'd nearly finished *Assassin's Creed*.'

'What had you done wrong?'

'I was late to my mum's cremation.'

I shrug. I look at him and see a boy shrouded in swaddling clothes. With the pirate eyepatch, he looks like he's stoned. His one open eye is squinting and moving slowly across his peripheral vision.

'Have you played *Assassin's Creed III*?'

'No.'

'Dude, you should. It's totally rad.'

'I haven't played a computer game since ... I was a child.'

'Too busy reading ... I bet the girls find that sexy, dude.'

'Sexier than playing computer games in cum-crusted pyjamas.'

'Dude, I don't want to leave England a virgin,' he says as I get up to go. 'I have to go back soon, before I run out of money. I can't go home a virgin. I can't.'

There's something pathetic in his voice that reminds me of me when Aziz and I were young and he was going out with a girl called Becky from a local school, and I was desperate to be kissed. 'Dude, I don't want to die a virgin.'

Aziz had replied, 'It's during our successes that we discover our true desire for failure.'

'What does that mean?' I'd asked. He shrugged. 'Dunno. Sounds cool though, right?'

I take my leave of Kitab 2 but promise to return the next day. In the last hour, he has ingratiated himself to me. I like the kid. He's a nice boy. He should have opened with his life story, I might have been more amenable to letting him stay. Maybe I feel a kinship for the fact that we're both mourning mums and we're namesakes. Maybe I'm just a softy. I am happy to swiftly forget the identity theft, the tweeting as me, the weird taking over of my personal space and the lies. Apart from that he's not all that bad. I mean, it's not like he stole my passport.

I head home. I try Aziz's mobile, but it just goes straight to voicemail. Once I'm walking from the train station to my flat, I phone Hayley to see if I can recapture some of the magic. I can't. She won't be interested in me after I shut down our make-out session. I owe her a phone call though. Just as a courtesy.

I dial her number. Her phone goes to voicemail and I don't leave a message. While I'm feeling benevolent, I call my dad. He answers almost immediately, like he was staring at his phone hoping for messages from the outside world.

177

'Kitab-san,' he says, happy as ever to hear from me.

'Hey, Dad.'

'I've been sitting here thinking about you,' he says. 'I think you're unhappy.'

'I am unhappy, Dad. I told you last time we spoke.'

'About what?'

'I dunno. The flat feels very empty at the moment.'

'I know, son.'

'So, yeah, I dunno, whatever,' I say, staring at myself in the reflection of a newsagent. I realise I'm looking at a poster for an Indian wedding magazine. 'It's fine. I'm fine.'

'I do not like this. I have realised I am not being a father to you. I am being a friend. A father would see that his son is suffering from writer's block. I found this site called Wikipedia and I started reading about writer's block. Have you heard of Wikipedia?'

'Yes, Dad.'

'You should get on it. I looked you up. You do not have a Wikipedia. How can you expect people to buy your books if you don't have a Wikipedia?'

'I'll get on it.'

'Did you know JK Rowling had writer's block?'

'No, I didn't.'

'Well, she did. And she has her book in Tescos.'

'Thanks, Dad.'

'I am here for you, son. You can talk to me about anything. I will listen.'

I deflect immediately and ask him about his latest dates and his latest stock triumphs and failures. Mostly failures – we are in a double dip recession. He tells me about a new company on the stock market that is marketing a revolutionary new breast cancer medicine and how he's dipping into his savings (also known as THE REST OF MY INHERITANCE) to invest in it, because my mum died of breast cancer and he feels that

178

investing in this experimental drug will give him some sort of karma.

'Not great, kiddo. Not great. Double dip recession.'

'Oh yeah. Well, buy low … sell high …'

'I might need to take some of the money back. Put it into the house. I can drive up the price of this house and all that money you have saved goes into equity.'

What money? There's not much left. I feel my phone vibrate with another phone call coming through. It's Hayley. I fob Dad off with an 'I'll call you back', and he grunts.

'What's wrong?' I say angrily, thinking I'm questioning my dad's grunt.

'Angry Kit. Such a turn-on …'

'Hayley … hey.'

'You rang?'

'Yeah. I was just …. Well, we got unfairly interrupted earlier so I thought I'd phone up and see what you were up to.'

'Were we?' she asks, sounding distracted.

'You know, when we were …' I put on a cheesy American accent. 'Making out.'

'I was with you until you said making out. This isn't *Dawson's Creek*, Kit.'

'Yeah, that wasn't very well played. Sorry. Anyway, what are you up to at the moment?'

'I am sedating myself with alcohol to stave off the pain of just having my first tattoo done. It fucking hurts, man. I had the most boring-est of boring-est days, Kitab, my ol' chum. I spent it in a caf researching Victorian etiquette at parties. It's really boring. All for a blog, too. A BLOG, KITAB. A blog I wrote for free. You know the *New Yorker* pays $10,000 or something for a short story. I've spent the best part of my week researching this. It'll take me a day to write. For free.'

'Really?'

'A. Blog. About. Victorian. Etiquette. Can you believe it?'

'Sounds dull.'

'Yeah. After you left me to go and check on some random dude in the hospital who really sounds made up, and I spent ages being quiet and reading books, the only remedy was to go out and get really drunk and I decided to get a tattoo done.'

'Cool. What of?'

'Some text: "Fiction Reprise". It's a Belle and Sebastian instrumental.'

'Right, cool.'

'Is it that? Or is it 'cause I'm hammered?'

'Where are you? I'll come and meet you.'

'Atta-boy. The pub at the end of your street. You'll have to extract me from the women's toilets. Good luck, my sweet.'

I hear the click of her hanging up and make the 5–7 minute walk from the train station to the end of my street in record time. The pub is empty – it's a Tuesday, the pub's worst day. Only the strong inhabit these walls: the die-hard darts players, the odd down-and-outer interested in rolling sports news, and Mitch – the wettest man in the book world. His Twitter profile describes him as 'Book obsessive. Often found in the pub.' Reliably so.

He sees me enter and beckons me over.

'I did a tweet. Did you see it?'

'No. Sorry, man,' I say, distracted, looking around the half-empty pub.

'It said, "Bolano knew his way round a metaphor like a conquistador knows patatas bravas."'

'Ha,' I laugh absently. I don't understand it.

'Wait, you don't follow me back.'

'Sorry, man.'

'Still languishing in cock-gate?'

Mitch laughs at his own joke.

'It wasn't my cock. It was someone else's cock.'

'You posted a picture of someone else's cock?'

'No, someone else put up a picture of their cock. You met him, the Indian guy at the reading the other night.'

'What, you?'

'No, the other guy.'

'What was he called?'

He fiddles with a cigarette packet when I don't respond.

'Oh ... you know that Hayley skirt,' he says.

'Skirt – Mitch, this isn't the 60s. We say muff now, or something else equally demeaning. Yeah, what about her?'

'I may have upset her.'

'How?'

'I think I said something bad to her.'

'What did you say, Mitch?'

'I can't be 100% sure. I'm pretty pissed. But I definitely coined a new entry for Urban Dictionary.'

'Mitch, just to clarify ... you may have said some sexual things, but you're too drunk to be sure?'

'Well, it's the only reason she hasn't come out of the shitter in an hour.'

'Right. Not cool, Mitch. Not cool.'

He shrugs and returns to a beaten copy of *The Great American Novel*, his favourite, lovingly annotated with his own personal edits.

The pub's not busy enough for anyone to notice me sneak into the women's toilets. I find Hayley on the toilet, dressed, checking her phone. She looks up at me. She holds out her hand and drops something into mine when I go to receive it.

Lacy and hottest-of-the-hot pink and barely present – it's her pants. She smiles.

'I forgot to put them back on,' she laughs.

They're damp, maybe something to do with the sodden floor. I can't be sure so place them in my coat pocket. The frills send electrical impulses up and down my spine.

'You here to rescue me or what?' Hayley snorts.

181

I grab her hands and pull her up and out of the cubicle. She falls into my arms.

'I don't love my new tattoo,' she says. 'I may have made some questionable decisions this afternoon.' She shows me the inside of her arm. In a typewriter font, it says 'Fiction Reprise'. I kiss her cheek. 'What is the maximum number of dances that a lady can dance with the same man?' I shrug. 'The answer is 3. At some balls, each of the ladies had a little card with all of the dances listed on it. In asking for a particular dance from a lady, the gentleman would write his name in the desired slot on the card so that they would both remember which dance he was promised. I learnt that fact. The day is not lost …' She laughs. I laugh with her.

Her drunk slur is emphasising the verbs in her sentences. She doesn't slur but she talks extremely slowly. She starts playing with the back of my head where my hair fades into an extreme short back and sides. I try to pull back and towards her for a kiss but I'm clamped into her. It smells of toilets in here. Oppressively so. It's spoiling the mood. I manage to grab her free hand and pull her towards the door, so forcefully she kicks the door onto my hand against the frame. I don't wince because I yell 'This is an extraction' in my most military voice. She slaps my bottom and we leave the pub.

The darts players notice our exit and nod at me. 'Good work,' the pinkest one says. The odd down-and-outer interested in rolling sports news barely notices. Mitch looks up at us and then down at his book coyly. As we walk past him, Hayley points and says with venom, 'Disgusting man.'

Outside the pub, with the world swaying to the beat of a gentle breeze, I try to work out the best place to take her, home for attempted seduction (downside, I need to do a food shop and she probably needs coffee, which I could choose to get from the good coffee place in the market about ten minutes away) or to a café to get sobered up (downside, it's hardly sexy sitting in a builder's café drinking instant coffee, or worse, in a douchebag hipster place where the music and irony are cranked up and there are more seats than there is space).

I take her home. We're in silence because I can only think of things I want to tweet her. I have nothing to say.

There's a who now under the train?

I didn't say anything to the driver, cos what can you say, but I was worried now. There was people under the train. What the fuck? I cracked open the door a little and he tried to stop me but I pushed him back. I pulled Teddy Baker into the driver's cabin and Bob followed him. I closed the door behind them.

'Dude hit some people. Did they jump?' I asked the pig man driver. He nodded. 'A woman jumped in front of the train carrying a baby.'

'We have to save them,' Bob said.

'Yes, Bob. That is the can-do attitude Aziz likes. Teddy Baker?'

'What about the train people?'

'Radio's broken. I can't get through to them,' the pig man stuttered.

'Are you ready for your first rescue mission?' I asked.

Teddy Baker nodded.

'Who made you boss?' Bob asked, like the douche he is.

184

'The English accent puts me in a natural position of authority.'

I had no idea what to expect. I don't do well in hospitals. They make me feel knee-queasy. Was it going to be the same with some mangled corpses under a train? I'm not going to lie when I say, I hoped the police and rescue turned up very soon. But seeing as they hadn't and all the spectators were happy spectating instead of aiding, I opened the door of the train carriage. I turned to the pig man. The bow tie was itching under my stupid spandex.

'Is the line electrified?'

He shrugged.

'Isn't that, like, Driving Trains 101?' Teddy Baker said sarcastically.

The pig man shrugged again.

I stepped out and down onto the tracks. I assumed that if these things were electrified I'd hear them buzzing. I peered under the train, my shoes slipping on the gravel and I could see 3 rails, 2 for the wheels and 1 for something else, but no bodies.

I looked up at the other guys to see what they were doing. Teddy Baker was on his phone.

'You fucking tweeting this, man?' I asked him.

'No way, dude. I'm on the MTA NYC Passenger Safety website. It says that the middle rail's carrying like 600 volts of electricity but the rails for the wheels are safe.'

'Safe? Safe. Right, okay. Maybe we should wait for the cops or something? Call the cops, Bob.'

'Don't fucking tell me what to do man.'

'Come on, don't be an arsehole.'

'It's pronounced ass-hole, asshole. Anyway, you wanna be a hero, be a hero.'

'There's 600 volts of electricity near my toes man. Is that a lot?'

Teddy Baker turned to the pig man and asked him if 600 volts of electricity was a lot or a bit more than a static shock. 600 volts was a lot. It had to drive an entire train.

Oh.

I was about to move forward towards the bodies when Bob jumped down onto the tracks from the carriage and pushed me out of the way.

'Outta the way, limey. I'll see about these guys. You don't speak their language.'

'What, English?' I asked but Bob ignored me. With 600 volts of electricity near my junk, it was probably not best to be a smart-arse.

I followed Bob to the front of the train. You could see where this woman jumped in front of the train but you couldn't see her. There was a trail of cloth on the tracks. Suddenly, through all the traffic and arguing, Bob and I turned to each other cos we can hear crying.

'There's a baby under there,' he said, over and over again, so I dropped to my knees, man of action me, to see if I could see what I was supposed to be seeing. Sure enough, I could see the bundle of cloth under the train, not too far, where the mum or woman or whoever the fuck it is lay there curled up. Brown cloth. There was a baby crying inside. The baby's alive.

'The baby's alive!' Bob shouted to Teddy Baker who I heard drop down from the carriage onto the train tracks.

'Word?'

They both stooped to my vantage point, but I was reaching under till I touched cloth. I wanted to see how lodged under there the mum was. I didn't want to touch the 600 volts of electricity third rail so was careful. Luckily, she was nowhere near it. She landed on the right side of the train and fell immediately underneath. The baby was curled on the other side of her, perilously close to the third rail.

Once I realised this, I yanked at the cloth harder. She wasn't stuck at all, just heavy. Teddy Baker saw what I was doing and he pulled the cloth too. Just as she started to unwrap from the brown cloth, I managed to pull at an arm. She was heavy. You could feel it in the mutton chop of her forearm. She was nearly dislodged when we saw the baby, in a sling at her front. No wonder she didn't really manage to jump far. She was heavy and weighed down by an 8-pounder. I wrenched at her arms and Bob reached down and picked the baby up and out of her chest sling. Teddy Baker put his ear to her mouth and I looked for a pulse.

I couldn't feel anything other than my own pulse pushing all that delicious adrenaline around my body. I felt amazing. It didn't feel right. It felt addictive.

Aside: rescue someone. If you're one of those fools who needs constant validation and the feeling that you are somebody, find someone to rescue and rescue the shit out of them. You will feel amazing.

I ran my thumb up and down her arm but I couldn't feel anything. Teddy Baker looked at me and shook his head.

'The baby! The baby!' We heard voices shouting about the baby. The spectators saw Bob's prize and started applauding him. Bob was holding the baby up to the windows like it was the lion king and he was Mufasa. We looked up from the corpse and to Bob and then to the crowd. Someone was shouting 'the baby' with a lot of urgency.

I saw a man running down the platform with a gun – a fucking gun! My first thought was, what the fuck, why has he got a gun near a baby? He started pushing through the applauding spectators and I turned to Bob.

'Bob! Look out!'

'Fuck you, Limey ...'

'Bob!' Teddy Baker shouted. 'Get back inside the train!' We jumped back inside the train carriage and closed the door just as the man with a gun ran through the crowd towards the edge of the platform.

'You need to drive the train,' Teddy Baker screamed at the

pig man. He was rooted to the spot. Shocked.

Teddy Baker punched him and spied a start button. He pushed it and I whacked down the accelerator lever. We felt the bump of the dead mum as the train started up. We were moving slowly. People were confused. The platform's spectators dispersed thinking the train was coming into station.

CRACK! The side glass of the cabin cracked with multiple stings.

'He's shooting at us!' Bob shouted.

We were being shot at, dudes!

Aaaaaaaand that's enough for today's blog. Tension, tension, tension – I am the master of tension. But let's just say, if I let this sit with you now ... when you hear what happened next, oh my, you are going to shit yourselves all over the internet. And there's enough wankers on there enough as it is.

There are 6 comments for this blog:

df325: Aziz, this is too funny.

AZIZWILLKILLYOU: Funny? Babes, did you not read it? I was shot at.

Gus Gustofferson: Lies. Lies lies lies. LIES.

AZIZWILLKILLYOU: Hey buddy, I'm back from America soon. Google 'The Little House' pub. Meet me there this Saturday at 3pm so I can knock the fuck out of you.

Gus Gustofferson: That definitely sounds like a threat.

Flately McBlackly: Did any of this happen in slo-mo? Like in the movies?

History:

If I delete Facebook, is it ever truly deleted? – Google
AzizWillKillYou blog hits – Wordpress
Kitab Balasubramanyam Call of Duty – Google
Chandler Call of Duty – Google

While Hayley sleeps off a hangover, I change my online passwords. My Twitter, my Tumblr, my Instagram, my Pinterest, my Reddit, my YouTube, even my Myspace. I stare at Tom, my first friend on Myspace, and wonder who he really is, that goofy avatar so ingrained in his user's spaces. Then I change the passwords for my current email address, my defunct email address, my email address with the ill-advised name (it was 'dogging@hotmail.com'), my online banking, my spur-of-the-moment Blendr account, my Amazon login, my iTunes, Guardian Soulmates, OkCupid, Guardian Jobs, my council tax, my gas and electricity – anything I can think of, anything that I do online. Which is everything, because who knows in this day and age where to even buy a stamp? I change them all back to something that used to be my password when I was in love with a girl called Giselle at school (G153LL3) and trawl around the internet verifying Kitab 2's tale.

I go to the Bangalore University website and look at the photo of Kitab 2's dad, trying to project the sternness of his face into the stories I've been told. I'm surprised by how familiar the dad's photo feels. He's caught in a portrait, but as if he was talking to someone then asked to crane his neck to the left and be photographed. He's smiling a rictus grin that says 'screw you and the camera you used to interrupt this superior conversation'. He looks like an intellectual. He looks like he knows his stuff. He looks like he would be stern in the classroom. These are all things I glean from a man who, despite an obvious fake smile, looks intensely serious in a bad moustache.

Now I've confirmed that certain elements of Kitab 2's story check out, I check my email. Nothing interesting. I check Facebook – I've missed 2 birthday parties, and some other people I vaguely know are engaged. A cursory look through their events and I'm caught up on the lives of others. This way I don't need to see them. I 'like' a few things at random, just to stay connected to these thumbnails I call friends and family. I check Twitter. No one has sent me anything of note. There's still the ends of the whole dickpic-gate thing being commented upon. I want to be disassociated from sex and penises as soon as possible. There's also links to things I might like about American sitcoms. Someone has sent me some gifs of my favourite character in *Parks and Recreation*. This distracts me for a lot longer than it should. Repeating animated loops of video are hypnotising. I've never figured out what they should be used for but something in me has always found them electric to watch. A related search leads me to a page of porn gifs, looped penetrations that never end, moans of pleasure in a circular infinity of for ever.

I 'like' more Facebook things – pictures of people's children, sarcastic political opinions and motivational quotes. I'm engaging in my friends' lives.

I link my Twitter and Facebook to some YouTube music videos I like. Just so I can feel like I've engaged in the world.

I've said more about my state of mind with the videos I choose than just saying, on Twitter: 'I miss Aziz and I wish this doppelganger would fuck off and that wasn't my dick.' Somewhere in this vanity is a genuine desire to communicate with the people who follow me. But on my terms. Where the things I rate create a demonstrative illusion of what I'm like as a person. In my head, this is exactly the message I wish to send out about social media me.

@kitab: 'What if I told you I can only emotionally respond to something by finding a corresponding video on YouTube?'

@kitab: 'I got nothing to tell you this morning.'

@kitab: 'how do you wake the person sleeping next to you without making it look like you're waking them up?'

Hayley is slumped across my bed, on her front, hands crossed under her head. She wiggles her toes and purrs. I wrench the cover out from underneath her, nearly stirring her, nearly pancake-flipping her, nearly bouncing her into the air, and I cover her. She grips the cover and turns over, grunting.

She grunts a lot in her sleep. She looks amazing.

Hayley's sleeping lump has taken up the whole bed. I go into Aziz's room and head to his bed. His bed stinks of someone who should have washed his sheets before pissing off on holiday, especially if you were rutting the morning of your departure. The smell of dried semen of for ever ago is comfortable; it stinks of interaction. I put my head down on his spare pillow and close my eyes. My feet are touching some papers so I push them to the end of the bed.

Then it hits me.

Kitab 2 slept here. Maybe they're his.

I snag the papers with my toes and pull them up the bed.

There are 2 passports and a handful of papers. The 2 passports – one Indian and one English – are Kitab's and mine. His Indian, with the laminated white turtleneck photo I came across when I first found him, and mine British, with me unsmiling looking like a stubbled man racked with guilt. Also, the papers include: his flight details; one of my bank statements; a list of computer shops, and a printout of a set of writing tips I wrote on my blog. They were meant to be funny. They contained sarcastic advice like, '6. No one cares how many cats or children you have. Adjust your bio accordingly.'

#WTF

His passport is new and shiny. He doesn't have any stamps except the one to the UK, which states it is a tourist visa, rather than a student or working one. He had no intention of anything other than coming here to appease his father. The piece of paper with the flight details only lists a single outbound flight to the UK, rather than a return one. It's been booked by his dad.

Annoyingly, he's picked the bank statement that involves a payment for a 20-minute phone call to Babestation, which came one night after the pub and a particularly celibate attempt to try to seduce a girl I liked that ended up with her saying nothing made her hornier than getting stoned, me buying some hash in the toilets, even though I hadn't smoked for years, and her taking it back to my flat to smoke it with me before falling asleep. Aziz watched from his room, laughing to himself. I went to my room, switched on the television and saw there was a redheaded girl with 2 bad tattoos and a South African accent. So I called her and asked her for love advice, which she was happy to give me. The visuals of her simulating finger-banging herself and cupping her breasts and rubbing them frantically only gave the backdrop of her advice about girls, depression and feelings of loss and ambivalence a bizarre context. Now, whenever I feel depressed, I feel horny. And I only have a redheaded South African who poses naked on television for money to blame.

And my passport? It's all been bullshit, the niceness and the declaration of love and the goofy intent to get laid – this is some serious identity theft. It was one thing to steal my Twitter login, that feels like a transience I can get over, but this is more serious. This feels more illegal. So, if he's intent on stealing my online persona and my official administrative one, who the fuck will I be in this scenario?

I jump out of bed steeling for a fight.

*

I write Hayley a note that says, 'I've gone to see a doppelganger about getting my life back. Sorry, this isn't cryptic. It's surprisingly literal. I have to go see this other Kitab. Sorry. I know. Sorry. Shall I say sorry again? I will be back before you can crack the wi-fi password. Sorry. Kit.'

I head back to the hospital to confront Kitab 2. On the way to the hospital, I try reading Aziz's blogs but give up with his ebullience. Online, people are polemicising against the latest round of cuts by the government and sharing their favourite 'humblebrag'. I'm momentarily distracted by a pun game involving reappropriating book titles to sound dirty. It's called #bookporn.

'Harry Potter and the Philosopher's Boner #bookporn'

'A Tale of Two Titties #bookporn'

'Bellend of a Suicide #bookporn'

'Even the Dogging #bookporn'

'Life of Creampi #bookporn'

'A Visit from the Poon Squad #bookporn'

I fire these off before I go underground. Underground, staring at my warped face against the train window, I wonder what that feeling is within me. It feels unfamiliar at first, but then the clenched fists, the sweaty brow, the inability to concentrate on anything, plus the bubbling rage inside me, the way it pulls at me – I'm angry. I haven't felt angry in a long time. I've barely felt anything but horny or upset in a really long time. Bless you Kitab 2, you weirdo.

Rach moved out of the flat the week my book came out. Because I was booked to go on a campaign trail, write articles and blogs, do library appearances and book readings, and because it was my first big thing and I kind of liked the attention and this was what I had been waiting for all this time, I didn't cancel anything. The week before she left me, I had gone on the radio to plug the book. Because the presenter was attractive, I flirted with her on the air, much to the annoyance of Rach who was sitting on the other side of the glass in the studio.

Instead of one of the funnier anecdotes about Aziz and me as teenagers, the presenter had picked out a passage to read back to me. It involved the main character, opaquely based on me, arguing with his girlfriend, a version of the worst things about Rach.

On top of all the tweeting, the Facebooking, the Q&A email interviews, the politics of getting my name out there, the obnoxious arrogance growing inside me, I'd made fun of Rach on the BBC, the most holy of all places. And she hadn't even read the book yet.

That last coffee we had, she was crying and looking into the space between our mugs and said, 'Is that what you think of me?'

'No, Rach. It was just satire. Fun. It wasn't based on you.'

'Now everyone who listened knows that was me. Thank you. For writing me so horribly.'

I told her off for not being supportive, for not understanding the difference between fact and fiction, for daring to say I was anything less than a man with integrity promoting his work. I told her off for having a go at me for things that were my career. Rach just shook her head and said, 'You used to write me the most charming text messages when we first met. Now I'm lucky to get more than one word.'

She then told me she was moving out.

Kitab 2's welcome to that identity if he wants to steal it.

On my way from the station to the hospital, my phone rings and it's my dad.

'Hey pops,' I say aggressively, trying to hurry him off the phone so he doesn't ruin my stride, my inertia, my anger.

'You busy?'

'Yes. I am.'

'Too busy for your old man? What you doing?'

'Being busy,' I say, high-pitched, like a teenager.

'Fine, I'll go. Just quickly, Kitab-san – I've got this girl who loves Mexican food. I want your recommendations.'

'Try the internet, Dad.'

'What? You expect me to trust strangers over my friends? Kiddo, you do not know how I operate.'

'Goodbye, Dad,' I say.

'What restaurant?' he asks, hurried.

'I dunno, Dad. Honestly, I don't know anything.' I look at the station I'm stood outside. People stream past me in either direction. I have nothing to tell my dad.

'Okay,' he says. 'I guess I can look online. How are you, kiddo?'

'I've got to go, pops,' I say, and I hang up the phone.

I find Kitab 2 sitting outside the hospital, on a bench, smoking. He nods at me and smiles and I'm immediately disarmed. How could this goofball plan this identity theft attack on me? Look at him, smoking like a one-eyed sailor. It's almost comical. Without wanting to, I smile at how silly he looks and he taps the space next to him, placing an arm up on the back of the bench to welcome me.

I sit next to him. We don't talk for a minute or so. I breathe in and out, controlling my anger, counting to 10, remembering a grief counsellor once informing me that things that were out of my control were things I shouldn't lash out at. Kitab 2 offers me a cigarette. I take one just to take one and stare at it.

The cigarette looks delicious, mostly because I haven't smoked in a few years. Rach and I gave up together. She'd be so mad.

Before I can intellectualise sign-offs and permission slips for the cigarette, Kitab 2 has flared a light for me. I accept it, cupping the flame into my neck. The light breeze distracts the first attempt. The second gets me all the way lit. Immediately, the smell and taste and sensation is sending a chill through my legs. My lungs feel acrid and warm. It's a confusing process for my body. How can something so amazing feel so unnatural?

'What's up, dude?' he asks.

I remember why I'm here and the cigarette in my hand, sending toxins into my brain is making me feel angry again. I drop his passport in his lap. I shake my head. He looks up at me and smiles with all the charm in the world. 'Dude, where did you find this? I thought I had lost it.'

'You stole my passport,' I shout. 'You left it in Aziz's bed.'

'No, I didn't,' Kitab 2 says, laughing and looking away from me, spluttering away the *j'accuse* with his lips.

'You did,' I say, feeling angrier. 'You fucking did. Don't deny it. I leave my passport in the kitchen drawer, with my bank statements. I also found my bank statement. In Aziz's bed. Where you were sleeping. Not in the kitchen drawer where they belong. Why did you have it? What the fuck were you doing with it? Was stealing my online identity not enough? Seriously, Kitab, this is serious shit. I could report you. You stole my passport. What were you going to do with it? What the fuck were you going to do with it?'

'I wanted to see what your date of birth was,' he says, smiling. The cigarette burns in my hands. It doesn't taste like it used to.

'Kitab,' I say, steel-like. 'You're really messing with my life right now …'

'What life?' he asks.

'What does that mean?' I say, pointing the cigarette at him, dropping a mound of ash between us. 'What the fuck does that mean? You stole my passport because I have no life?'

'Dude, calm down. I was just having a look. I was just trying to help. I wasn't stealing it. I promise,' Kitab 2 says, cocking his head like a puppy. Either he's that cute or he knows he's appealing to my sense of brotherly love.

'Look,' I say, sitting back down on the bench properly and looking at patients ambling by. 'Between my dad and his stupid dates, and this girl I'm seeing, and writing, I've got no time for silly buggers.' Kitab 2 sniggers at the word bugger. 'So why are you doing this to me?'

'I haven't done anything to you,' Kitab 2 says. 'Nothing, dude. I'm just being there for you. You need me to help you have fun, right? We've had fun. I didn't do anything. I just had your passport and statement. You have been so nice to me. You let me stay at your flat. You fed me non-veg pizza. You took me to university and made me end up in hospital because I was buying drugs. You. You are a cool dude, dude.'

'Kitab, you're going to have to stop fucking with my life,' I say calmly. 'Whatever you're up to, stop it. I've been nice to you. I don't appreciate being fucked with in this way.'

'Dude, I'm in hospital because of you. You owe me. Please dude, you owe me.'

'You're here because you got beaten up.'

'I'm here because you wouldn't be my friend,' he whines loudly, the declaration clear: this is the reason we're at this place now. Because I wouldn't be his friend online.

'Why would I?' I say, my voice rising.

'You just click "accept" on Facebook. It's easy. That's easy.'

'Kitab, man, you're delusional.' Neither of us say anything for a few seconds. 'We've got nothing.'

'But I like you. And I love London. And I love your life. I want your life, dude. I want to be like you. You have such a cool life. You live in London. You go out. You meet girls. It's awesome.'

'Yeah, and? You can go and do all that yourself, you know. You don't need me.'

'It's easier to find a job and an apartment with a British passport,' he finally says, quieter.

'So, you were going to use me for a job? What? You were going to pretend to be me?'

'Dude, you are not as cool as I thought.'

'That's not really the point is it?'

'If you were cool, you wouldn't have such a problem helping a friend.'

We fall into silence. I watch the cigarette burn in my hand. I don't need another drag. My hand feels so comfortable. I don't want to ruin the equilibrium with another drag.

'Dude, why are you always quiet?'

I don't answer him. I shrug with the barest of shoulders and stare at buses going past, men entering and leaving a sex shop opposite the road, and the shoes of passers-by.

'Dude, you need to say what's on your mind. I'll tell you what's on my mind. Here's what I'm thinking. I like you. I want to be friends because we're the same person. I want your life. But also, I think you're rude. You wrote this book and now you think you're a super cool man, but you're not, dude. You're just a moody rude dude. So maybe I feel like you don't like me. But also that you don't like anything. Except this Aziz. Are you in love with him? Dude, seriously, you're a loser.'

I look at him and smile.

'You nailed me in one,' I say flatly.

'Sorry, dude. Just wanted a reaction.'

'Why did you take my passport?'

'You can get a new one, right? If I take your passport, I can stay in the UK and get work, dude. "We all look alike, right?" That's the first line of your book. I can work here and it'll all be cool. I never have to go back. Ever. It's boring there with my dad. You don't live with your dad. You don't have to study all the time. You don't have to go into a certain job. You have freedom. I have nothing. So I want to stay here.'

I never wanted to be the voice of brown England. I never wanted to be the Buddha of Suburbia for my generation.

'Dude, your book is like *The Buddha of Suburbia* for our generation.'

'Thanks,' I say, absently.

'So what if I borrowed your passport. I was going to photo-copy it and take down all the details so I could apply for things. That's cool, right? We're brothers.'

'We're others.'

'Brothers,' he says. 'Only 2 people in the world with our name. We all look alike, right? Dude, I'm sorry I said those words, did those things. I like you. I want to be like you. You're cool. I lied. You are super cool. Dude, listen to me – you're awesome, dude. Really awesome.'

More tolerable silence follows. A mutual respect based on a rapport finally found. I feel hypnotised and strangely comforted by his words. Like helping him is a natural thing. I smile. This guy's a charmer.

'Thanks,' I mumble.

I ask if he wants anything. He says a beer. I go off to buy us teas. When I return, I sit down and we're in silence. I feel sore about the passport thing but don't want to bring it up again. It's done with. I want for Kitab 2 to break the silence as he inevitably will do.

'Are you on Tinder yet?' Kitab 2 asks. I nod, because we're friends now. 'Let's see if we can find a girl to visit me in my hospital bed,' he says and giggles. 'I need to get my dick wet, dude.'

'No, man. That's weird. Also, I don't think they'll let you bring girls in.'

'If she's close, I can pop out. No one would notice. I'm in a room full of 3 other Indians. We all look alike. Your words.'

'I'm not going to do that.'

'Okay, I understand. Can we at least look at who is on there right now?'

'What if your nurse is on there?'

'It's better if I know, dude.'

I sidle next to Kitab 2 and load up Tinder on my phone. I

press refresh and it updates all the girls geographically close to me. There are 15 girls.

'Why have they all got their tongues out?' Kitab 2 asks.

'What do you mean?'

'All these girls, they're sticking their tongues out. It's not sexy, dude. Maybe it's because they're all fat.'

'That's unfair,' I say. 'People get self-conscious when they have their photo taken. This is what they think we think is sexy, I guess.'

'I'm not fussy, dude. I'm lost in a strange country, I've been beaten up and I'm a virgin.'

'Well, let's find you someone.'

We search through the 15 girls, but Kitab 2 doesn't like any of them. He dismisses them as too fat, not blonde, too fat, piggy eyes, too fat, too young, too old, not blonde, hairy, too fat, too fat, not my type, Indian, black, and not blonde. I close my phone.

'Sorry, man, them's the breaks,' I say. 'It can't be 100% accurate bikini-clad Playboy bunnies all the time.'

Kitab 2 looks at the ground. 'I know,' he says. 'I just thought …' Another silence follows. 'Do you do internet dating?'

'I tried it once. I didn't get anywhere. Aziz told me I should. He said it's like a meat market for casual sex with ugly people or boring silent dates with quiet people who are funnier online than in real life. I didn't meet anyone though.'

'I should sign up,' Kitab 2 says. 'I don't mind casual sex with ugly people, dude.' He smiles. Kitab 2 draws in a big breath. 'Dude, I want to go to a sex party,' he says after stubbing out his cigarette.

'Pardon?' I ask.

'A sex party. I want to go to one of those sex parties they have in London, where you wear masks and people have sex on round sofas with chubby blonde girls. I have seen it on the internet. When I was coming here, I looked up the local blue movies, dude. Britain loves swingers. And doggers. And sex

202

parties. They're all doing it. Everyone wears masks and you can stick it wherever you want. And the girls all sound like Ross's wife from *Friends*. It'll be cool, dude.'

'Cool, man. Have fun.'

'You have to take me. I do not know how to find one.'

Kitab 2 has mistaken me for a deviant. It's hardly the decadent noughties anymore. Hasn't everyone grown up and got cats? That's the first sign of slowing down. Pets first, sensible job second, put all your homemade 'art' in storage third … then maybe accidentally have a kid as you hit your 40s. Modern city dwelling.

'Neither do I, Kitab. I don't know what sort of guy you think I am but I'm not a "sex party" man. I can barely look at myself in the mirror let alone prance about in just my penis, thrusting it into any orifice that takes my fancy.'

'Oh,' Kitab 2 says. 'This is disappointing. I have made it my personal odyssey to have sex with a British woman. And where better than a party where everyone is doing it? And if it ends up on the internet, I can have a mask on my face but I will know it's me.'

I point at his pants area. 'I'm surprised you're so proud.'

'I saw one of your Twitter followers is a lady who organises sex parties. Her name is @partyorifices. Tweet her and ask.'

'Mate, I have over 2000 followers. I'm not going to tweet someone I don't know and ask them to invite me to a sex party,' I say, folding my arms. 'That's not cool. I don't want to do that on my account. Everyone already thinks I'm a sexpest.'

'On September 4th, she tweeted to you that she loved your work and you were welcome to come to one of her parties anytime,' Kitab 2 says, leaning towards me.

'Right …'

'You don't remember.'

'Not really. I probably thought it was spam. Mate, I'm not doing this.'

'I can make life very difficult for you,' Kitab 2 says, mirroring my folded arms.

I think about it and shake my head emphatically. 'No, you can't, Kitab. Seriously ... I've half a mind to report you to the police. Or email your dad. I found him on the Bangalore University website. I bet he'd be troubled to know that you weren't spending his money how you told him you would.'

I can play hardball too, I think. Not very successfully admittedly, but in this game of wits, we're both twits.

'I set up a webcam in your bedroom, dude. I got some video of you jerking off. I can put it on YouTube.'

'No, you haven't.'

'No, I haven't. You're right. I don't want to blackmail you, dude. I just want a favour. A favour, please ... '

'A favour aside from letting you stay at my place, eat my food, helping you with stuff?'

'A final favour. I'm going to go home, I think.'

'Home meaning where?' I ask.

'I am going back to India next week. Going to say there was problems with my visa, and I'll reapply next year. I just want this trip to end with a beautiful time. Come on, I will leave you alone. I promise. You go back to your life and I go back to mine.'

'You said you didn't have a return journey.'

'I do. I changed my ticket. I used your credit card to pay the £100 extra.'

'You did what?' I say. 'Fuck's sake, Kitab. That's dark. You're paying me that back. When you get back, I don't care how you get the money. But you're fucking paying me back.' He nods, embarrassed. I make a mental note to start checking my credit card bill once in a while.

'Come on, take me ...'

'I don't know, man. It's not my thing ...'

'My mum's dead and I don't know anyone in the city and

I'm alone … take me … My final wish to you.'

I get up and leave him there. I drop the cigarette on the ground. I've taken one puff.

Teddy Baker pulled the train driver down below the dashboard because he was slow to comprehend the situation. The screams from the platform and the screams and bangs from the passengers in the train didn't alert him to the fact that we were being shot at. And just when the train cleared the station and geared into speed, the stupid baby started crying. Teddy Baker thrust it at me. I took it and looked down at it. It was a fat white baby.

#Azizhatesyourkids

I shushed the pink big-ass baby by bobbing it gently against my sweating Lycra chest.

'You are a heavy fucking thing ... yes you are ... yes you are ... you heavy little thing.'

'Teddy, what do you make of this?' Bob asked. Teddy Baker was driving the train while the train driver composed a text.

'We saw some fucking action, eh boys?'

'Yeah, Teddy. We saw some action.'

'It's the Aziz effect,' I told them. They needed to recognise that I am Aziz, bringer of chaos and party-hard fun.

I am Samson. No, I am Hercules.

The rush that I was feeling holding this gangster's baby and fleeing from a gunfight dressed as a motherfucking superhero was like nature's Viagra. Shitbirds, I suggest you try it.

Then there was the unmistakable sound of another gunshot.

BANG.

Like that. BANG. Just BANG. No announcement. It wasn't like a movie, so there was no trumpet stab and no building of tension. It was just matter-of-fact, a bullet was fired.

We all ducked and that caused Teddy Baker to wrench the accelerator then pull it back too far before Bob stopped the train. We were in a tunnel. The lights shone out into nothing.

The only sound was the baby crying.

'Should I call 911?' the train driver asked. 'Never mind. No reception.'

A knock came in the door.

'Hello?' Teddy Baker asked meekly.

The train driver took a fire extinguisher to the window in front of him. The glass shattered, scattering outside. He pulled himself out of the train carriage and ran off into the darkness. Bob ushered us to follow him. I shook my head.

'What about the people?'

'Fuck the people.'

'Fuck you. You're a superhero.'

'Yeah, an unarmed one.'

Bob leapt up onto the broken window frame. I pushed the baby towards him.

'Fuck that,' he laughed and jumped down, disappearing into the darkness.

'Hello?' Teddy Baker asked again.

'Open ... the ... fucking ... door.' The voice that replied to Teddy Baker was too muffled to be chilling, but I still felt like I might shit myself, baby-style.

'Why would we do that?' Teddy Baker shouted back.

'Because I'm out here with a train full of people I'm happy to kill one at a time until you do.'

'That sounds pretty unreasonable, mate,' I shouted. 'What's the point of that?'

'Are you British?' the muffled voice asked, incredulous.

'Yeah,' I said back. 'And what?'

'I don't understand your accent man. Put the American back on.'

'Right. What ... do ... you ... want?'

'How about we start with my baby?'

Teddy Baker knocked on the door. 'Are you the baby's daddy?' he asked.

'What the fuck do you think, Einstein?'

'Can you tell us any distinguishing features as proof?'

'Distinguishing features? What the fuck? It looks like a baby. A fat fucking baby. Open the fucking door, you wiseguys.'

'The baby IS fat,' I said to Teddy Baker, whispering.

'We can't give him the baby.'

'We can't let those passengers die though.'

'Why did the mum kill herself? To keep the baby from this guy?'

'He's going to kill those passengers ...'

'You guys do know I can hear you, right?' the muffled voice reminded us.

I mouthed 'shit' and Teddy Baker mouthed 'fuck'.

CLUNK.

Something spanked the door and it rattled in its frame. And again. And again. Like a fire extinguisher. CLUNK. CLUNK. RATTLE. RATTLE. The baby cried again.

The muffled voice shouted, 'He needs feeding. Come on. Think of the baby.' The CLUNKing was boring into my brain. Teddy Baker started whimpering.

I turned to the dashboard of the train and pressed go, whacking the accelerator up as sharply and far as it would go. The train lurched forward and we stumbled into the dashboard as the train picked up a momentum that sent it careening into the tunnel. The CLUNK stopped while the momentum of the train was pulling us all forward but started up again when we hit optimum speed.

Teddy Baker whacked my arm because there was a station coming up. Just before the train could hit the station I slowed it to a sudden stop. Teddy Baker and I fell into the dashboard. I pulled myself up, baby in one arm, and through the broken glass pane and stepped down onto the very bare edge of the platform.

Teddy stumbled up and followed, jumping down onto the platform as the door to the cabin thundered open. We ran.

Whistles blowing and commotion followed us up the corridors and tunnels so when we hit the ticket office, Teddy Baker perfected a smooth leapfrog up and over the ticket barrier. I handed him the baby with such force that there was a moment when it was suspended in mid-air. I pulled myself over the ticket barrier and we ran to the stairs. Whistles, calls of 'stop, police' and screams all clattered behind us. I looked back and it hit me: we were being chased by policemen. Why were we being chased by policemen? This realisation made me pause, which gave a police pig the opportunity to jump on top of me from the stairs. I crashed to the floor and was turned over and my arms grabbed — knee in the back, proper force — as I was wrenched back. I screamed.

911 is a joke. You called it, Flav.

I turned to the policeman holding on to me. 'Am I being arrested?' He laughed. 'What does that mean?' I asked. 'Seriously, I know about you New York City cops. Am I being arrested? Can I get a witness?'

'Hey,' the cop said to me. 'Are you British?'

I nodded.

'Hey guys,' he shouted to the people around him. 'It's fucking Harry Potter here. Harry Potter here cracked the case, got the Sterling baby back. Motherfucking limey Harry Potter!'

'Are you sure he's British? He looks too dark.'

'Hey buddy,' the cop said to me. 'I'm going to need to see some identification. Are you really British? Not ... Indian? Middle Eastern?'

New York City Cops. They ain't too smart.

There are 17 comments for this blog:

GustaveGrime: Kill yourself. Now.

AZIZWILLKILLYOU: Do I know you, homey?

GustaveGrime: What does it matter? This is terrible stuff.

AZIZWILLKILLYOU: Listen, man, if you need to talk, air out some issues, I can give you my email address and maybe we can squash this beef.

GustaveGrime: There's no beef, man. I just think you're an idiot.

211

AZIZWILLKILLYOU: And I think you're an asshole. Where do we go from here?

GustaveGrime: Fuck you.

AZIZWILLKILLYOU: There, there, little one ... get it all out in the open. Cry yourself to sleep.

GustaveGrime: Don't patronise me. I know about you and your shitty little attitude towards up and comers. When it comes down to it, this blog is bullshit.

Anonymous: Dude, Gustave, chill. Man is too funny.

AZIZWILLKILLYOU: Thanks, Anonymous. Whoever you are?

DF325: Hey, Aziz. When you back? I am DTF.

GustaveGrime: When it comes down to it, there are people smarter than you, more talented than you, more better-looking than you, but you'll always win because you're the bigger cunt than all of them. What's it to you what I think?

Anonymous: Fuck off this blog.

AZIZWILLKILLYOU: Co-sign.

GustaveGrime: Idiots.

AZIZWILLKILLYOU: I think you're all missing the point. I was shot at! That not cool enough?

History:

Sex tips – Google
How to last longer – Google

I catch Hayley poking around Aziz's room when I return. She's holding some photos of us, printed before the digital revolution. I'm dressed as Spider-man and him as Batman in one. In another, we're laughing at Dad burning meat on a barbecue. She looks at me and places her index finger on her cheek, screwing it lightly, her knee cocked.

'How's the booze head?'

'So bad I cried off travelling up to Liverpool to do a reading. Terrible, aren't I?' she says before pointing to the shelves. 'This room's like a guest room …'

'Aziz has a Nintendo Wii and some t-shirts. Everything else he borrows,' I say. She lifts up his Clash t-shirt.

'This is tiny. I'm guessing he's one of those guys who wears everything he likes on his t-shirts so people can form personality profiles of him?'

I nod.

She walks towards me, her arms behind her back. She's wearing one of my flannel shirts and her long legs peek out of them. She has thick calves and slender thighs. She has legs like Popeye has arms and I feel nothing but lust.

I walk into the room and Hayley puts her arms up to hug me.

'What you doing in here anyway?' I ask.

'Sorry, I dropped a contact lens,' she says, shrugging. 'I heard a noise. I thought this was the bathroom.' She pauses. 'I was being nosey. Okay?' She sighs, then laughs to herself. 'I borrowed a shirt. My clothes smell of booze, man.'

'Yeah, no problem,' I say, reaching my arms out towards her. She hesitates, keeping herself just out of my reach. 'Look at you, all knight in shining armour-y …'

'It had to happen once in my life.'

Hayley moves past me and walks out into the main bit of the flat. She picks up things, much like Kitab 2 did when he first came here. This time, they are picked up and replaced in an ordered way. She picks up a photo and points it at me.

'That's my mum. She died when I was young. A small child. She's with Aziz.' The photo is of Mum holding Aziz's hand. He's dressed in that Batman outfit. 'I know next to nothing about her. Like, I know her favourite song and what she smelled like. But not much else, not much useful. She's barely 3D in my head. She's just a bunch of static images.'

Hayley sits on the sofa and looks at me. 'Remember the first time we met?' she says. I shake my head even though I remember it well. She was dressed in a summer dress, her hair was in plaits, she had an ice cream stain on her brogues. And she was late for a reading. I was halfway through reading a short story and she entered, with bluster and noise. And the stage was right by the door.

'"Carry on"', I bellow like she did that night.

'Yeah, I still think about that night. You were so funny. When we were sitting at the back, after the thing was finished, on a bench, our heads against the wall, telling jokes. I know it's stupid but your repeated "that's what she said" and "that's a good name for a band" jokes, they had me in stitches.' She stops. 'I was so annoyed you had a girlfriend.' She screws up her nose. 'You haven't done those jokes this last week.'

'That's what she said,' I offer weakly.

I move closer to her and she looks away, then back to me. I place a hand on her knee.

'I'm still me. I think,' I say.

'I know,' she says, kissing my forehead. 'Anyway, that guy I first met knocked his pint into my handbag.' She laughs. 'You ruined my phone and a cheque I hadn't cashed.'

'It was partly revenge,' I say. 'For you coming in late.'

Hayley leans forward, rubs her forehead against my lips. I pull her mouth up to mine.

We laugh. We kiss. Our kisses carry weight this time.

I get a tweet from Kitab 2. He's signed up for an account as @kitabtwodeetwo. It says, '…'

I don't reply. Hayley is snoozing across me and I'm respecting the body warmth and the end of my purdah (the messy, quickly finished end) by checking my phone as silently as I can. This is nothing like the videos I stream everyday. This is nothing like being alone. For the first time in months, I don't miss Rach, but I do understand what made it work. It's been a long time since I've been this intimate with someone. I fall asleep.

I wake up 2 hours later and hear that Hayley has put the kettle on so while she makes us a drink, I check my phone. I notice that Kitab 2 has tweeted me again. This time, he's changed the handle to @k1tab.

He tweets: '@kitab Come dude … I get out of hospital tomorrow.'

10 minutes later, he tweets me again and says: 'Come on dude. I need answers.'

I check his account.

10 minutes later: 'Hey @partyorifices. You're following my namesake @kitab. I'm the real @k1tab. I want to cum. To a party.'

2 minutes later: '@kitab don't bother dude. i sort myself out.'

1 minute later: '@kitab dude, still come with me.'

1 minute later: '@partyorifices thanks for following me back. I'll DM you.'

20 minutes later: '@kitab I explained the situation to @partyorifices. They're having an ethnic night for us.'

He's doing this all in public. Not that he has any followers. But it's uncomfortable for me given our recent episode with the porno-graphic picture. It looks crass. Days after my dickpic, months after I decided I was a 'serious' novelist, he's making me look a fool. Indelibly so. @partyorifices has a lot of followers. A lot more than me. I feel uncomfortable. Kitab 2 doesn't get it. He lives his entire life online. He is not bothered by the self-censorship of holding yourself back for emergencies, of not tweeting your loca-tion, making you less susceptible to stalkers, thieves and snipers. I try calling the number he's left me. I don't get through. I'm about to phone the hospital when Hayley brings us coffee in bed.

'Coffee for the bad boy?'

'How am I a bad boy?'

'All boys with tattoos are bad boys.'

'What are you up to today?' I ask, sipping the coffee. It's too milky. I pull a face.

'What's wrong with it, you fusspot?'

'It's fine,' I say, wincing through a reassurance sip.

'Would you prefer masala chai?' she says, smiling.

'Yeah, and a mango.'

Hayley rests her elbows on my hips and balances her head on her hands. 'We should go out. On a date. With wine. And dinner. And conversation where we don't moan about publishers and depressing book sales. We could talk about lots of things, dead relatives, dysfunctional families, special skills – did you know I know how to weld? That's not even a first date revela-tion, but I would tell you. Just so you know.'

'I'd like that.'

'I mean,' Hayley says, jumping up, spilling coffee on me. 'How will you ever know the answers to the following ques-tions: Hayley's food phobias; places Hayley has travelled to; Hayley's guilty music pleasures; and the charming story of how I once saw Michael Fassbender in an East London hipster pub drinking Guinness by himself.'

'You tweeted that one,' I say, smiling.

Hayley plops herself back on the bed, the vibration springing hot coffee onto my skin. 'Damn you, internet, there's just nothing left to know about anyone anymore.'

'That's not true,' I say. 'The more I've spent time with you, the more I've realised I barely know all the good stuff.'

Hayley lies on me and tells me about all the places she's visited while I finish my coffee.

Her presence distracts me from my screens.

Hayley is sleeping. She can fall asleep anywhere. Dad says this was my mum's greatest trick. I can't stop thinking about Kitab 2 and his open door policy, embarrassing me. But there is a girl I like a lot lying on my chest. Kitab 2 has crossed a line. I don't want him to associate himself with me anymore. But as Hayley stirs and her hand gently rubs at my stomach and starts to make tentative moves under the covers, I'm quickly informed by my body where my priorities lie.

Hayley leaves me 2 distracted hours later to go read from her novel at a library in Goodmayes. I joke that she will be asked 'Where do you get your ideas from?' a lot. She jokes that as I'm of the ethnic persuasion, I'll probably be asked what my parents think of my work.

'One's dead, the other's a douchebag. I don't think they think anything about my work,' I reply. She grabs my forearm and bites it, kisses me on the lips and leaves.

I wait 30 seconds, to avoid an awkward walk to the station, and then run out on my way back to the hospital to find Kitab 2. This time I am seething with war.

War doesn't take public transport, though. I stop at the taxi rank and get a minicab back to the hospital.

So what happened was the po-po eventually got up off Aziz, pulled me up and took me to one side and said they had to bring us in for questioning. I asked if I'm being arrested. They said no, I could call a lawyer. I asked if I could call the embassy. I was concerned because I'd just rescued a baby not kidnapped one. Brown man caught with white baby ... I've seen this movie. It ends in a bay in Cuba.

#keepyourpromisesObama
#stopthedronestrikesObama

The dude told me it was just procedure, but something wasn't quite right when Teddy Baker and I were shoved into the back of 2 separate cop cars and driven off in separate directions. We were being separated and I wasn't too sure why. As far as I was concerned, I did the cops' work for them. I cracked the case. I did a sterling job on the Sterling case. I kept asking the po-po in the front of the car where I was being taken but they didn't answer me. They straight up ignored me. They hadn't taken my stuff off me or cuffed me. But I couldn't call anyone cos I'd left all my shit in that weird house of Bob's. Fucking Bob, where was Bob?

When we got to the police station, the cop opened the door quietly. He didn't say anything to me, even as I nodded at him. He just pointed me towards the door. I wanted to ask him if I was going in as a free man or not but I didn't say anything too Aziz-y, cos that's the sort of shit that gets you interned or Guantanamo'd. I was walking with skin issues here.

Inside, I was met by the original detective who called me Harry Potter. Except my nickname had mutated in transit. 'Look,' he said to the room, pointing at me. 'Osama Bin Potter.' He laughed. People rolled their eyes. I saw Teddy Baker down the corridor.

'Yo, Teddy,' I shouted.

'He's fine,' the detective said. He held out his hand. 'Detective Alverton.'

'Wassup, man,' I said and slapped his hand. He looked at it and replaced it in his pocket.

'So,' he said, pointing to my Lycra. 'This looks like a girl's costume. What's your name supposed to be? Brown Lioness?'

I smiled sarcastically, but I thought he was talking like he thought the whole thing was funny. He led me down the corridor. My hands were clasped together, like I thought I'd been arrested already. But I hadn't been. I needed to keep remembering that. He took me into a room called Examination Room 2. I wondered if Teddy Baker was in Examination Room 1. What a fucking doppelganger, eh? We hung out one night and he got me arrested wearing Lycra so tight you could see the last time I manscaped down there.

Examination Room 2 was exactly how anyone who has seen a film with a scene in an examination/interrogation room would imagine it. There was nothing in it except a plastic table and a pen and pad. Detective Alverton pulled a dicta-phone out of his pocket and sat down. He gestured to me to sit down. I sat down and placed my hands on the table. They were still magnetised like I was cuffed.

'So, how does a British citizen find himself wearing a girly superhero outfit in the subway rescuing the baby of one of the city's most eminent bankers?'

'I have no idea, mate. Life's crazy.' Somehow, I found some swag back. It was like my bowels wanted to run, but my mouth wanted to run too, so they were both fighting impulses to shut up and flee.

'Nice tattoo,' Detective Alverton had noticed my sick bow tie tattoo and pointed to it. 'What is that?'

'It's a bow tie.'

Detective Alverton stood up and left the room for 5 minutes. I was not sure what kind of game he was playing. Whether this was an intimidation method or he needed a piss. He eventually returned, smiling to himself. Then he looked at me and smiled more.

'Nice tattoo,' he said again.

'Innit,' I said. Cos what more could you say? It's an awesome tattoo.

'Matching tattoos. Are you guys, like, together or something?'

It didn't occur to me that this might seem weird, 2 guys

running around New York dressed as homemade superheroes with matching individual tattoos but it was weird. I shrugged.

'Does that matter?'

Detective Alverton shook his head.

'You're not lovers?'

'Nah man, just ... you know. Whatever. It's just a tattoo.'

'Cos the last thing we need is 2 weirdo gay lovers with weirdo matching tattoos running around my town solving my cases.'

'Sorry, dude. What's with all the homophobia, mate?'

'You don't belong to a cult?'

'What kind of cult gets matching bow tie tattoos?'

'A weird one.'

'You don't know me, detective. But I run cults. I don't belong to them.'

Detective Alverton's tone had changed. He was looking at me differently now he knew that Teddy Baker and I had this weird connection. He couldn't quite understand something but, typical cop, he wasn't telling me anything, he was just sitting there judging me in whatever way he wanted to. It unnerved me. I wasn't sure what I was supposed to do at this point.

'Am I under arrest? Because I'm not sure I did anything wrong.'

221

'Let me see here: trespass on New York Transit Authority property, absconding with a baby, running away from police officers, resisting arrest ...'

'Hey, I came here willingly because you told me I wasn't under arrest.'

'Fine. Not resisting arrest.'

'You're still making it sound like I did something wrong.'

'Paint me a picture, if you will, As-Is ... I mean, I gotta ask ... what were you doing tonight?'

I don't know what possessed me to give all my cards away or risk my words and actions being mangled but in that situation what could you do? You think the truth will set you free. So I started at the beginning. I told him about the Google image search, the tattoo, the Facebook stalking, the first meeting, meeting Bob – all of it. The social media treasure hunt.

And I led Detective Alverton, who, the entire time had a weird grin on his face, towards where we're sitting now. The problem was as I told the story, his grin got more fixed so I lost faith in my story and tripped over myself. I mean, I'd live-blogged all this so it wasn't like none of it wasn't public record, was it? Why would I lie to you? My most loyal of peoples.

'Tell me about this Bob guy. I'm interested in him,' Detective Alverton said when I'd finishing telling him my frankly awesome tale.

'I dunno – he lives above some dive bar in Brooklyn. He's a bit of a shit.'

Detective Alverton grabbed a pencil and made a note. He looked up.

'As-Is, say that again – I want to get it exactly right. He's "a bit of a shit"? Or is he a whole of a shit? Or is he just a shit? Come on, say it again. Be specific.'

'Dude's a wanker. I'm not a fan. "Unlike".'

Detective Alverton wrote something then looked back up at me and smiled. 'Thanks, As-Is,' he said, and he left the room.

'Wait, detective – don't I get a phone call?'

'Why do you need one, son? You're not under arrest, are you? Unless you feel you need to be.'

Detective Alverton returned a few minutes later, smiling. He put a folder on the table, one of those plain brown paper folders that people in CSI shows carry when they're about to pin something on you.

Comments are disabled for this post.

History:

Sex party etiquette – Google
Ways to last longer – Google
Peter North cumshot – YouPorn

In the cab over to the hospital, I trace the letters on my forearm. The tattoo artist has done a quick job on the 'ook' of 'book'. I marvel at my tattooed skin's ability to highlight some of my own inadequacies. I haven't written in days, weeks, months. I haven't done anything of worth. The irony of the tattoo brings a smile to my face. It hasn't turned out to make the statement I intended it to.

The taxi stalls in traffic round the corner from the hospital and I feel the nervous energy in my legs beg to spring into action, so I ask the driver to pull over and I run unnecessarily but urgently to the front door. They're closing for visiting hours but I claim an emergency and am allowed up to Kitab 2's floor. I run up the stairs. My legs run out of enthusiasm for bursts of energy at the first floor. I push through and I run to the room where he's holed up, ready to unleash the fire of 'respect the social etiquette' on him, but the lights are off and the beds are all empty.

I run back to the reception desk and a nurse shrugs. 'Visiting hours are over, darling.' I am sweating and not even my closed mouth can disguise my desperate pants for air.

'Where's Kitab, the guy who was in that bed today?'

'Oh, the sweet Indian guy?' she says, smiling. 'With the permanent erection?'

'Yeah.'

'Visiting hours are over.'

'I'm really sorry, but where is he? I was supposed to pick him up and I got waylaid. I'm here to pick him up.'

'Oh, right. Well, you're very late. He left 4 hours ago. Said he was discharging himself. Then he laughed. And said, "that's what she said". He left. And before you ask, I don't know and don't care where. He was silly to discharge himself, but as long as he sticks to his prescription of painkillers, he should be okay.'

'Right … thanks.'

'And he should have that priapism checked out …'

'Thank you,' I say, making a mental note to tweet something about the word 'priapism'. I don't know what yet but put a pin in it. Not the priapism. The idea. I laugh to myself.

'Are you alright, love?' she calls after me as I turn to leave. 'You're very sweaty. You should get that checked out.'

I stand outside the hospital and shield my phone in my jacket from potential muggers. I check Twitter: nothing. A girl who looks attractive has just retweeted my link to my article about the tattoo. I reply, 'THANKS FOR THE RT!!' to her. I check out her avatar in closer detail. I feel like a creep and close the window down. Nothing from Kitab 2. People are talking about welfare cuts. I don't have time to formulate a pithy opinion. I check Facebook to see if Kitab 2 and I are still friends.

The top news stories: Cara changed her profile picture to a photo of a sonogram. Rach is 'in a relationship'. What the fuck? She's in a relationship? Already? With who? I scan through her profile, distracted, unable to decipher who she's in a relationship with. She's working quickly. Kitab 2. Nothing from him. I email him. I text the phone number he left me. Nothing.

I think I know where he is. He's off somewhere being disgusting. At a sex party he found on Twitter. There's something so creepy about the whole affair. I've watched the videos on YouPorn and RedTube, I've seen the masks and bellies and the kneading of a placid girl's breasts. I've heard the gruff

Benson & Hedges voices cooing and grunting. The bellies flopping over their genitals, the translucent white skin. The stroking of the penises while waiting turns. The grimaces of pain and pleasure from the women. The men, 5 to 1, the sweaty backs, the realistic girths, the grunting and writhing and silence, the deafening silence. I've seen the American college parties where the frat boys call in hookers and the hookers bang everyone on the beer pong table whilst upperclassmen *oi-oi* and coo and shout words of encouragement in the background while the uninhibited girls take control of the nervous boys buoyed by the pack mentality. I've even watched bukkake, which I've never seen the titillation in. All of those films are about domination by the ugliest of men. I've watched the videos and I've felt a wave of self-loathing towards myself and the internet for allowing me to be able to search for them, snatching 30 segment buffered fragments as I skip through the highlights of 4–16 minute videos of acts that were once intimate and the imagined landscapes we created to turn ourselves on as teenagers. The mystery, the power of imagination's all gone now we can search for whatever we want. How this could result in something beautiful and sexy like @partyorifices claims, I don't know. It'll just be full of fat white people too rich for conventional banging. I have to stop him live-tweeting this. I want no association with it. Also, it's for ever. If he's going to be applying for jobs, for university, for anything, that digital footprint of his needs to be clean.

The internet is both transient and eternal and there's nothing you can hide from it once it goes online.

I have no choice but to head over to where this party is and call for him at the front desk. Do sex parties have front desks? Do they have receptions?

I look at the @partyorifices Twitter account and at their website and there's nothing on there to even hint at a location for tonight's orgiastic festivities. I suppose that's sensible given this is supposed to be elite and word of mouth and undercover. Husbands, wives, colleagues – they shouldn't be made aware of your disgusting whereabouts, should they?

But if we are to subject connected social animals to our every whim, even ones best kept private, then everything should be on display. Your location should be traceable, so people can see that when you Facebook about travel problems, you're still in the pub and covering up a late arrival for dinner with the wife. Your porn history should be matter of public record. Mine would never show a consistency you could look at and know my 'type'. Your real likes and dislikes should be in a separate list, just underneath your social likes and dislikes, so people can see that you secretly prefer Coldplay to whatever hip band is out there right now. Unless you don't mind people knowing you like Coldplay.

And if you're the type of person who goes to sex parties you find on the internet, by golly, your friends and family, your colleagues and acquaintances, accountants and clients, should all know about it.

I stand on the street outside the hospital and run through my options. This is ridiculous. A social media chase around London. A high octane chase all on a 120x60mm screen.

If only he used Foursquare, that would make all of this a lot easier. I check through the various sites under my own name but find nothing. I do a Twitter search for Party Orifices. I do a Google image search. I email *info@partyorifices.biz* (awww, they could only get the .biz. This makes me sad for a split second).

I check through my notifications. I see that about 6 hours ago, Kitab 2 accepted my friend request. I click onto his account. It's bare except for YouTube trailers of video games and updates on his score on *Mafia*.

My hunch is that he's the kind of guy to 'check in' at places and let you know exactly where he is, even if his dad is friends

227

with him or his friends are prudes. No matter where you are or what you're doing, there's that innate compulsion to tell people that's where you are and that's what you're doing.

I look at his timeline. Kitab is 'checked in at Wilmington House'. A building called Wilmington House is exactly the type of place where people would be having a sex party. I look the address up. The house is across town. I have to brave public transport.

I head to the station.

Wilmington House is on a cul-de-sac in one of the better-off ends of town. This is where the rich can afford to own housing. All the bankers and MPs, all the socialites and tenuous links to royalty. I never come here. I never visit this part of the city. It is far removed from my life. It's not where I come from and it's not what I aspire to be. I keep it real in East London. Not south or west where the stinky winds don't visit. There is a quiet in the air that feels like nothing I'm used to. It feels like the stillness that every rich person needs after a long day. I hear clichés, like the wind whistling through trees, kids playing in gardens and dishwashers, as I walk through the streets.

Wilmington House is nondescript in its appearance. It's 3 storeys and has shut blinds in the windows. Ivy bushes obscure the front walkway. The door isn't illuminated. Everything screams no one's home. I ring the doorbell and nothing happens.

I ring it again, twice. Nothing happens.

I ring it again. Nothing happens.

Then twice again. And I see a flicker of light behind the opaque window pane. The door opens and a woman with a wild mess of curly blonde hair, in her 40s and smiling with a cigarette-stained line of teeth, answers the door. She is dressed in a tight black dress. She is barefoot.

'Yes?' the woman says, dismissively.

228

'Party Orifices?' I say, confidently.

'Excuse me?'

'I'm here for Party Orifices,' I repeat, less sure.

'I don't know what that is.'

'This is Wilmington House, isn't it?'

'Yes, it is.'

'So, this is where Party Orifices is, isn't it?'

She pauses. I'm nervous. I don't want to go in. I don't want to see the sweaty writhing of flesh unless it's through the filter of a screen. I feel a burning pit of sweaty anxiety in my stomach, splooshing around like downing water when you're hungry. I am not ready for this type of thing. Like Seinfeld said, 'I'm not an orgy guy.'

'Is this your first time?' she asks wearily. I nod. I'm nervous. My bowels are aching. My stomach is churning. She shakes her head and picks up a clipboard from the side. She looks at it.

'Name?'

'Kitab.'

'Kitab what?'

I give her my full name. She looks down the list.

'You're already here.'

'Yes, I'm here. Standing in front of you.'

'But you're already crossed off the list.'

'There's 2 of us.'

'Excuse me?'

'2 people with the same name. Believe it or not, that name's like John Smith back in India.'

'There's no one here called John Smith.'

'No, I know. My name's Kitab Balasubramanyam.'

'I'll be right back.'

She closes the door and the dim light is shut out. I wait there. I check Twitter – 3 rappers with mixtapes have spammed me with links to their downloads, the girl I tweeted thanks to earlier favourited and retweeted my tweet, a model called @sammyk has tweeted me a picture of his penis. I check Facebook. Rach is mysteriously no longer in a relationship. Her basic profile info says Rachel Calaver, London. Maybe she has hidden me from certain updates. There is no sign of Kitab 2's debauchery being made public just yet. Probably because he's currently involved in it. There's time for tweeting later. Hopefully no Instagrams.

I watch a couple pass behind me. They're talking about his day, his boss, until they notice me in the garden, then they're awkward and shhh each other. Like they're embarrassed for me. Because we all know what happens at Wilmington House. The girl flashes me an awkward smile. The man opens the door to the flat next door, a rictus grin of embarrassment on his face. I wish I was wearing a hoodie.

The door opens while I'm distracted and the woman is standing there again, looking annoyed. I wonder if she's annoyed at having door duty when there's all this fucking going on elsewhere, or if she's wishing she had a different temping agency, one which sent her to offices instead of orifices.

'Come on then ...' She gestures to the gangway next to her. I squeeze in through the doorway into the hall. There are candles illuminating white walls. I can see the folds of tapestries on the walls but not their contents. Probably some offensive reappropriation of the *Kama Sutra*. Or something else equally 'tits-everywhere' masquerading as erotic art. 'This way,' she says, with air in her voice. She leads me into the next room and points to the right door. 'You can get changed in there.'

'Oh, right.' I'm not sure what I'm supposed to do but I imagine I have to play some sort of part. I walk into the room. It's a toilet, a functional small toilet. There are masquerade masks on the back of the door. I look at myself in the mirror and wonder what I'm supposed to do next. I can't emerge in what I'm currently wearing. Maybe if I strip down to pants, t-shirt and socks and put a masquerade mask on. I grab a classy-looking black one and slip it over my eyes. I take my shirt and jeans off, and bundle them into the sleeves of my jacket. I take my shoes off and fold them into the centre of the jacket before scrunching it into a ball. I look at myself in the mirror. The only thing that distinguishes me is my tattoo and my brown skin against the white of my Radiohead t-shirt that declares 'Kicking Squealing Gucci Little Piggy'.

I suck in and leave the toilet.

She is waiting outside for me and takes my stuff. She grabs my arm and writes '696' on my hand. She smiles at me and delivers the line she's been delivering all night: 'Don't sweat the number off finger-banging anyone or I won't be able to locate your things.' She pauses. 'T-shirt?' I shake my head. 'First time nerves? Don't worry, darling. Everyone's friendly. Second floor. There are bowls of these around but here's one for starters,' she says, smiling.

She hands me a condom. I hold it and stare at it wondering what my life has come to. I feel no arousal, no stirring, nothing that could give this rubber Johnny a chance to perform its life's function.

And with that she disappears into the bowels of the house, taking my t-shirt, wallet and my phone with her, and I feel more naked than ever.

I walk back towards the front door where I saw some steps. I walk up them.

Aziz once told me he thought the reason our friendship worked was because I was so repressed and he was so comfortable.

'You're so perverted in private, but whenever I talk about finger-banging, you get all prudish. Make your mind up.'

'No one needs to know the things I'm into.'

'Interracial redhead lesbians, bruv. I've seen your internet history.'

The day he caught me on the phone to a sex line, one drunken evening, I was so mortified, even in my drunken state, that he

231

knew never to bring it up. More than once a week I'd hear his room a-rocking. Whereas, whenever I was home with company of a sexual variety, I would squeak and mumble like the strong silent soldier. He was right – I was repressed. I couldn't bring myself to say the things he did in public. He would happily talk about sex with anyone. Even my dad was more comfortable with the idea of talking to me about sex than I was.

That was until my drunken curiosity made me call a sex line and he caught me, and knew. The kiss-n-tells stopped after that.

Is it so bad to worry about how you're presented in public? I'd tell Aziz things, in whispers in the confines of our flat, once I'd made him sign a verbal non-disclosure and confidentiality agreement. It was how I was wired. I didn't like being open about this stuff, and why would you? The hints of sex in my book were jokes, allusions to wanking and handjobs, and that was fine, that was enough to turn up the noses of my elders. I couldn't imagine being any more sordid than that.

The prude eagle has landed. The repressed viper is in the nest.

CA-CAWWWW. HISSSSSSSS.

At the top of the stairs I can hear different varieties of giggling, from the embarrassed to the hysterical, from the deep-voiced male to the squeaky-voiced male. That's weird. Mute girls at a sex party. I inevitably make a mental joke that maybe their mouths are full, then I agonise over whether that counts as sexist, because I would hate to be deemed sexist, especially within my own internal monologue.

Then I see a swinging willy walk past. It's jostling in its join, flip-flopping from left to right, pink and nestled in grey hair. Its owner is naked, save for his own masquerade mask. The mask covers up a greying face with greying male pattern-baldness. He points to the door behind me and says 'excuse me' so

I move and watch him enter another room. It's just a toilet. There are 2 room options in front of me. The doors are only ajar so I can't peer into them and get a lay of the land, get an idea of the type of activities taking place, or get a location for Kitab 2. I can feel my own willy shrinking in confusion and embarrassment. If at any point I'm required to remove my boxer shorts, I will die. Luckily, if that old man is indicative of the talent, I will probably not be confused by my cock into attempting my own act of mutual onanism with a stranger.

#circlejerk

I wait and muddle myself up into a head of worries. It's oppressive being in a room of people having sex with each other and not wanting to participate. It's like dancing. Whenever everyone's dancing and you don't want to dance they refuse to understand why you wouldn't want to dance, not even taking into consideration whether you could dance, certainly not bothered with such trivialities as whether you should dance. Dancing is like public sex parties. Everyone except me wants to get involved.

I need to find Kitab 2 though. He should be in one of these rooms. In theory.

The toilet flushes in the room behind me. I don't want to still be standing here when that guy emerges, so I duck into the nearest of the rooms. This is obviously not the guffawing room. The lights are dim except for a spotlight in the centre where a lady is dancing. She is a wearing a gag in her mouth and nothing else. There is no music playing but she writhes slowly and swirls her hands and arms about like a festival mum, like a geriatric twerk. She looks like an art teacher, with a thicket of curly hair, a mouth where the wrinkles of lips have disappeared into each other and saggy, small breasts with black nipples.

There are 7 men, all sitting on sofas, their legs crossed, watching her, naked, touching themselves like it's the breeziest

233

thing in the world. It's hard to see them in the dim light and I don't get any time to look because the writhing festival mum grabs my hand and pulls me towards her, angling her pelvis towards my naked thigh. Before I can decline this dance, the wiry mound of her undercarriage is causing a friction of Velcro with my thigh hair as she rubs herself on me. There is a trail of mucus making a home on the fringes of my boxers. I am too embarrassed to find this sexy so I pull away and shield myself with my upper arms, moving backwards towards the wall.

A screen, a screen ... my bandwidth for a screen.

The greying, bald toilet man walks back into the room, sees her and bends her over. She grabs her ankles. He condoms up and presses his dick into the canyon of her arse, exploring and then thrusts himself inside her. She makes an unnecessary porn noise.

I scan the sofas. It's all men, all white, one applauding, so I leave the room.

In the corridor, a man and a woman are dancing at the top of the stairs. They have their arms around each other but she is resting her elbows on his shoulders and he is nuzzling into her neck. When his hand moves towards her down-below bits, I realise they're not dancing. They're doing the penetrative lambada. I duck into an adjacent doorway, where I am met by the collective groan, squelch and smack of skin.

I find 4 mattresses in the centre of the room, and, instead of sofas, single beds line the wall. It's like the last days of Rome. I scan the interloping intersecting buddies all bent over each other grabbing whatever genitals are on offer. They're all white. They're all melting into one another with their skin. By the window, watching it all with a mask on, and a saree draped around his head is Kitab 2. He has a throbbing erection that he tugs at mindlessly and slowly. It's definitely him. I recognise

234

the pubic hair from the Twitter controversy. I start to cross the room, but realise I will be tugged at if I get near these folds of fat in front of me. There is no gangway. There are only elbows, only breasts and only the grunts of those dissatisfied by conventional love-making.

I wave at Kitab 2 till he points at me and offers a thumbs up. I beckon him over urgently. As he walks in between the bodies on the mattress, disturbing their equilibrium with his redistribution of weight on the mattress springs, people bang on his ankles. No one is interested in his penis. I wonder if he's disappointed.

He makes it over to me, stepping over frotting, squelching, writhing, sweaty, flabby bodies, and punches me on the tit, so I reciprocate, hard, on the arm that I know was bruised in his accident. He yelps.

'What the fuck, dude?'

'What are you doing here?'

'Look at it, dude. Everywhere. This never happens in India. Or if it does, then I don't know about it.'

'Mate, what are you doing?'

'Trying to get laid, dude.'

'Any success?'

'No. It's like they hate India or something. Every time I go and try to put my penis in someone's mouth they slap it away. I think the last girl bruised it.' He points downwards. When I don't look, he grabs my face and I pull away.

I tug at his arm and pull him out of the room. In the corridor, the lambada couple has moved on to doggy style. She is crouched on the floor as he mounts her from behind, his belly hanging over the curve of her bottom. She looks up at us and smiles. He offers me a thumbs up. Why is everyone giving me the thumbs up? Is that sex party code? She opens her mouth suggestively, looking at me, and reaches up to pull at my boxers, so I back away.

Kitab 2 notices her looking at me, and the guy pounding her from behind winks at us both so he reaches down and de-pants me. I'm too shocked to react and don't fully comprehend what's happening till I feel a rough hand tug at my penis. It's Kitab 2's hand guiding my cock to the girl's mouth. She's jerking forward with each pounding and eventually her mouth finds the tip of my involuntarily erect penis. I punch Kitab 2's hand away and push him back.

She starts blowing me furiously and I pull out and back away but my penis pulls forward because it wants this. I fight my horny impulses and turn my hip till the woman bangs her nose on my hip and it flings out a trail of snot. She smiles up at me. I bat her hand away and grimace at her snotty mouth. Kitab 2 pushes me out of the way and pulls his penis towards the woman's mouth, but the guy pounding at her pushes him back. The girl helps him. They both push Kitab 2 till he falls into me.

Kitab 2's penis explodes with white effluvium, beading into the thick dreads of his pubes and down his legs, dribbling dangerously near my foot, which is underneath him. Kitab 2 convulses with satisfaction.

While I push Kitab 2 off me, the couple change position and the girl straddles her man and rides him hard.

'My turn, dude,' Kitab 2 says to them both, holding up a condom like it's a badge and he's with the sex FBI. They ignore him. He says it again, louder, more insistent. 'My TURN, dude.' The copulating couple turns to him and they shake their heads.

'Looks like you're done there, Gunga Din,' the old man says.

'Racist,' I say. Kitab 2 looks at me like I'm embarrassing him. 'Fucking milk bottles.'

The girl doubles her rhythm and we fade away from their collective sex brain periphery.

I'm lying on the floor, stifling a laugh at Kitab 2's rejection, when a larger lady approaches and looks down at me. 'What an invitation,' she says, pointing at the involuntary erection I have. She sits on my chest with her back to me. I feel the gristle of her vagina against my belly button. 'This is okay, yes?' she says.

'No,' I reply.

She takes the condom out of my hand and tears it open.

'Seriously. No, thanks,' I say.

She turns back to face me as I wriggle into a half sitting up position, resting on my elbows. 'What? Not to your tastes?'

'I'm not here for the sex.'

Kitab 2 turns to us.

'What the hell, dude? Why do you get everything I don't?'

'You up for it, then?' the lady says to him.

'Not with you,' Kitab 2 says. Kitab 2 thrusts his condom at her as she looks at me trying to get away from her. She drops the condom on my feet and presses down on my thighs as she stands up, bum first, arching herself into a right angle. It'd be sexy if I wasn't terrified of human contact. And if I didn't have a girlfriend. I have a girlfriend now, I think. A girlfriend. I scramble out from under her and stand up, shielding my involuntarily erect penis with my boxer shorts.

'That was supposed to be for me,' Kitab 2 says and thwacks my arm with the back of his hand.

I pull Kitab 2 into the toilet. Inside the toilet, the candles smell like incense and it makes me feel sick. My mum used to burn incense every morning in the kitchen, the room beneath my bedroom and I'd know that it was time for school. I hated school so the smell of incense automatically makes me feel like I'm 20 minutes away from getting punched in the ribs.

'Why are you telling the internet that you and I are at a sex party? You do realise we have the same name, right? You do know people can see stuff when you put it online, right? I thought you wanted to find a job.'

'Chill, dude. Who cares? How many other Kitab

Balasubramanyam's are there in the world? Maybe everyone will think it is like John Smith in India.'

'We're not in India, mate. We're here. Where I live. And you're associating me with you. All the time. Saying we're going to sex parties. What would my publisher think? What would my readers think?'

'Blah, blah, dude. All you're thinking about is yourself. And your fans. You're not Salman Rushdie. You're not Mick Jagger. You're just Kitab Balasubramanyam. From London. Fuck you.'

I'm not a violent man.

That is my proviso for when I grab Kitab 2 by the neck and force him against the toilet cistern. He looks panicked. He did not expect that. I hold him for what feels like hours, but it's probably 5 seconds before I remember myself and let him go. He grabs his neck and looks at me. He punches me in the ribs. The smell of incense burning my nose makes it all the more poignant. It doesn't hurt as much as shock me. He doesn't seem the punching type. I don't react because in the cramped bathroom, his pullback means the punch is more symbolic than effective. I look at him and shake my head.

'Why don't you get it?' I say.

'Get what?'

'I don't want to be your friend. I just want to be left alone.'

Kitab 2 looks at me with widening eyes, then cries. He holds his hands to his face. There's a knock on the door.

I open the door a crack and peer round.

'No sex in the bathroom,' the woman from reception says, her blue eyes wide with concern.

'We're just talking. Sorry. Pep talk and all that. First timers,' I say, by way of excuse.

'Get out of here, dude, you're hurting me,' Kitab 2 suddenly says behind me. 'Ow, seriously, get off me.'

'What is going on in there?' the door lady asks.

'Nothing. We're just talking.'

'No, we're not.'

I reach out behind me and try to punch Kitab 2 quiet, but I hit air and something crunches down on the fleshy bit of my wrist. I spin round and Kitab 2 is biting me as hard as he can. I wrench my hand out but it hurts, it's clamped. I squeal a throaty but high-pitched AGHGAG. I judo chop Kitab 2 in the neck and he releases me. I rub my hand.

The door is thumped open.

One of the burly naked men from the writhing girl room, the one I'd clocked for being better built than his chubby naked cohorts, grabs me and pulls me out of the toilet by my hair. It happens too quickly to process it but I fall into his frame and smack my cheek against something hard – I hope his hip bone. He reaches down and pulls me up with fists in my armpits. I hear the door lady ask Kitab 2 if he is okay. He is fine, he says. Scared though. I am pulled towards the stairs and ushered down to the lobby. The door is opened and I'm pushed out into a slightly frosty September night. I bang on the door as it closes. I want my stuff. I need my stuff. Kitab 2 has gone too far. I wonder whether I can call the police. Except, my phone's in there. So's my wallet. I bang on the door again.

I see the light crack in the glass so I ready myself in fighting stance in case the naked hard man with the fists is coming out. The door opens and my things are thrown at me. A shoe lands on my bare toes and I yelp. The door slams shut. It's cold so I throw myself into my clothes and go to pick up my wallet and phone off the ground when the door opens again and a completely naked Kitab 2, bundling his clothes into his crotch, is pushed out as well.

He falls back into me and I push him forward. He spins round and sees me.

'Fuck you, Kitab, you fucking idiot,' I say.

'They threw me out. I accidentally tried it on with that girl. I thought she was part of it, dude.'

'I don't care, Kitab. I'm going home. I never want to see you again.'

He starts babbling as he throws his jumper over his head but I'm not listening. My chest is pumping, the anger has manifested. I'm shaking. If I don't walk away from Kitab 2, I might cry. The stomach churns of grief and anxiety peel through me. I need to keep moving. I jump up and thump a sign that says 'No through road' with the vigour of a thousand high-fives. I decide to walk home because it's a nice night and Aziz would have said, when you need a pilgrimage to have a long hard look at yourself, why take the bus?

Detective Alverton leant back in his chair and burst out laughing. He stood up and held his belly. I didn't know whether I was supposed to laugh too so I was doing awkward smiles the whole time, trying to work out if this was a maniacal 'I am going to fuck you' laugh or a 'you are fucking funny' laugh. Either way, this was getting to the point whether he either arrested me or sent me to the pub with a pat on the back. I was considering calling my brother to sort me out a lawyer or something. There was some fucked up atmosphere in this place.

He eventually calmed the fuck down, sat back down at the desk and looked at me. He shook his head.

'You're a funny guy,' he said. 'I like you.'

'So what's happening now?'

'Oh, right ... yeah, sure ...' Detective Alverton slid a file over to me. I opened it. It was mugshots of some serious-looking white dudes, all thick necks and evil eyes dogging me up. 'Recognise any of these people?' I shook my head. 'Well, they were the guys shooting at you in the train.'

'Oh right, okay.'

I looked at the photos of these shooters. They were generic

241

angry white men with neck tattoo types. I shrugged. I didn't recognise any of them.

'Who are these guys?' I asked.

'Oh, it's quite complicated. Sterling's a banker, whose investment portfolio included a complex of car factories. He ran the business into the ground and collected a bonus for selling the land because it was the site of a Civil War battle. Anyway, all these families lost all their money. And so, one of the people, this guy here ...' Detective Alverton pointed to someone weedier than the others, his eyes sunken into his face, greying thinning hair hanging on for dear life on the top of his dome. 'He lost everything. His wife died of stress. She was pregnant. So he must have flipped. Turns out, his cousin's a capo in a local crime mob so they decided to kidnap the guy's baby and hold her to ransom.'

'Not the best plan.'

'No, especially seeing as the nanny thought they were immigration and ran.'

'Really? How do you know?' I said, sitting back, my arms folded.

'Because she was also being chased by immigration officers when she started running,' Detective Alverton said, leaning forward and shaking with barely restrained mirth.

'That shit cray.'

'That shit cray indeed.'

'So, in all, we're lucky.'

'No, you guys are idiots. The baby's lucky. Because, hey, no one needs to be kidnapped, whatever age.'

'Cool, so what happens now?'

'Nothing, we let you go, you go. We can call you as witnesses when this case goes to trial. I've got your official statement.'

'That's it? What was the good cop/bad cop thing about?'

'There's only one of me ...'

'Okay, the bad cop shit.'

'Oh, you know ... fun. It's been a slow night and Detective Martinez is with the actual punks who kidnapped the girl.'

'So, you drew the short straw?'

'If you call a couple of heroic fucktards in leotards the short straw, then yes. Yes, I did.'

'Fair play, mate.'

'I'm sorry – indulge me, I gotta ask ... what made you think this was okay?' He laughed.

It turned out Detective Alverton was alright. Had loads of stories about weird New Yorkers, like the guy he arrested for shitting in envelopes and sending them to publishers, like the band who always recorded vocals in a jail cell for an

authentic sound so the lead singer had to keep finding ways
to get arrested and then phoned his vocals in, to people like
Teddy Baker and Bob, but who did actual weird vigilante
shit like beat purse-snatchers to within an inch of their life.
He blamed Kick-Ass and the internet. He supported Man U,
which was okay I guess, they are the Gooners of the North.
His barbecue chicken was to die for. And his wife's going in
for a boob-reduction this weekend.

We sat there chatting for an hour before he finally let me
go. We swapped emails. He told me to stay away from Teddy
Baker, but didn't tell me why. I nodded sagely at him and
we went our separate ways. I headed out of the police station.
I needed to head back to Brooklyn and try and get some of
my stuff back. Outside the police station, Teddy Baker was
waiting for me.

He smiled at me and shrugged.

'Every night something new, eh?' I said.

'What was all that about?'

'Cops just being cops.'

'You've been in there for hours.'

'Yeah, come on, man. I need a beer, my balls are chafing in
this Lycra and I wanna get my phone and stuff from
Disappearing Bob.'

We started walking to the subway and I asked Teddy Baker
what the deal with Bob was. He told me that Bob was a
good guy really, just not very good with confrontation or

244

making decisions. He was one of those guys who prided himself on a moral code, but often that moral code didn't involve anything happening in real life to question it. I said he sounded like a massive dickhead.

'Man, that wasn't cool what he did, just leaving us like that.'

'Teddy Baker,' I said. 'I have to ask you. We look alike, right? We both have similar facial features, similar build, similar skin tone – Teddy Baker, why the honky name, brother?'

Teddy Baker thought about it, then shrugged. 'I'm just racially ambiguous, I guess.'

'Where your parents from?'

'My dad's from New York, upstate. My mom, she's from Pakistan.'

'Jeezus, that solves a few mysteries, why didn't you say that before?'

'Cos she's whiter than me.'

'Oh, right. Why do you think Detective Alverton told me to be careful of you?'

Teddy Baker stopped walking at the subway entrance and faced me. 'He said what now?'

Yes, I shouldn't have said it, but sometimes you want to know that bit of information so bad you end up splurting shit you're not supposed, you know?

'I thought they said that incident was irrelevant,' he said to himself and then shut down, big time.

Teddy Baker looked crushed. He just stared at me and then walked down the stairs to the subway. At the bottom he turned back to me and gestured for me to catch up.

We didn't talk for the rest of the subway journey to Brooklyn. We didn't talk when we got to Bob's house. We didn't talk as I gathered my stuff. And we didn't say much beyond 'laters' when we said goodbye.

I got back to my hotel at 3 a.m. and fell asleep. As I lay in my hotel room and thought about all the crazy shit that went on tonight and the person who it all thundered around, I knew that the next day I had to see Teddy Baker and get to the bottom of who this guy is. Because we still had a journey to go on, him and me. It's beyond our tattoos. We'd started something. Something nuts is in the air and it's pulling us together. I felt it as we both ran along that train platform up the stairs – I felt changed, people. I felt it as he and I were carted away in cop cars. I felt something.

All my life I've been waiting for the greatest adventure and right then, I felt like I was only at stage 1 of it. I'm being unfair, I was shot at last night. Maybe stage 4 or something. I don't know. But look, right, here's the thing – I'm addicted to this shit. I spent the night trying to think about what my mum, god rest her soul, would have said about this all. They would have called me nuts. But there you go, you live and you definitely don't learn.

All these nuts scenarios passed through my head as I watched the flicker of various chat shows on the mute television in my hotel room. What if his Pakistani mother actually recruited him for a terrorism thing and that's why I should stay away? Maybe he stole Detective Alverton's girlfriend once and that's why I should stay away? Maybe he's just a deviant and this was all part of some ploy to get into my pants and that's why I should stay away? Does Detective Alverton know this guy? But mostly importantly, do I want to know him beyond the weird week we're having?

Either way, there's more to be discovered with this guy.

There are 18 comments for this blog:

Anonymous: too funny. new york city pigs eh?.

Gustave_the_Great: Just one thing: why would that detective tell you all those things? sounds like you made it up. surely he can't tell you those facts. They're part of an ongoing investigation.

AZIZWILLKILLYOU: Well he did.

Gustave_the_Great: Oh really? Because I did some Googling and I couldn't find any reference to this case. I spoke to a buddy of mine in a law firm in New York and he couldn't find any reference to this case. Certainly no reports of trains getting shot at. Are you so sure this actually happened?

AZIZWILLKILLYOU: Just because it didn't get in the papers, doesn't mean it didn't happen.

df232: Hey Aziz, it's Della. We met in Whole Foods. Call me.

AZIZWILLKILLYOU: Yo, Della, I'm flying back soon. Next time eh?

df232: I just found you on Facebook. I'm coming to London in the spring. Let's hook up then.

BrightStar: Just found this blog on StumbleUpon. It's too dope man. Hilarious stuff.

Gustave_the_Great: All I'm saying is, if you're writing non-fiction, there's 2 rules: 1) Make it real. 2) Make it good. You've achieved nothing. Why don't you come and read my blog: **www.alexdoesfood.wordpress.com**. I got loads of stuff on there that would put this turgid shit to rest.

AZIZWILLKILLYOU: Wait, so this entire time, you just wanted me to look at your blog?

Brightstar: Hey man, so, I sent this to aLL MY FRIENDS. Can't wait to happen next.

NB_Tony: Hi Aziz, mind giving me an email on **tony@nbc. com**. I think we can talk about taking this blog to the screen.

Gustave_the_Great: What the fuck? This guy? SERIOUSLY? You people have no fucking idea. I work everyday as a lawyer and I spend hours writing this food challenge blog and this cunt gets a comment from someone at a television station? Fuck you Aziz. I'm going to stab you if I ever see you.

AZIZWILLKILLYOU: I've just forwarded that comment on to the police my friend. Trolling can be tolerated. Death threats? You gots to go.

Alvy_CHickenz: Yo, Aziz, you make me sound like a chump in this. Douchebag! Email me back. Alverton, son!

df232: AZIZ! What the fuckkkkkkkk?

AZIZWILLKILLYOU: one more instalment my friends. Get ready. Especially if you're wondering what happened to Bob.

History:

Track lost phone – Google
How to stop identity theft – Google

I get 100 metres down the road in my outraged stomp before something hurtles into my back and sends me crashing to the ground, chin first. I feel the tarmac graze down my face at high speed.

It lands on me and starts pounding my back like a massage gone wild. I fling myself from side to side and eventually shake it off. I flip round to find it's Kitab 2, half-dressed, trousers in his hand, no underpants on. He throws more punches and I fend them off in a way Mr Miyagi would have been proud of. Wax on. Wax off. He isn't deterred and throws harder punches. I catch one wrist, then the other, like a ninja master, and I push him off me. I try to pull myself off the pavement without the use of my hands. It's harder than it looks. I struggle up to a crouch, consider a sucker-kick to his unhindered groin, but rise to standing instead.

'What the fuck are you doing?' I say, letting go of his wrists, hoping he has calmed down.

'Dude, why did you ruin that?'

'I didn't ruin anything.'

'You did … you did. I was going to have sex with a girl. Now I'll never have the chance. You ruined it. You ruin everything.'

'Of course you will. Man, calm down!'

'You get what you want. You always get what you want. This was for me. This was my thing. You were winging me, dude.'

'I didn't want any of that,' I say, as Kitab thrusts his wrists at me and I bat them away.

'No, but you got it. What did I get? They all laughed at me. All of them.'

'Sorry man. You were just so …'

'So what? So Indian? So bud-bud-ding-ding? You hate your own kind that much?' I feel dizzy. I'm surrounded by fresh air. Where's my phone? I need to live-tweet this.

@kitab: 'My doppelganger just punched me in the face.'

'No. It's nothing to do with that. It's you. Me. We don't know each other. Kitab, man. Look … you embarrassed me by even going there in the first place …'

'Whatever, dude. You got everything. I got nothing.'

I check in my pocket for my wallet to give Kitab 2 some money to go away.

'No. No way,' I say. Kitab 2 holds something up. It's my phone and my wallet. I forgot to pick them up after they threw Kitab at me. They're usually the first things I check I have.

I lunge towards him but he dances back.

I run towards him.

He socks me in the face and sprints back towards the sex cul-de-sac. I watch him run off, stunned. I consider chasing after him but I'm tired. And I can't run anymore. I rub my face where he punched me. I'm screen-less. It doesn't feel right.

I then decide maybe I should get the tube, so duck into a train station. I have my Oyster and keys still. I hobble into the station and limp down the stairs to the platform. I wait 3 minutes before a train turns up. 3 minutes of dead air. No internet, no music in my ears, just my thoughts. I sit down in a train and realise my chin is cut and I've bled all over my nice jeans. A necessary sacrifice to the god of self-preservation. If you could call 2 wimps brawling in the street that. If you could call it brawling. That's if we'd even qualify as wimps. All I have left of my identity is my Oyster card. I live through the journeys I have made in the past. I am laid bare.

Have I just created a nemesis in my own name?

The train journey is painful as it waits at all the stops for longer than necessary, and it takes me an hour and a bit to do a 30-minute journey. I walk down my high street, up my road to my house. I call my dad from my landline as I enter the flat. It takes me a few minutes to get used to pushing buttons again, so used am I to touchscreens.

He answers on the second ring. 'Balasubramanyam speaking.'

'Hey Dad.'

'Kitab-san. Where have you been?'

'You know, just hanging out.'

'At sex parties, I see. Do you have to make them so public? Actually, you are lucky you did this time because I was thinking of going. Don't want to go to the same ones as your children, eh?'

'No, I suppose not.'

'Is it any good?'

'What?'

'The sex party.'

'No, Dad,' I say curtly.

'You okay? You sound down in the dumps.'

'Yeah, I'm okay.'

'Want a drink with me? My treat, kiddo.'

'No. I just want to watch something crap on television and go to bed. I've been out too much recently.'

'Fine. So … what's your new book about?'

'I don't know, Dad. Not yet.'

'Maybe you should write about a writer. Write about a writer doing things out of his comfort zone.'

'Sounds like a cliché.' I fire up my laptop. I wonder what I've missed online.

'Well, if you haven't got any other ideas, I will give you that for free. Just dedicate your book to me for a change.'

'Thanks, Dad.' I don't know if he can hear it, but there's a lump in my throat stopping me talking at a normal pitch.

'You know, I love you, son. I may not show it and I may be preoccupied with my own life, but you know I love you, kiddo.'

'I know.'

'Death, it forces us together in a way that isn't natural. If they were around, we wouldn't be meeting up and talking about sex parties and social lives, you know? But we're forced to because we're scared of death driving a wedge. I love you. That's all you need to know.'

I miss Aziz.

'Me too, Dad.'

I need Aziz around. I feel formless without him.

'Come home soon. I miss you. Maybe we can watch cricket.'

He hangs up the phone. Against my better judgment I have tears in my eyes that sting because I let them linger longer than they should. I wipe them on my jacket and take it off, falling onto the sofa.

I tweet.

@kitab: 'I should have listened to my dad more in life. Maybe I'd have been punched in the face less.'

I go on Facebook to see what Kitab 2 is doing. Nothing, so far. He has been quiet since he checked us both into Wilmington House and said we were there for Party Orifices. 68 of his friends and mine 'like' the check in. I try to work out how to de-tag myself from it but manage only to share it on my own Facebook wall. I try calling my phone again but it goes straight to voicemail. It's the first time I've used our landline in months. I nearly fall over walking away from the receiver, forgetting it's corded. I leave him a message asking him to call me. I message him on Facebook. Time to clear the air, I think. I need my wallet and phone back. A day wasted furiously pushing buttons, clicking, trying to fix my life through a screen, I keep seeing myself in my mind's eye sweeping the laptop off the table onto the floor and stamping on it. I don't dare tease out that impulse. On a loop, like a pixellated gif, me sweeping my laptop onto the floor till it smashes, the subtitle reads 'I can haz meatspace?'

I notice, just before I fall asleep, that Hayley has updated her relationship status to 'it's complicated'. I also see she was checked into Nandos with her agent earlier. *It's complicated ...* I pretend I hope she's not thinking about me. Aziz would have a field day. Consummate relationship material, he always calls me. He jokes that the second date is always the moving truck date, even though I've never lived with anyone but him, a long-term girlfriend and my parents. I fall asleep where I fell, on the sofa, in my clothes and wake up late the next morning from a nightmare where Kitab 2 is standing over me, straddling me, with his penis in my face, laughing and tweeting from my phone while squeezing my neck tight. I sit up and check for my phone. It's still gone. I reach for my computer and work out how to report it stolen.

It takes a surprisingly long time.

The damage Kitab 2 has caused to my online reputation gives me cause to re-evaluate the point of having one. I only joined up to Facebook to keep tabs of photos and events in friends' lives. I only joined up to Twitter for the attention. Neither satisfied me. A few hours later, I find myself 1000 words into something new, with 'delete account' windows open on both sites. I stare at my email, at the many unattended-to messages and notifications. I only exist in other people's ability to reach me. The 1s and 0s of our personas. I stare at the delete account screens and old pictures of Aziz and me arsing about. I look through Kitab 2's Facebook account and his tweets. I have assimilated him in my mind. I know exactly who he is. Who we are.

Flicking through my emails, I see that there are 4 that have been marked as read even though I haven't seen them. A couple are from my dad, forwards of cheeky messages from girls, they're unanswered. One is from Hayley. It's an email from her asking how I am and where I am and whether I want a drink.

According to the reply I don't remember sending, I've written, 'Dude, am thirsty. Let's get a drink and then some dick-time. Where you wanna meet?'

Hayley hasn't responded to that. I send her an email saying, 'Ignore that last email. It's not me. Will explain.'

It's a bit weak, but how else do you explain the situation succinctly when you don't have a phone and people don't read long emails anymore?

The email after that is a Google calendar request about an afternoon event round the corner where I was supposed to be reading from my book at 12.30 p.m. It was paying, too. £25. Plus beer and food. I'm late. It's 1.30 p.m. I grab a book, put my shoes back on and rush out of the house.

I leave my screen hovering over the 'delete account' screens for Twitter and Facebook.

I run down the street, worrying about being late. I live by my Google calendar. I'm dumb without my phone.

I reach the pub that the reading is above and clatter through commuters, sweating. I'm halfway up the stairs when I stop. All this for £25. I catch my breath. I can hear the hush of a room of people upstairs and the low mumble of someone reading in a soporific rhythm.

I walk slowly up the stairs, trying to be quiet, trying to not be the late guy who clatters in. At the door, there's a guy in big glasses and tweed sitting next to a square tin of money. By the little in there, I judge that there's perhaps 10–15 people at the reading.

'5 pounds,' he says, not looking up from his phone. He's streaming football.

'I'm reading,' I say. 'Kitab Balasubramanyam.'

'Balasubramanyam …' he says, slowly, like he's double-checking every syllable against his brain's data records. 'Nope. You've been and gone.' He looks up. 'You're not him.'

'What are you talking about?'

'You finished your reading 10 minutes ago. Said you were leaving, that you had some drink and dick-time coming up.'

'No. I'm Kitab Balasubramanyam.'

'No,' he says, repeating my frustration, with 20 times more sarcasm. 'You're not. You look nothing like him.'

'Where's May? She's running this, isn't she? She knows me.'

'Look, it's only 5 pounds. Okay? Just pay the money if you want to come in.'

'But I'm reading ...'

'Kitab's done,' he says, looking back down at his screen. 'Oh, now I've missed a goal.'

'He already read?'

'Yeah, and he was hilarious too, judging by the guffaws.'

'Thanks,' I say and turn back towards the stairs. I stare down into the pub, processing what's just happened.

I walk down the stairs feeling a chill of nausea around me. I walk into the toilets and I'm about to sit down on a toilet seat just to steady myself and calm my nerves when I realise this is one of those pubs where they distrust the men to keep toilet seats clean by not pissing all over it, so have removed them. I remain standing, feeling my spine unaligned, the usual weight not distributed evenly through my body. I have no phone in my left pocket. I take a breath and walk back into the pub. I scan for Kitab 2 in case he's lurking. I can't see him anywhere. I stand in the doorway and let the silky rush of a light breeze cool itself on the cold sweats at the fringes of my face. I'm so nervous I need a poo. But the toilets have no toilet seats.

He read in my place. I don't wait around to go up to May and clear the air. If she didn't notice, then more fool her. There's nothing I can do. It's done. This is what he wanted from me? He can have it. I feel strangely free. Without a phone and without the obligation to fulfil, to muster up the strength to entertain for money and validation, I feel fine. I feel okay. Standing in that toilet, the thick gristle of piss welding itself to my nasal hairs, I think, 'Well, that's okay then,' and I leave the pub.

I walk back in the direction of home.

Via my local.

I spend 2 pints with Mitch talking about his new girlfriend, someone I didn't even know he had. He tells me about her job, her likes and her dislikes. He regales me with stories of old-fashioned dates, how he romanced her and where they're going this weekend. I sit and listen and laugh at the relevant bits and awww at the soppy bits. He soon takes his leave of me to go and see her. They're off to see a film tonight. He read a review of it in the paper and it sounds up their street because there's a colour in the title, and it has subtitles and is only showing in one art house cinema. It sounds like a slam dunk for Mitch.

I take up Mitch's stool at the bar and order another drink. I take the book he's left for me and open it at page one. It's Wodehouse. He says it's the funniest book in the world, some-thing for me to aspire to. Despite alluding to being well-read, I've never picked up a Jeeves book. I read the back – it sounds like it'll make me laugh.

I feel a tap on my shoulder some minutes later and look up. It's Hayley.

She smiles at me and I lean forward to kiss her. She offers me a cheek then her lips. I smile at her.

'What you been up to, cryptic email man?'

'Ha,' I say. 'Funny story ... I got stalked by my namesake off the internet. Remember I told you about him?'

'Yeah ... but yeesh, really? Really? Tell me everything,' Hayley says. She orders a drink first and while she does, I regale her with stories about Kitab 2, from his add request to him staying with me, thinking I can help him cut loose in London. Mitch steps back into the pub to pick up the card he's left behind the bar by accident and she stares at him awkwardly while we wait for him to settle up and leave again. We retire to a table in the corner. I continue my story of Kitab 2, filling in the blanks of the last few days with the full thing, from the add request to the appearance to the dickpic to the sex party. It sounds insane. It sounds like it didn't happen. It sounds like fiction. When I'm done, and she's given me an appropriate amount of laughing and 'wow, that's incredible' and 'tell me about the sex party' we decide to go home for dinner.

As we leave the pub, she stops and asks, 'Wait, did you have sex with anyone at Party Orifices?'

I shake my head.

'Not willingly and not completely.'

'Unwilling at a sex party.'

'Physically, and emotionally,' I say. 'Unwilling at a sex party … good name for a band.'

Hayley is silent as we step away from the pub. She is silent for 20 yards. She slips her arm into my hand and we walk back home.

It doesn't feel old-fashioned. It feels just right.

Then Hayley's phone rings. And it appears to be me phoning her.

Today, I had just met Teddy Baker for brunch when we got attacked with a knife.

It was Bob. He didn't announce himself like that. IIIIIIIT'S BOOOOOB (that looks like someone is saying Boob not Bob but whatevs). He jumped out from a stairwell and jabbed a knife in the air between Teddy Baker and me.

We were both tired but we felt we owed it to the internet to meet up and record a viddy-cast about our meeting, try and sum up the evening we'd had, try and sum up the feeling of making that connection.

We had been talking about the weather and then rehashing the events of last night and suddenly, we were being jabbed at by Bob.

'Teddy,' he shouted. 'Get away from the sand nigger.'

'Bob, what the fuck are you doing?'

'Teddy Baker, get away from the sand nigger.'

I obviously took offence to this. Who did this cracker redneck city motherfucker think he was? So I grabbed the wrist of his hand with the knife and pulled it down to the pavement and stomped on his fist with my boot (thank you, Ted Baker) and he let go. But this cracker redneck motherfucker wasn't going quietly. He uppercut me. On the chin. And I stumbled backwards.

Sand nigger? It wasn't even factually accurate. It's double-racism against anyone from the Middle East and black people and I am neither of those things. Fucking idiot. Got me using words I'm not comfortable with on my own blog. Don't flame me, bros.

He fell over, clutching his hand, but kicked out at my legs and caught me on my bad knee, from an old bike accident. I fell over, but on top of him, so I attempted an elbow drop, but he punched upwards and caught me in the stomach. I couldn't breathe. Teddy Baker just stood back and watched. Was this who he was? A coward? I leaned into Bob and tried some close punches. He tried the same. We were rolling around and throwing in as many small punches as we could.

Bob smacked me around the temple and pushed me off him. He stood up and looked at me, on the floor, winded and bleeding, my hair a mess.

'Teddy, come on, buddy, let's go.'

'Sure, Bob ... I ...'

I tried to get my breath back. I spluttered like I was trying to talk, and they were very gentlemanly in waiting for me to spit out what I wanted to say. 'I ... Te .... Ted ... ...
Tedd ... ... TED ... ... TED.
TED ... TED. TED. Teddy Baker, you are nothing like me,' I said. 'You were supposed to save me. You were supposed to be my doppelganger. I even got a tattoo to cement the

deal. A copycat doppelganger tattoo. You were supposed to change my life. You're an idiot. You know that. I realised something, just now while your mate was racially abusing me and punching me in various marine pressure points, like he's been training to take down darkies professionally for a while now. I don't understand how you could possibly have that cool-ass tattoo and be the most boring anti-awesome person I have ever met. Matter has anti-matter. I am Aziz. You are anti-Aziz.'

'That detective told you I got arrested for making home-made explosives didn't he?'

'No. What the hell?'

'I was young. I was an asshole.'

'Still ... what were you planning to blow up?'

Bob threw his whatever hands at me. I pulled myself up onto a stoop. He tugged at the skin around his tattoo, straightening his skin bow tie.

'It was a drunken bet,' he said, playing scuffed toes with his trainers. 'I was out with Bob and some girls that we were into and they all kept calling me straight-laced. They all dared me to get a tattoo that would get me fired. So I got this because ... I don't know, I can't remember the exact reason. I was drunk. But yeah, I got it. And I got fired for having it. And ever since, I've been trying to take control of it. Ever since I got this tattoo, everything's been going to shit for me. I got fired, I had to move back in with my mum, I lost 100 followers on Twitter ... lots of shit stuff, man. I hate it. When you showed up, I thought my luck would change. But you're rocking that tattoo. I'm going to get mine removed. It's brought me nothing but trouble. You have swagger. I have a tattoo I hate. You see, this tattoo changed my life. It became a curse for me. For you, it seems to be your life-blood. I hate it.'

'You can't actually get it removed just yet. Not for 3 more years,' Bob said. 'Remember?'

'The contract. But isn't the contract void? We didn't sleep together in the end.'

'But ... come on.'

'COME ON ... Bob. No one cares what you think,' I said.

'Don't talk to Bob like that,' Teddy Baker said, indignant.

'Oh my god, you're not the guy I want you to be, Teddy Baker,' I said. Bob ran towards me screaming but I was ready and I held out the heel of my palm at the optimum time and caught Bob on his chin. He dropped to the floor. 'What's his fucking deal?' I asked.

'Bob's mum ... her cleaner died on 9/11.'

'Right, okay ... shit. Wait, what? What's this got to do with me? And his racism?'

'Oh, he's just a racist. A really nasty racist.'

'His mum's cleaner. Fuck me, that's tenuous. North tower?'

'No, heart attack. On 9/11. A couple of years ago.'

'So, what's his problem?'

Teddy Baker shrugged.

'You're a dullard,' I said to Teddy Baker. 'But it was nice meeting you. I believe the rest of New York has a lot of swag to offer me so I'm going to leave you be now.'

I shook Teddy Baker's hand.

'Stay in touch, homeboy,' he said.

'Whatever, homeboy,' I said.

But Bob was not done. He stood up and socked me in the mouth with a knuckle duster on his fist. I fell back to the ground and cracked the back of my head on a stoop.

Bob laughed and they both walked off together in the direction Teddy Baker and I had been headed. I lay there for a few minutes and wondered exactly what had happened. Maybe meeting people off the internet isn't what it's cracked up to be. But then, while I was lying there recuperating, I checked my Blendr and realised I was on the stoop of a girl looking for 'whatever'. I messaged her. She messaged me. I messaged her that I needed some medical attention urgently. She came down and helped me up to her apartment. There she fixed me up. She put cold compresses on the back of my head and cleaned up my cut lip. She gave me a happy ending while I told her my story and this girl, this Della, well, she ruined my only pair of jeans with my own spuzz because I was so tense and came so hard, it went everywhere. Girl can tug, ya get me. So that's a win for meeting strangers off the internet.

There are 17 comments for this blog:

GustaveGrimes: I'm going to meet you at the airport tomorrow with a screwdriver and rape your arsehole with it.

AZIZWILLKILLYOU: You're taking all the romance out of it.

GustaveGrimes: You should have killed yourself out there.

Teddy Baker: Hey Aziz, So much for state secrets, eh? Anyways, I was just letting you know I'm getting my tattoo removed. I've got job interviews in the next few weeks and I think it's time to be more professional. Anyways, thanks for documenting the good times. Boring though?

GustaveGrimes: Teddy Baker, fuck off.

df232: Hey Aziz, I'm in London. Call me. I'm at the Old Street Travelodge. Room 323.

AZIZWILLKILLYOU: Teddy Baker, my friend, it's been a journey. If there's one thing I ask, keep the tattoo. To remember me by. And boring? Come on. Have a long hard look at yourself. @GustaveGrimes – go fuck yourself.

Teddy Baker: Fuck you Gustave. At least I use my real name.

AZIZWILLKILLYOU: Keyboard warriors, mate. It takes all sorts.

Teddy Baker: I got the job by the way. And the guy didn't mind the tattoo. I work in web development now. Need a website? I'm not cheap but I can sort you out.

264

AZIZWILLKILLYOU: We'll talk. ps give Bob a kiss from me.

Teddy Baker: Bob says you have unfinished business.

df232: Fuck you Aziz.

GustaveGrimes: Jeez-us Aziz, you really do write shit, don't you? That's why we're not in a band. But every fucking day I have to hear about your bullshit from people. You will not leave my life and I'm fucking sick of it. Look, just take this paltry time you've been given and fuck off okay?

df232: I hate you, Aziz.

AZIZWILLKILLYOU: Not as much as I hate myself, darling.

Jimmy329: Hi, I'm a literary agent and just wondered if you'd ever thought of turning these blogposts into a book. I think there's something here. Would love to talk some more about it. How do I get in contact?

History:

<folder empty>

Hayley answers her phone call from me, confused. I whisper that it must be Kitab 2 so she puts the phone on speaker. We hear heavy breathing, then, in a cod English accent,

'Uhhhhh, uhhhhhh, hey baby, it's Kith-ahhhr-buh.' His Indian pronunciation of Kitab betrays who it is. Not like me. Kit like football kit, ab like abdominal crunch. I make the motion to keep him talking.

'Hey, Kitab?' Hayley says, confused.

'Yesh. That'sh my name. Don't wear it out. Let'sh meet up,' he says, almost Sean Connery-ish. 'I want to dick you hard.'

'Oh, okay,' Hayley says. She mimes a WTF. I stifle a nervous LOL. 'Sure thing. Where are you?'

'I'm at home. Come shee me. You have keysh to my plache, yesh?'

'Now?'

'Now.'

Kitab 2 hangs up the phone.

'What was that all about?' Hayley asks.

'I think he thinks he can have sex with you.'

'Well, at least I now know you weren't making him up,' she says, nodding her head.

'Did you really think that?'

She ignores my question. 'Why does he want to meet me at yours?'

'Maybe he has plans to do you in front of me, as the ultimate revenge. In my bed with the webcam on.'

'It's a foolproof plan.'

266

'It's not a foolproof plan. I don't even have a webcam.'

'He nearly had me fooled. I mean, do you 2 look alike?'

'We all look alike, racist.'

'Having sex with me in your bed. That would teach you a few life lessons,' Hayley says, smiling. 'And to think, all I wanted from this day was a Nandos and live-tweeting *X Factor*. I really wish I hadn't texted you a picture of my breasts.'

'Did you?'

'Yeah. It took me hours to get it right too. Brelfies are hard.'

'What's the deal with "it's complicated" on your Facebook?'

'Oh, you know, sending an FU to an ex-boyfriend. But you know, given this second Kitab ... I'd say things have got very complicated.'

Hayley and I are waiting in my bedroom, for what, we don't know, when I hear a window smash. I usher her to stay in the bedroom and open the door slowly, peering into the main room. She is standing behind me.

Nothing seems amiss.

I can hear the crunch of feet on broken glass. I creep out from my bedroom. Hayley follows me. I can't see anything that shouldn't be how it is. There is no broken glass. There isn't a smashed window. It's empty, as I left it. I turn to Aziz's room. The door's closed. Which is strange. I didn't close it before. I hold the handle and close my eyes, channelling a modicum of bravery from somewhere, anywhere, then I burst into the room.

The curtains are closed. There's a lump in the bed.

'Fuck off, I'm jetlagged. We'll talk later.' It's Aziz, mumbling. The dry lump of panic in my throat oozes back down towards my chest.

'Sorry,' I say. I turn around as I close the door. 'My brother,' I whisper. 'He's asleep.'

Hayley nods and turns back around towards the bedroom. She walks in. I hear a door thump behind me. I turn round.

There's nothing there. I'm imagining things. There was no glass. It's just the sound of other people in the flat. I'm not used to it.

I walk back into the bedroom. Hayley's sitting on the bed, flicking through her phone.

'Well, this is boring,' she says. 'I was hoping for a showdown.'

'There's nothing to showdown. I just want my phone back,' I say. 'And for the guy to leave me alone.'

'You've made it,' Hayley smiles. 'Your very own stalker.'

'And he turns out to be a doppelganger. Wait, phone my phone.'

Hayley picks her phone up off the bed and dials my number. I can hear the faint bings and bongs of the church bells I've chosen as my ring tone.

I walk out into the main room and peer through the net curtain. I can see him in the front garden, staring in. My phone's in his hand. He's watching the screen, letting it ring off. Hayley's in the doorway of my bedroom, her phone clamped to her ear. When she gives up the ringing and puts the phone down by her side, I pull the curtain tight and mouth to Hayley that he's out there, what's our plan? She shrugs. She says she didn't prepare for such a situation.

'Just go out and talk to him. He's hardly a guy with a weapon, is he?' she asks.

I can feel the echoes of blows over my body from our last tussle, but she's right. I look out of the window. He's searching in the front garden for something, stones, rocks, maybe to break the glass. I walk to the front door.

In the corridor, I can hear my upstairs neighbours listening to Kanye West. It's the first time I've noticed their noise since Rach left; she used to complain about their mid-week parties and how they made it impossible for her to fall asleep. I've tuned them out since, obviously.

I walk to the front door and open it quietly, stepping outside into the overcast dreary day, looking out over my street and my front garden as Kitab 2 raises a rock over his head and gets ready to strike at the window.

'Kitab,' I say, and he stops. He looks at me and drops the rock, backwards over his head. It bounces on the ground and smacks forward into his heels. For a second, I see him wince. He keeps his hands up and faces me, like he's surrendering, laughing, surrendering. I run forward.

I jump at him, my arms ready to clamp. A mid-air rugby tackle, successful, sends us both to the ground, me on top of him, his arms still aloft, the weight of my body pushing all the air out of him. He makes a noise like a strangled seal, a wispy brown, barely-no-longer-a-teenager seal. I sit on him in cowgirl position, straddling him.

I raise my fist to slam down into his face. I've forgotten myself. I've forgotten who I am. I don't know this man. I've never seen him before. I look down at Kitab 2. For a pregnant second, he looks like I was when I was a teenager, running around, pretending I could take the world on, only on occasion letting the mask slip.

He cries.

With no air in his body and the weight of me, his tears are shallow and punctuated by seal gasps. My fist is still raised as I watch him try and fail to cry. His failure to cry is what makes me punch the ground by his head in frustration. It hurts but I pull the punch at the last second, realising it looks a bit silly and aggressive. The fear in Kitab 2's eyes as he turns his head to my fist resting on the concrete next to him is palpable.

'Kit,' I hear, and I look up. It's Hayley. She's standing in the doorway, her arms folded. 'Stop,' she says. 'Just stop.'

I stand up and offer a hand to Kitab 2. He takes it and stands up next to me.

*

269

'You're very pretty,' Kitab 2 says to break an awkward silence in the flat, while I make an ice pack for my hand with a bag of peas.

'Thanks, buddy,' Hayley says, pulling a face. I shake my head. My skin is still fizzing.

'Thanks for saving me,' he says.

Kitab 2 runs up to Hayley and embraces her. She struggles to unpin herself from him. I rush over and grab him under his armpits. Kitab 2 giggles but then presses his face into Hayley's mouth. His nose strays too close to her and on impulse, she bites down.

Kitab 2 lets go, squealing and clutching his nose. The bite isn't hard enough to make him bleed, but is enough to shock him backwards. I lift him up and he laughs.

I pull Kitab's arm and drag him into my bedroom. I push him onto the bed.

'She bit me,' he says, strained. 'What an animal. I bet she's a dynamite in the sack, dude. What do you say? Kitab sandwich?' I want to tell him that technically it'd be a Hayley sandwich on Kitab bread, but I don't.

I hold out my hand. 'Where's my wallet?' I ask.

Kitab 2 shakes his head so I tickle his armpits. He giggles till it's too much. I push my hands into his pockets, pulling out wads of tissue, paper, some bank notes and, finally, my wallet, shrouded in the fluff of snotty tissues stewing in hot pockets.

I hold it up to him. He stops giggling and looks at me.

'It's the end now,' I say.

'We had fun, didn't we?' he says.

'What do you mean?'

'I've had the best time in London. All this fun. I have to tell you, dude. I've met this girl. She wanted me to buy her a beer, and cigarettes and a Big Mac. Then she let me kiss her. It was wild. All 5 minutes from here. People round here are cool. We're

270

meeting later. She's taking me out. "All the best places", that's where she wants to go.'

'Anything else of mine you got there?' I ask.

Kitab 2 shakes his head. I tickle his armpits again, straying up towards his chin/neck lines. Out of his other pocket, he pulls out a wad of paper. It's old bank statements, a photocopy of my credit card and passport and a flyer for a prostitute.

'What's this?' I ask, waving the flyer at him.

'I phoned to see if she takes credit cards ...'

'Kitab, enough now ...'

'Dude, we are just getting started. I did your reading last night. It was amazing. We can double up. Do twice the readings. Meet twice the girls. I talked to a couple of girls after the reading. They didn't like the story but they thought I was cute. Digits, Kitab. Digits. Maybe I should stay.'

'Kitab, no ...'

'Come on. You meet all these girls. You have to take advantage, no.'

I shake my head. 'No, Kitab. It's time for you to go home.'

'I don't want to go home. Not to that dad. He hates me. He won't let me bring girls home. No way. I want to stay with you. We're going to have the best time. About Hayley ...'

I interrupt. 'You need to go home and see your dad. You need to go back to school and get a degree. You need to pull yourself out of this. You need to call all your old friends up and say you want to see them. You've had a difficult thing happen to you. I can't be the person to help you through this. Okay?' I am getting higher and higher pitched. 'I can't be your guy. I can't look after you. And stop messing with my life.'

'Sorry, dude,' Kitab 2 says. 'I thought it was funny.'

'It's not.'

'When I read your book, and I read about all the stuff you and your brother did – how you were always making fun of each other and getting each other into trouble … I wanted that,' he says. His face falls.

Kitab 2 cries. He holds a finger to his nose and tears fall down his face. I cuddle him. 'I'm scared,' he stammers.

'I know,' I say. 'Me too.'

'As soon as I read your book, I thought we were the same. I thought we could be friends. We grew up the same. Except you had a brother. Then when I found out about your brother, I thought I could replace him.'

It hits me. Everything that's got me about this guy, everything that has pushed me towards something I never wanted, something I never could accept – that static was not working for me. By pushing me and pushing me towards meatspace, by giving me this endless chase outside my flat, I've had enough, I realise that maybe I'm not the pacifist who is scared of conflict I always thought I was. I want to kill the boy. I want to destroy him. He has damaged me, online and offline. He has cheated me of a chance to be who I choose to be. He has tried to be me. He has been me.

I push him onto the bed. 'How dare you?' I say. 'How dare you? How …' I say it again and again, I am going to beat the living fuck out of this kid, I am going to beat him like he has beaten me. He has given me the thing I've avoided all this time – a reason to be angry. I don't want to be this man, but I am and I will.

For the second time in an hour, I raise my fist. I grab Kitab 2's neck and I get ready to pummel him.

'Kitab, stop,' I hear Aziz say behind me. And like an automaton who respects his elder brother, I stop, drop my arm, let go of Kitab 2 and turn round.

The door's closed. It's just me and my other. I turn back to Kitab 2. Everything has melted from his face – the childishness, the pervy leeriness, the swagger, the lip curl of the boy in control. He looks like a little boy again. I shake my head at him. It's time to let him go.

'Look, it's going to be fine. Okay?' I say, reassuringly, reasserting myself as the adult in this situation.

'How do you know?' he says.

'Because you have a family. Family's important. Go be with your family.'

'My dad never wants to see me. He's always going on about himself and his career and his life.'

'They surprise you, parents. He'll want to see you.'

'How do you know?'

'When's your return flight booked?'

'Tonight, dude. But I was hoping to leave a man.'

'You are, whatever that means … you are. I'll call you a cab to the airport. You'll get on that flight and you'll go be with your dad. Okay?'

'Yes.'

'Good,' I say and extend my hand.

'I just really wanted to have sex with somebody, dude,' Kitab says. I nod. 'That girl said to meet me later. Can I text her and say we can use your spare bed?'

I shake my head.

'No way, man,' I say.

'It should be easier, yes?'

'No,' I say. 'It should be harder.'

'That's what she said …' Kitab 2 said, and we laugh. For the first time, in unison, we laugh.

Kitab 2 shakes my hand. I keep holding him and walk out of the room.

Hayley is standing there, her arms folded, looking annoyed at Kitab 2.

'You okay?' she asks me. I nod. I turn to Kitab 2 and gesture to her at him.

He shrugs.

'Say sorry,' I say.

'Sorry,' he says. 'Sorry I tried to do you.'

273

Hayley smiles like it's fine but it's really not.

Kitab 2 looks at me. 'Wow, dude. I gave you advice about cheering up. You give me advice about responsibility. Peas in a pod, dude.'

He smiles. I smile back. This time I mean it.

'Kitab,' Hayley says. 'Should I go? I feel like I've walked in on something.'

I grab her hand and shake my head. 'It's complicated,' I say. She smiles.

I order a cab and set about making tea. Hayley leans against the kitchen counter, her arms folded, like she doesn't want to be here. I don't blame her. She looks beautiful angry. Kitab watches television. My weird family, I think to myself. Aziz's door is still closed. I should wake him, I think. I flick through my social media streams at great speed, expecting an ease to overcome me. It's just a whirl of scrolling. None of it means anything. I put my phone in my pocket.

The taxi arrives.

He says goodbye and cuddles me. 'I like that,' he says one more time as he gets in the car. I give the cab driver the fare upfront. Kitab 2 is returning to India with half of what he came with. He rolls down the window.

'Dude,' he says. 'I think you changed my life.'

'Dude, don't oversell yourself.'

'You got me half a blow job, beaten up, famous on the internet and I had a ham sandwich too. It was the best holiday ever. When I reapply for university, when I come back to the UK to study gaming, you'll take me out?'

'Maybe,' I say. 'Wait, you ate meat?'

'I am non-veg now. I ate the ham out of your fridge the other day. Bloody tasty, dude.'

I shake his hand and bang on top of the car to show I'm finished talking to the other Kitab. The car pulls away.

I go back into the flat. Hayley looks at me. 'That was Kitab?'

'Yep. That was Kitab. The other Kitab.'

'From Facebook and the sex party and the university?'

'Yeah,' I say, looking at the front door.

'I don't like him.'

'Me neither,' I say. I make a move to cuddle her, feeling out whether her annoyance is with me as well. She unfolds her arms to let me in when the doorbell rings.

Thinking it's Kitab 2 having forgotten something, I buzz the front door in without thinking and open the door to my flat.

In walks Rach, followed by my dad.

'Hello, Kitab beta,' my dad says softly. 'Hello, sweetie.' He winks at Hayley. 'Bad time?' he says to me. 'Sex party?' he stage-whispers. I shake my head.

'Rach, what are you doing here?' I ask, confused.

Rach looks at Hayley then at me. 'I'm not sure, to be honest. Your dad called me. Said he was worried about you. And I need to return the keys.' She holds up her ring of keys. She still has the Bart Simpson key ring I bought her.

'Okay, but, guys, I'm a bit busy right now. Why are you here? This is Hayley, by the way. Hayley, this is my dad, Rasesh. And Rach, of "my ex-girlfriend Rach" fame.'

'Hi,' Hayley says, embarrassed.

'Kitab beta,' my dad says, switching to the affectionate Gujarati of my ancestors. 'Why is there a blog called aZiZWILLKILLYOU?'

I feel my skin tense with a fizzing burn. 'What are you talking about?'

'Kitab beta, you retweeted a blog you said was written by Aziz. What is it?'

'It's Aziz's blog,' I say.

'Darling,' Rach says, cocking her head sideways, in classic Rach sympathy pose. She folds her arms. 'What are you talking about?'

'Aziz?' Hayley asks, confused. 'Your brother, Aziz?'

'No one,' I say defensively. 'Aziz,' I repeat. 'He …'

'Oh, Kitab,' my dad says and walks over to me. He has his arms outstretched. He wants to give me a cuddle, not a fist bump and shoulder bump, a proper cuddle, like a dad should, an arm around the neck and an arm around the back. I look at Hayley; she doesn't know what to say.

Rach pipes up. 'Rasesh, aren't you mad with him? Jeez, Kit, why are you doing this to your poor dad?'

'I don't need to explain myself to you, Rach. We're not together anymore. I need to go to bed.'

'No,' my dad says. 'You're going to sit down.'

'What? Dad, not now. I've got company.'

'I am your father. I don't say this enough, Kitab beta. But I am your father. So sit down.'

I shake my head: no. As in, I need some space, and I head to the toilet. I close the door and I sit on the loo.

'What's shaking, bro?' I look up. Aziz is leaning on the edge of the bath.

'When did you get back?' I say, trying not to show my happiness that he's back.

'That doesn't matter. Thanks for retweeting my blog. I got quite a few hits.'

'No worries,' I say. 'How was your trip?'

'Listen,' Aziz says. 'That's why I'm interrupting your toilet time. I need to tell you something.'

'What?'

'I'm moving out. I'm moving to America. Teddy Baker and I are going into business together.'

'What are you talking about?'

'I'm going.'

'Okay,' I say. I look away from him. He moves closer to me. I look up and he's simulating thrusting his hips into my face. I smile. I don't mean it. I want to ask why but that seems redundant at this point.

276

'You're not going to make this a thing and cry, are you? I swear, I've known you since you were born and yet I've never seen you cry more than you have in the last 3 months. You didn't even cry when Mum died.' Aziz leans down to my eyeline. 'Who are you and what have you done with Kitab?'

I hear Dad call my name in the next room, telling me to hurry up.

'Sounds like you're in trouble,' Aziz says. I smirk. 'I don't miss that.'

'You can't go. I need you.'

'You don't need me. Just remember me. Just remember how fucking awesome I am.' He scratches at his scar, furiously. Now the bow tie's not there, I'm reminded of how dark it is. It looks inflamed. Always has done. Like it never stopped healing.

'What happened to the bow tie?'

'It couldn't hide everything for ever, Kitab.'

'You don't need to hide. Come on, come say hello.'

'I can't do that, Kit.'

'Why not?'

'You know why not. Just … remember. In that brain. Remember me. It's important you remember me. Don't be me. Remember me. Memory is important, Kit.'

'Okay,' I say. I gulp. I stand up and turn to the sink. I run cold water out of the tap and splash it on my face. I turn the tap off and look in the mirror.

I'm alone again. Aziz has left the building.

I open the bathroom door and step out into the lounge. Hayley looks uncomfortable. She's sitting on the sofa next to Rach. There's an empty canvas bag next to Rach's feet, waiting to be filled with the remaining remnants of her life here, I'm guessing. Hayley's sipping tea from Aziz's favourite mug, the white one with red polka dots.

'Hi,' I announce to the room, limply.

277

'What's this about?' my dad says. 'What is this aZiZWILLKILLYOU?'

Rach stares at me and shakes her head like she's here against her will, trying to save me from a pit of chaos, against her will. She speaks first. 'I don't know what happened to you when that stupid book came out, Kit. But you changed. Really badly. You changed.'

'No, I didn't.'

'You did,' she says, shaking her head. 'You gave up on real life.'

'I was just trying to make a name for myself.'

'Yeah, but at the expense of everyone around you. In real life …'

'Meatspace,' I say to myself.

'Kit, please … it was you and that book and those updates. But you've gone too far this time. What are you doing to your dad?'

'Rach, just … look, I don't know why you care. We're not together anymore.'

'Doesn't mean I don't care. I mean, you've changed so much. You don't go out. You don't do anything. And yet you are living this life that's not real. It's not real. None of it is real.'

'It is real.'

'Kitab,' my dad says. 'What is this about Aziz? Why are you doing this to me? He's dead. I have accepted this. Why not you?'

Hayley looks at me. 'What?' she says, lightly.

'I'm sorry, Dad.'

'What is going on, Kit?' Hayley says, standing up.

Rach turns to her. 'Aziz is Kitab's brother. Was. He died.' She shakes her head like Hayley should be on page 265 like everyone else.

'Shut up, Rach. Listen, Hayley, I can explain. This isn't … it's all very confusing.'

'Why,' my dad says. 'I don't understand, beta.'

'Remember the day you bought Aziz and me that modem? On 14.4 dial-up?'

Dad smiles. 'The phone was always engaged. All those pictures of that girl ... What was her name?'

'Pamela Anderson ...'

'You dirty boys.'

Rach looks at me and my dad. 'No, Kit, it's not okay what you're doing. You can't just laugh about it with your dad like it's some big joke.'

'I have to remember these things,' I say.

'You did. In that book,' she says. In *that* book, like the book was the thing that broke us up.

My coming-of-age book was about me and Aziz. It was about our teenage years, a fictionalised memoir of me and Aziz growing up without a mother, taking care of our dad and getting jobs to help pay bills, the capers we used to get up to, how we relied on getting into scrapes together to get by, how we rinsed each other all the time, how Aziz looked after me, saved me from beatings from older kids, how we were against the world. How we had this hustle at the pool tables. How he knew how to cook. How Dad lost his job. How we had nothing. And how we survived. No money, living in a one-bedroom flat with a manic depressive father. Finding all the joy and fun we could in the world. Making money through scams, odd jobs, doing silly things for dangerous people we grew up near. All the mixtapes of indie B-sides we'd sell for a pound. The stupid stuff. Our attempts to mother our dad, our dad's cack-handed attempts to father us. The crap advice he gave us. The Vedic lessons from his brother that made no sense. It was about men and how having a strong female around shapes you, but for us, we didn't have that, we only had each other, and with stoic men in one room, it was a mess of taking the piss to stop yourself saying something meaningful.

I made stuff up. I filled in blanks. I fictionalised it. I made everything a hyperreal version of what happened. Because that's what Aziz and I would do. We used to make up stories, adventures, us as superheroes vs gangsters. He'd dictate and I'd type them up on Dad's computer. We had a story about Aziz going on holiday to New York, his ultimate dream to walk the streets shown in those gangster films, and Aziz would be on the subway when shit would go down and he'd have to rescue a baby from the jaws of death. Then he'd meet the girl. Then he'd be a national hero. Aziz and me. And I wrote about it. New York was his dream. He had posters of Mean Streets, the builders on the Empire State Building, New York Yankees over his bedroom wall. It was a totem for him, of freedom. Of having made it.

He never got to go.

With the novel, much as it mostly happened, it also mostly did not. The difference between memory and memoir, fiction and non. That's where I walked a thin line, mis-remembering things about Aziz and me on purpose, to help the narrative. But it was mostly everything – us making up stories, us in our indie band, us dealing with my mum's death, us fighting local bullies, us dealing with our ridiculous family. Us bringing each other up. He was the eldest. And thus my hero. Everything seemed possible when he was around. The book was about him. And me.

'So, how did Aziz Will Kill You come about?' Hayley asks. I don't know what she makes of me now. She probably thinks I'm crazy.

I wrote a blog, as him, to promote the book coming out, on the insistence of my publisher, imagining who he would now be. What he would look like. What our relationship would be.

I still have these exercise books of all the stories we wrote. Under my bed. I re-read them to channel us. Us together. This was us in unison, communicating with the world. I read the case of the missing baby, where super-heroic Aziz chases after a baby in the New York subway. I found that the voice of Aziz was too wrapped up in how I remembered him and not necessarily who he was.

Aziz and me.

Writing about him back then, about our teens, before the accident, it had brought it all back for me. I never knew my mum. I was too young. Losing Aziz was something I didn't ever really get over. It seemed like he should just be there. Like he had realised his dream and gone to New York for 15 years and was just there. It didn't feel real that he didn't exist.

When I sat down to write that blog, the him now, who Aziz was now, it was like he was standing over my shoulder, pacing the room, throwing his hands about, dictating it to me.

And I wrote it down because who knew Aziz now better than Aziz?

All I knew was, I thought he would probably have a bow tie tattoo.

It was something he had joked about with me and Dad when we were growing up. Him, desperate for a tattoo, me and Dad telling him it was pointless, they were permanent. I would never get one, I told him. Dad said they were ugly, they weren't smart. 'Then I'll get a tattoo of a bow tie,' Aziz bellowed, laughing hysterically. 'I'll be the smartest guy in the room.'

Before writing the blog, I'd Googled bow tie tattoos. And I'd found a guy who looked how I imagined Aziz would. He had his build, his arrogance, his shit-eating grin, his teeth, his nose, his complexion – he was the doppelganger Aziz had never had because we didn't get to see who he would become. Except now I knew. He was there, in the flat, and he looked like some random dude off the internet, called Teddy Baker.

Before, I couldn't channel his voice. I'd spent months writing a novel about him, but now I had to write about him *now*, I couldn't get it right. But, with this guy – who I researched, and

281

found his Facebook, his Twitter, his Linkedin – as my inspiration, the blog flowed. And didn't stop. I wrote more. Like he was stood over me, dictating the stories. Like when we were younger. The first blog was meant for the publisher's website. I finished it quite quickly once I had the totem of who he could have been staring at me from Google image search.

At the same time my publisher was insistent I help out on as much publicity as I could. This was the life now. The connected author. Gone were the days of hammering your fists down on a typewriter in isolation with a bottle of some Glen or some Jim for company. Now, it meant blogs, tweets, Instagram, videos, Spotify playlists, book trailers, email interviews – my entire life as content to promote thinly-veiled fiction. While they got me reviews in broadsheets, I tackled the community aspect of the connected writer, and nothing was sacred then. If I could write about it on the internet and get those delicious, addictive interactions, I did.

There was one guy I knew could get me an interview on the radio. He presented a show on a community radio station and my publisher thought it would be good exposure for me. I went to school with this presenter. Aziz used to tease him mercilessly for carrying a briefcase. I looked through all my contact books, through Facebook, through Twitter and I couldn't find a contact for him. I tried mutual friends and I couldn't find a contact for him. I even called his parents' house and they wouldn't give me a contact for him. He was on community radio. That meant he was too famous to give old school friends his details. I started looking through old defunct email addresses, trying to find emails we had exchanged, hoping that I'd stumble across an email contact for him.

And in my first email address, one I'd set up on a 14.4bps connection, with Aziz, on our first modem, a month before the accident, the very first email I'd been sent … it was from Aziz. I'd set up KitabWillDestroyYou@hotmail.com and Aziz had set up AZIZWILLKILLYOU@hotmail.com. And when we'd set them up on our 14.4 dial-up connection, he'd sent me an email.

To: KitabWillDestroyYou@hotmail.com
From: AZIZWILLKILLYOU@hotmail.com
Received: \<redacted\>
Subject: test

Yo Kit,

Test email ...

If you are the Captain of a sinking ship, the best example you can set is to get off that ship as soon as you can. Really, you should be the first off.

AZIZ.

I'd forgotten about that. The only email he'd ever sent me. The only communication. The only representation of his voice I had. I only had memory and a few photos and his pay-as-you-go mobile phone, which he got to help him sell stuff. I never threw it away. I kept it all these years. I find it comforting to call. Now we live in communications, missives, tweets, statuses, emails, likes, aggregated search filters, recommended videos, round robins, listicles, sparrowface, duck lips, selfies, event invites, texts and I had none of these from my brother. None to remember what kind of person he was, only the barest fringes of my memory. You can construct entire people out of everything they've ever done digitally. But not Aziz. I only had that email.

Then, when Rach moved out, it was like he'd lived with me all along. He told me he was going to coach me through my break-up, 'stick with me kid and you'll be fine', and the spare room, the office where Rach worked from home, it was his, and he was there. I didn't question it because if I did, he could leave, he would leave and I'd lose my brother again. And, it's only now, telling my dad and my ex-girlfriend and my new girlfriend this that I realise I've tricked myself into believing he was here.

I don't tell them that. I tell them about the blog and how it became easy, like he was there, to update this one story we had written, and make it him now, because him now, he should be able to exist electronically. He pre-dates social media, he never lived to make his mark and fuck it, he deserved it, he deserved to make his mark. He deserved his presence.

He deserved to live for ever, tweeting and blogging and Instagramming. Not me. Him. Because if he was doing all that, it meant he was back in meatspace. What I don't say is that room next to mine, it would hum with the sounds of him bringing girls home, watching television till 3 in the morning, working out, whistling to himself. The flat was filled with Aziz. And that made it so much easier to accept that Rach wasn't there anymore.

Aziz was in the building.

But Aziz doesn't live here anymore.

'Kitab, beta … that sounds … crazy,' my dad says.

'Memories eventually lie,' I tell him.

'This,' he sighs. 'This is a bigger lie.'

'He's my brother. Don't you dare take this away from me.'

'Life goes on, kiddo,' my father says. He shakes his head. I can feel Rach and Hayley both looking at me with pity in their eyes.

'Aziz is dead,' I say, almost as a question and almost as a reminder.

'How did he die?' Hayley asks.

'He was always riding that bloody bike too fast,' Dad says. 'Always too fast.'

'He was cycling down the high street where Kit grew up,' Rach says, the pragmatic objectivist. 'Fast. He swung onto a zebra crossing to get across the road and a car hit him.'

'Were you there?' Hayley asks.

I shake my head. I wasn't there so I still don't feel like it happened. If I didn't live-tweet it, it didn't happen. I don't have a timeline of events. I look around the flat. It feels half lived in. It doesn't feel like our place anymore. I look at Rach. She definitely doesn't live here anymore.

Where's Aziz? I need him.

The sad truth of it is, that guy from the radio, he contacted my publisher directly and told them he was desperate to have me on the show. I said no.

'You don't need me. Just remember me. Just remember how fucking awesome I am. Just remember. In that brain. Remember.'

'You need to shut that blog down,' Dad says. I nod my head. I think about Kitab 2. The weirdo did me some good. He got me out of this flat. Out into the world. Away from the chutney.

'I've got nothing left to say, Dad. That blog's done. It was Aziz's story. I just wrote it down.'

'Hayley,' I say. 'I'm not crazy.'

'Okay, chico,' she replies. 'It's okay. We can talk later, okay?'

I walk over to the fridge, I grab a tote bag that's hanging off a drawer. I open the fridge and I pull out the 5 remaining jars of chutney. I place them in the bag and thrust my hand out to Rach. 'Here you go,' I say. 'You're finally all moved out.'

'Thanks,' Rach stays. 'Look, I …'

'I'll be fine,' I say. 'I'll just go running or something, get out more, that sort of thing.'

'I was gonna say, I'm going to delete you from Facebook, I think. It's too easy to stalk people. Is that okay?'

'Whatever,' I say.

'I'm going then,' Rach says. I nod. She turns around to leave. She shakes Hayley's hand, firmly, like they've struck a business deal and she kisses Dad on the cheek.

'Rach,' Dad asks. 'Isn't your mum single?'

'Not for you, Rasesh,' she laughs, opening the door. 'Not for you. You're trouble.' He giggles to himself as she closes the door. Rach has left the building. I am no longer in a relationship.

I look at Hayley. It's complicated.

'Dad,' I say. 'I didn't mean to hurt anyone.'

'You did,' he says. 'I was hurt. I was really hurt. I still am. But I realise I am not innocent in this. This is my fault as much as yours. I should be more of a father, and less of a friend. Eh, kiddo?'

'No, Dad,' I say. 'I should be more of an adult.'

There's an awkward silence. Dad shuffles his feet. 'Look,' he says. 'We will talk about this properly, but I do have a date. A third date, with a girl called Madhur. I really like her.'

'Third date?' I say, surprised. 'You should go.'

Dad's already half out the door before I get to finish my sentence.

'Double date?' he says, looking at Hayley.

'We'll see, Dad. We'll have to see about that.'

He walks out of the door. I follow him. I close the door behind me. It's just him and me in the communal area. He looks back at me. 'I don't need the money,' he says. 'I think you need to take some time, think about things. Use that money to buy you some time.'

'Thanks, Dad,' I say. 'Are we okay?'

'No,' he says. 'No, we're not. I'll tell you something about Aziz, that you never ever got right in any of those blogs. Something you forgot. And in your book too. I read your book. I never told you but I read it. And you know what you missed? Aziz was never good with the ladies. He tried. Oh, he tried. He could talk to any man in the world, about anything. And everyone was his best friend. But with girls, he would go silent, and he would go giggly and he could not get a word out. He was shy. Not that you'd know because all you saw was loud Aziz. There was a shy Aziz too. He was a sweet boy. He was such a sweet boy. Anyway, son, we are going to spend more time together. Proper time. You and me. We could go for a walk. We could go on holiday. Not always dinner. Not always the same place. And you're going to talk, too. You never talk. So I just keep on talking about nothing, about girls, because that's the only thing I have going on. Because you sit there, wishing you were somewhere else. I'm your dad, beta. You have to tell me things. You're broken up with Rach, fine, that's sad, she's a nice girl. Talk to me. You're upset about a bad review in the *Telegraph*, that's annoying. Talk to me. I have a Google Alert set up on my son's name. I love him. I'm proud of him. He should know that.'

I'm crying.

Dad wipes a tear from his face.

'Thanks, Dad,' I say.

'This other Kitab, Aziz, this new girl – they get your attention, your interactions. What do I get? One dinner a week? Come on, beta. There's only you and me. Let's make a change.'

I make a weird noise, a horse neigh. I've never heard it before. Dad walks over to me and he cuddles me. I cuddle him back. We stand there for a few moments. I can feel him drying his eyes. I wipe my tears into his jacket.

'Hey,' he says. 'I have a hot date tonight. Don't ruin my clothes.'

'You should get going then, Dad.'

He lets go of me, wipes something off my cheek, pats it and goes to leave. He stops, facing the door. 'Yes,' he says. 'It will be hard work, but as long as that's enough, we'll be fine.'

He opens the door and is gone.

*

Dad has left the building. I walk back into the flat and it's just Hayley and me. She walks over to me, her arms folded, and buries her nose in my armpit. I giggle. It's ticklish.

'You think I'm crazy, don't you?'

Hayley nods. 'Yeah,' she says. 'I do. Do you want to go for a walk?'

I grin. That's exactly what I want to do. I take my phone out of my pocket and leave it on the counter. 'I'm ready. Let's go.' We walk towards the door.

History:

Writing tips – Google
Get motivated to write – Google
10 essential tips for writing – Book
Writers handbook – Book

I choose meatspace. I start waking up early, eating properly, spending a minimum of 4 hours a day out of my flat. I allow myself an hour of internet 3 times a day. I build a routine, something I've sorely lacked.

I find a job copywriting for an ad firm near me. They let me work from home. I choose to hot desk with them. I get up early each morning and I sit at my desk and write for 3 hours before I have to be at work. The feeling of being surrounded by people again, on coffee rounds, talking about *Game of Thrones*, standing over each other's desks and picking apart the finer details of full stops, punchier headlines and puns – it feels electric.

The sounds of my alarm clock barely register over the heavy purrs of Hayley as she lies next to me. I take my laptop into the other room and start writing. It feels forced, then it feels easy, then it feels like the worst thing I could be doing but I'm getting it done.

I get the occasional email from Kitab 2. He asks for me to provide him a reference to reapply to school with. He's doing an English Literature degree in Bangalore, much to his father's disdain and wants to write a novel based on his week in London. I reply that I'm happy to. He's grown on me. My mentor.

I see Dad regularly. He moves into a flat nearby, out of my childhood home. We sell most of the contents and he sets himself up with an Ikea catalogue-style place. Near me, he sees me more often and he's able to enjoy what he describes as 'the carnival atmosphere' of where I live. We go for walks, to the cinema, sometimes to concerts – old Bollywood song evenings where we sit on cushions, sip red wine and listen to the songs of Dad's for ever ago. He tells me stories about Mum. I tell him stories about Aziz, ones he has never heard.

My news channels become just that, news channels. I close my Facebook account and sign up for a new email address. Before I delete my Facebook account, I do a search for my name and find a third Kitab Balasubramanyam. His avatar is a photo of his torso. We're growing in legion. I'm not so much a 'me' anymore. Time for me to leave. I click delete.

I open the fridge, trying to make a cheese and something sandwich. I notice there are no chutneys. Just a jar of Branston pickle. Perfect, I mouth to myself.

Hayley spends a lot of time at my flat. She doesn't like her flatmates much. A collection of different herbal teas comes with her, filling one of my cupboards up with box after box.

One afternoon, Dad is over and I'm showing him how to make roast potatoes. We're sitting at the kitchen table, drinking beers and he looks at me.

'How is the second novel coming?' he asks.

I tell him all about it. I talk him through the plot. He asks questions, I make up answers to disguise the fact I haven't thought of that yet. He gets me to define my audience. He laughs at the right bits, he gasps at others.

We talk for 30 minutes about the book and during a natural lull he puts his elbows on the table. 'I'd like to see those books, the ones you and Aziz wrote,' he says. 'It would be nice to read my 2 sons' adventures.'

'Yeah,' I say. 'Sure.' I go and get them. We spend the rest of the evening acting out the stories in Aziz's voice and gestures, remembering how he relayed details with his entire body. It feels good to talk about him like he's not there anymore.

As we remember him, he feels more alive to me than he has done in years.

I'm walking down the high street and a car passes, music blaring. It stands out because it's not grime or hip-hop like it usually is in this area. It's a song from the 80s. It's by Elvis Costello. It sparks a memory. Aziz and I are riding bikes through my old neighbourhood. The roads are empty because it's the middle of the day. The sun is shining and I'm wearing a t-shirt with Shaquille O'Neal on it. Aziz is wearing a Clash t-shirt Dad hates. Because they're loud and obnoxious, according to him. And probably have lots of tattoos.

He's going faster and faster and encouraging me to keep up. I feign a lack of fitness but it's because I'm scared of speed. Aziz lifts his hands off the handlebars to the sky. He is graceful and in command of that bike. He is practically flying. He turns round to me and I'm close enough to see him wink. He steadies himself and then brakes suddenly swinging the bike round to face me. He starts bellowing at the top of his voice, semi in tune, I join him when I know the words. It's our favourite song, a tape we found amongst Mum's things, 'Shipbuilding' by Elvis Costello recorded over and over again on one side of a blank C-90 tape … both Aziz and me, with all the will in the world,
  'Diving for dear life
When we could be diving for pearls.'
Some memories will for ever be 3-dimensional.

Aziz vs the True Death

<Sorry, the blog you were looking for does not exist. However, the name aZiZWILLKILLYOU is available to register!>

Acknowledgements:

ābhāra #1: wife Katie for the 'two brain' theory, for making me laugh more than anyone and for teddy dog.

ābhāra #2: my agent Jamie Coleman from Greene & Heaton, for being a hard taskmaster, good egg, giver of notes, calming navigator and curer of 'Second Novel Syndrome'.

ābhāra #3: Scott Pack, Rachel Faulkner, Cicely Aspinall and everyone at The Friday Project for making the book possible and for letting us send some meat into space.

ābhāra #4: Nick Dogg, the Sophisticated Party Robot for designing the book cover, spending dedicated hours cutting up small pieces of meat and creating something so disgusting and beautiful and fitting and for making the lapsed vegetarian in me feel sad. Chris Lawson for the photography.

ābhāra #5: first reader James Smythe for telling me it was okay; Gavin and everyone at Quartet Books for unending support; Vanessa Pelz-Sharpe and Mark Bray for instructing me on tattoos; my uncle Mukesh and my dad Jitu who unwittingly provide me with a lot of material; Josie Long, for giving me The Golden Game, and for once doing a project called 100 Days to Make Me a Better Person, where some of the writing I did seeded ideas for characters in this book; Riz Ahmed for asking me about my line between fiction and non-fiction; Georgina Ruffhead and Gemma Addy from David Higham Associates; my honey Sathnam, for the walk and the ice-cream; Katherine Woodfine, Hannah Davies, Anna McKerrow and Will White for WriBooWiBoo.

ābhāra #6: Gautam Malkani, Teju Cole, Nerm Chauhan, Kunal Anand, Suze Ázzopardi, Niven Govinden, Stuart Evers, Lee Rourke, Anjali Bhatia, Katherine Solomon, Chimène Suleyman, Rupa Bhatti, Joe Pickering, Krupa and Leena Shukla, Salena Godden, Lucy MacNab, Alan and Mary, Anita Rani, Evie Wyld, Mimi and Bobby Etherington, and Rukhsana Yasmin for various words and acts of kindness and support over the years.

And, finally, an ābhāra to Rob Lingham for that night in the pub when we found your internet doppelganger, The Boy with the Bow Tie Tattoo.

Shout out Arts Emergency and Roy Castle Lung Cancer Foundation.

The writing of this book was supported in part by Arts Council England and the Authors' Foundation.